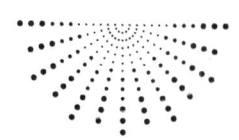

ROSIE SWAN

PUREREAD.COM

Copyright © 2023 PureRead Ltd

www.pureread.com

All rights reserved. No part of this publication may be reproduced, distributed or transmitted in any form or by any means, without prior written permission.

Publisher's Note: This is a work of fiction. Names, characters, places, and incidents are a product of the author's imagination. Locales and public names are sometimes used for atmospheric purposes. Any resemblance to actual people, living or dead, or to businesses, companies, events, institutions, or locales is completely coincidental.

CONTENTS

Prologue	1
1. Blood, Sweat and Tears	5
2. A Shameful Shilling	10
3. Mr. Pillar	14
4. Haunted	21
5. In His Sights	30
6. A Grisly Opportunity	33
7. Time To Cry	39
8. Gentlemen and Factory Girls	42
9. Falling Foul	47
10. What People Say About Factory Girls	52
11. Bonner's Gate	56
12. The O'Briens	62
13. Bleak House	72
14. Hearts of Stone	75
15. Out of the Frying Pan	79
16. The Dipping Room	87
17. One Bright Spot	90
18. Red And White	94
19. Peter	97
20. Uneasy Alliances	102
21. The Music Hall	106
22. A Dark Light	110
23. Back At The Paragon	113
24. Against the Rules	117
25. Matchwomen	124
26. Keeping Secrets	127
27. White Slavery	130
28. The Reading Room	135
29. An Inconvenient Truth	145
30. True or False	148
31. Trouble	152
32. Mile End Waste	155

33. A Great Choking Weed	163
34. Hidden	168
35. The Spark	175
36. A Forgotten Dream	178
37. Lost	181
38. Not The Only One	186
39. Short	190
40. A Lady's Honour	194
41. Carpet Bag	196
42. Wimpole Street	200
43. Boycott	203
44. Strike	206
45. Innocence and Experience	208
46. To The Editor	214
47. Exploitation	216
48. Never Come Down	220
49. Outside The Gates	225
Chapter 50	228
51. Escape	232
52. Blackleg	235
53. Eliza	239
54. Sisters	242
55. Into The Dawn	245
56. Black and White	248
57. Memories	253
58. Standing Up	260
59. Impossible Dreams	267
60. Glasgow Hands	273
61. Highbury	280
62. Trampled	285
63. Ghosts and Shadows	288
64. Lofty Figures Fall	291
65. Empty	296
66. Regrets	300
67. Hand In Hand	305
68. March	310
69. A Missing Peace	313
70. We've Come A Long Way	316

71. The Fallen	325
72. There is Nothing Lost	327
73. Christmas	337
Love Victorian Romance?	343
Have You Read	345
Our Gift To You	367

PROLOGUE

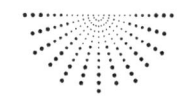

The Victorian match factory girls were a group of young women and children who worked in Britain's heartless match factories. The history of their plight is closely associated with the working conditions prevalent in such factories, particularly the exposure to toxic chemicals and the dismal lack of workers' rights.

In the 19th century, match manufacturing involved the use of white phosphorus, a highly toxic substance. Matches were commonly referred to as "Lucifers" during this time. The process of making these matches involved dipping the matchsticks into a mixture that contained white phosphorus. As a result, the female workers were exposed to the hazardous effects of the chemical and a condition known as "phossy jaw" which often resulted in disfigurement and death.

The plight of the match factory girls gained attention and sparked public outrage. The grim working conditions and the detrimental health effects of white phosphorus led to a movement advocating for the welfare of these workers. Activists, including notable figures like Annie Besant, campaigned against the use of white phosphorus in match production and pushed for labor reforms.

> **SAVE THE POOR MATCH-GIRLS**
> from "PHOSSY JAW"—a loathsome disease incurred by inhaling poisonous Phosphorus fumes—
> **BY USING ONLY**
> **SALVATION ARMY MATCHES**
> which are manufactured under perfectly healthy conditions, absolutely free from health-endangering processes.
> HIGHER RATE OF WAGES PAID FOR LABOUR THAN BY ANY OTHER FACTORY.
> **NOTE.**—Ask your Tradesman for **DARKEST ENGLAND SAFETIES**, and take no others. If you cannot obtain them easily, send post card for name of nearest shopkeeper and full particulars to COMMISSIONER CADMAN, 101, QUEEN VICTORIA STREET, E.C.
> Send for the new Illustrated Pamphlet on "Match-Makers' Leprosy," which will be forwarded FREE.

Their valiant efforts eventually bore fruit with the British Match Girls' Strike of 1888. Brave workers protested against unfair working conditions and the use of the killer chemical. Despite strong opposition, the strike was successful, resulting in improved conditions for the match factory workers, including the elimination of white phosphorus from the match production process.

The victory of these courageous women marked a significant moment in the history of workers' rights and industrial reforms that touched every sector of Victorian working-class society.

It is here in the fray of a fearsome female revolution that our story is set...

1
BLOOD, SWEAT AND TEARS

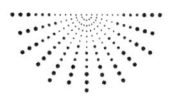

The company of Pillar and Perkins had been founded in Plymouth during the 1840s. In the twenty years that followed, they relocated to East London. They put up a lumber mill on Bow Common, demolished an old candle factory and built their own in its place: a long building of red brick with square turrets at either end. Steam engines powered the machines inside, and hundreds of employees made matches from sticks of poplar and Canadian pine wood.

Men mostly handled the sulfur, powdered glass and white phosphorus in which each match had to be dipped. Then the process was passed along to the women and teenage girls, who dried the matches, halved them, packed them into boxes and tied them in bundles. Their many hands built a hill of profits, at the top of which the factory owners sat.

The first troubling tremors came in 1871, after the Chancellor of the Exchequer proposed to introduce a tax of a halfpenny per hundred matches. The tax was withdrawn, in no small part thanks to the hundreds of matchwomen who marched to the Houses of Parliament to protest it, but the excitement had been too much for Mr. Arthur Perkins, and being of advanced years, he perished of a heart attack a few days after the good news had been announced.

Then it was just his partner, Mr. Richard Pillar, left to manage the company, at least until his son Edward came of age. Ever more grateful for his seat, now that the danger had loomed so close, Mr. Pillar clutched tighter and vowed that nothing would threaten it again. And so the years passed, like the pistons of the steam engines in the factory that went up and down: winter-summer, winter-summer, winter-summer, and Mr. Pillar's hill of profits grew higher and higher, until it began to blot out the sun.

∽

It was a March morning in 1888, and the London fogs hung low over the city. They mingled with the smoke gushing from the match factory's many funnels. Beyond it, past several long, straight rows of rooftops, the River Lea wound like a grey snake, its waters churned up by great black barges.

The Moss sisters were walking to work when the lady tried to stop them. Mile End Road was busy with early morning traffic, carriages and omnibuses rolling past, and she stepped out from Bow churchyard and onto the pavement before them. Rebecca, who was the eldest, thought at first, she must be some kind of zealot looking for donations, and tugged Eliza's arm so that they might go around. But then the lady spoke.

"Excuse me, but do you girls work for Pillar and Perkins?"

"Yes, ma'am," Rebecca replied, narrowing her eyes slightly. The lady was small in stature and looked to be in her middle age; her black gown had square shoulders which looked like those of a man's greatcoat, and her brown hair had been drawn back from her long, stern face.

"My name is Annie Besant," said the lady. She seemed altogether too calm to be a zealot, Rebecca decided, but that did not make her any less suspicious. "I wonder if I might speak to you about the conditions there."

Rebecca nudged Eliza, who had opened her mouth to speak, and turned back to Mrs. Besant. "Meaning no disrespect, ma'am, but I don't see how our work is your business. Good day—"

"If you change your mind," Mrs. Besant said, blocking the path again to hand Rebecca a card, "This is my address. Mind you don't lose it." Her eyes found Rebecca's, and the younger woman was surprised to see the kindness in them. "I don't know if you have heard of the Fabian Society, but at the moment we are organising a boycott against Pillar and Perkins for not paying workers like you a fair wage. We would be interested in hearing your side of things."

"Good day, ma'am," Rebecca said again, abruptly, and hurried Eliza on. She did not turn around until they had been walking for a few minutes, and by then, the lady's figure had disappeared, lost in the crowds behind them. "You were going to speak to her, weren't you?"

"I wanted to tell her what happened to Mum," Eliza replied, instantly on the defensive. "Is that so bad?"

Rebecca glanced at Eliza, and sighed. It had been a long time since she had seen her younger sister smile. In the last few months, her face had grown wearier than seventeen should be. "Listen to me. This kind of thing's dangerous, all right? You remember Bloody Sunday, a few months back? People who went protesting were run down by police horses, beaten with truncheons." She saw Eliza wince. "I don't want to upset you, but talking to ladies like that is only asking for trouble."

They had come up to the front yard of the match factory now, where workers were milling around. Rebecca looked up at the large, imposing building, so high that she had to crane her neck. More gently, "Remember you're still new. Things aren't so bad here." They stepped in through the gates amid the crowds of matchwomen, and before her voice was swallowed up by the din, Rebecca added, "You'll get used to it."

2

A SHAMEFUL SHILLING

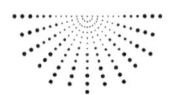

Eliza was on cutting today, which always made her nervous. The fact that she and a hundred other girls were packed together in the boxing room like sardines did not help matters. Somewhere behind her, Rebecca was filling the matchboxes, and meanwhile, Eliza had to watch the serrated blade work its way down through the splints of double-ended matches, slicing them in half. Every now and then, the metallic cord holding the top of the blade steady would come loose, and before it got tangled with the wheel, she would have to secure it again, her fingers quick and careful.

The fumes were not as bad up here on the second floor of the factory, but as the day wore on, the smell in the boxing room would generally get worse and worse. This was because it was impossible not to fire at least a few of the matches when you were handling them. Eliza had heard of girls losing half a day's work that way. When she was waiting for a new stack of splints to be brought up from the drying chamber, she snuck a glance at the next bench over from her, where Sarah O'Brien was working. Sarah was Rebecca's friend, and she almost never fired the matches. She was also, however, one of the noisiest people Eliza had ever met, and as long as the foremen weren't around, she was bound to be cackling or calling like a crow.

That was the thing about working in this place: the noise. Never mind what Rebecca said; Eliza didn't know if she would ever get used to it. She had been a maid before this, in a house where you were supposed to tiptoe and whisper and generally make yourself invisible. None of the girls in Pillar and Perkins bothered to do that. They sighed and cursed and sometimes even sang. Eliza, who believed in maintaining something of her dignity even if she had to be a factory girl, never joined in.

The grey clouds shifted past the small, high windows of the boxing room, and it was nearly lunchtime when a girl from downstairs brought Eliza one last stack of double-ended splints. Eliza secured it in the machine, and set the wheel going. Her eyes moved back and forth with the motion of the blade, watching in case the cord above came loose. When it did (as always), Eliza sighed, stretched out her right hand—and snatched it back again, just in time as the cord came completely loose, moving at a rippling, deadly speed, winding itself around the wheel tighter and

11

tighter until it snapped in half, and the whole machine ground to a halt.

Eliza had her right hand cradled to her breast. She could almost feel the little bones of her fingers, crushed and broken as they would have been. Her heart pounded against her chest.

"Now you're in for it," said Sarah, who looked quite sorry for her. Still breathing fast, Eliza glanced at her, and tried to distract herself from what had just happened by thinking about how dirty Sarah's hands were, by reflecting on the great pity that she wore her hair in that boyish cut with the dark, heavy fringe when her face was almost pretty.

A series of lumbering, heavy steps, and the foreman, Jem Wilson, was at Eliza's bench. "Well? What happened?"

She looked up at him. From her first day working here, she had known that Wilson was a nasty piece of work: his face was brick-red from drinking, and his small, closely spaced eyes zeroed in on his prey like those of a wolf or fox, lighting up at every chance for cruelty. Slowly, she lowered her hand. "The cord broke—I was afraid my fingers—"

"That's a shilling," Wilson said, surveying the debris of broken splints under the blade of the machine.

"A *shilling?*" Eliza's voice jumped up an octave, so that several other girls in the boxing room looked around.

Glancing behind, she saw Rebecca, her hands frozen over her work. Her sister shook her head and mouthed something. Eliza's shoulders sagged, and when the foreman cuffed her over the ear, she was resigned to the blow because she had been expecting it.

"Be thankful I'm not taking more. That's a hundred good matches you've lost." As Wilson strode away, he growled over his shoulder, "And in future, *never mind your fingers.*"

3
MR. PILLAR

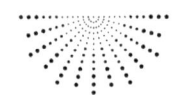

At lunchtime, everyone ate by the machines, because there was no separate room where they could take their meals. A strong garlicky smell always clung to the food, from the sulphur and phosphorus fumes. Mostly, the girls were too hungry to notice.

Rebecca wolfed down her sandwich even more quickly than the other girls around her and hurried out of the boxing room. The offices were in another wing of the building, away from the factory itself. It was a long walk through a draughty corridor on the ground floor. Through the many windows, the courtyard was visible, and the spire of Bow Church peered over the far wall of the factory.

The secretary, Mr. Lethbridge, sighed audibly when the clerk outside let Rebecca into his office. "Sir, I was told you could meet me today. I'm Rebecca Moss—"

"I remember who you are, girl." The secretary put down his pen and gestured for her to come in. He was thin as a rake, with wisps of white hair along the sides of his head. He looked as though a puff of wind might blow him away. "Esther Moss's daughter, yes? Sit down."

"Yes, sir." Rebecca halted before his desk, and brushed down her apron before she sat. As the secretary looked at her expectantly, she cleared her throat. "I've come to ask about the support that was promised me and my sister, on account of our mum's phossy jaw. It's been a month now since she died, and—"

"We were very sorry to lose Esther, of course," Mr. Lethbridge interrupted. "She was a good worker. Phosphorus necrosis of the jaw is a most unfortunate condition."

"Yes, sir." Rebecca looked down at her lap and twisted her hands together. She had taken care to wash them before she came, but some dirt still clung to her nails. "She was in a lot of pain—towards the end. At first, we got her sore teeth taken out, but then her jaw didn't heal proper, and we couldn't afford a doctor to look at it…"

"Just a moment." Mr. Lethbridge was rummaging in the drawers of his desk. He drew out a file and leafed through it. With one hand, he adjusted his spectacles. "Ah, yes. According to our records, for each week that your mother was no longer able to work for us, she received compensation from us of one pound." He raised his eyes to Rebecca, with a questioning look. "That seems to me a sufficient amount to afford a doctor's fees. Unless, of course, you and your sister spent it on something else…"

"We spent it getting her teeth taken out. Sir." Rebecca was sitting up tall in her seat now, her spine stiff, her jaw clenched. "The money stopped coming in after the first two weeks."

Mr. Lethbridge's gaze had returned to his records. "According to what I have written here, your mother continued to receive compensation from us right up to her death."

"But I'm telling you, sir, that she didn't." Rebecca couldn't help it: her voice rose in her agitation, and suddenly she could feel tears pricking her eyelids. As Mr. Lethbridge looked across the desk at her, she willed herself to be more like him: cold and calm. "And now she's dead, and we've still got nothing."

"According to our records—"

"I'm not a liar!"

"Rebecca, please: calm yourself." Mr. Lethbridge leaned his elbows on the desk and sighed again. "I am not calling you a liar. I am just saying that you must be mistaken.

What happened to your mother was unfortunate, but she *was* appropriately compensated. Anything further than that would be special treatment. Accidents happen in every place of work, and if our company were to give out a hundred pounds for every single person affected by them, we would have gone bankrupt a long time ago."

"I didn't say a hundred pounds, sir." Rebecca's eyes had grown wide at the mention of such an enormous sum. "It wasn't even on my mind. I just want enough to be able to pay rent for my sister and me."

"And how much is your rent?"

"Two shillings a week, sir."

"Well, your sister is now working for us, too, is she not?" Mr. Lethbridge raised his eyebrows. "And a piece worker for our company earns four shillings a week. Along with your income, that should be more than enough to pay your rent."

"But the *fines*, sir," Rebecca cried, her desperation growing as she felt her chance slipping away. "My sister was fined a shilling today—that's half the rent—"

"I would advise you both, then, not to incur any more fines." Mr. Lethbridge pointed up at the clock above his desk. "For example, if we carry on this interview any longer, you will miss the bell, and incur a fine for tardiness."

Rebecca rose to her feet, trembling. She felt like a stubborn child as she said, "I want to see Mr. Pillar."

Mr. Lethbridge took up his pen and began to write something. He did not look up as he said, "I believe he is in his office. You are welcome to go and check."

The door to the managing director's office stood ajar, and Rebecca knocked quickly, before she could lose her nerve. "Mr. Pillar, sir?"

"Yes, what is it," said a voice, and Rebecca pushed the door open. She halted a few steps past the threshold as she saw who was sitting at the desk.

"Beg your pardon, sir, but I was hoping to speak to the elder Mr. Pillar."

"Father's gone out," said Edward Pillar. He was sitting behind the desk with a pile of papers before him, but he had the chair sideways and his legs stretched out, gleaming black boots crossed at the ankle. In the corner of his mouth dangled a cigarette, which was nearly spent, and he had his hands propped behind his head. "I thought I closed that door." He cast a sidelong glance at her, and smiled, stubbing out the cigarette. "But it *is* good to see you, my dear. Rebecca, isn't it?"

"You know very well what my name is," said Rebecca, flatly. "And as I can see you're busy, I won't keep you any longer, sir."

"Busy, she says. Wit *and* beauty. No, stay a minute." Edward turned his chair around to face her fully. He was a man of about thirty, with black burnsides and pomade in his hair. He should have been handsome: his full lips, moulded cheekbones and long, dark eyelashes had certainly made him popular among many young women. But taken all together, his face had a hardness to it that Rebecca did not like. She watched him warily, as he continued, "Now, my dear, I hear your sister has come to work here."

"I don't see why that should interest you," Rebecca said frankly. Edward looked at her in surprise, and then laughed.

"No one else speaks to me the way you do, Rebecca. I've always enjoyed it."

"Sir, I will be late for work—"

"Just tell me, is she as pretty as you?" Edward leaned forward on his elbows, with one of his winning smiles. He had a row of fine teeth, that were whiter than anyone else's Rebecca had ever seen. "That's all I want to know."

"Eliza is a child," Rebecca said pointedly. She drew a deep breath. "Now please, sir, I'll have no more of this nonsense. I must go."

"So, *Eliza* is her name. I shall remember that. Wait, I can get the door." Edward hopped out of his seat and crossed the room in a few strides. As he drew the door out fully, he leaned close to Rebecca, and said softly, "My lady."

For the rest of the day at work, no matter what she did, Rebecca could not shake off the scent of cigarette smoke and eau de cologne.

4
HAUNTED

It was haunted: Eliza was convinced of it. She still woke up every morning with the sound of her mother's sobs fading away in her ears; she went to sleep every night and saw again that terrible, lurid glow through the darkness.

The room they rented on Greengoose Lane was small, but Mum had always kept it nicely when she was alive, and now the sisters tried to do the same. There was pretty blue wallpaper, now faded, with a few mould stains that they scrubbed at ineffectually once a week. An aged Queen Victoria stared from her frame down at the table. The oil lamp made things warm and friendly in the evenings. But the porcelain shepherdess, silver locket and framed daguerreotype on the chimney-piece were all covered in dust, because they had been Mum's favourite things, and now Eliza would not let Rebecca touch them.

It had been a horrible death. It was always on Eliza's mind. Her beautiful mother, with tear tracks on her cheeks and her jaw worn away to the bone. The factory had turned her into a night horror, to a thing that glowed in the dark. But at the very end, she had been sweet and patient, her hand caressing Eliza's face while Rebecca hovered in the background.

Having visitors over was always a welcome distraction from such morbid thoughts. Eliza only wished that Rebecca had invited someone other than Sarah O'Brien, who would not let up talking all the way home. When they got in, Sarah dumped her shawl on the old armchair where Mum used to sit and took up the worn volume that had been left on the cushion. "What's this?"

"*Oliver Twist*," Eliza replied shortly, as she went to light the lamp.

"Oh, Mr. Dickens! My pa used to read him to me." Sarah began to thumb through the book, running her dirty fingers over the pages. "I can't read much myself. I can make out people's names all right—ah, the Artful Dodger—I remember *him*…"

"Be careful with it," Eliza said severely, coming up to take the book back from her. "It was my Mum's."

The smile faded from Sarah's lips. Rebecca, tying an apron around her waist, rolled her eyes. "Never mind her. Eliza, help me cut the bread-and-butter." Her hair, which was a darker red than her sister's and much curlier, had been tied back with that garish pink ribbon which she thought was so pretty.

When they were all sitting down to tea, Sarah took up a new subject. "So, you saw her too this morning, I reckon?"

The sisters stared back at her from across the table. "Who?"

"That socialist, Mrs. Besant. She came up to me as I was going into work, wanting to hear my *story*." Sarah shook her head in disbelief, sending her dark fringe shifting back and forth over her forehead. "I tell you, I wouldn't speak to her if she paid me. Not on my life."

"We thought the same thing." Rebecca glanced at her sister, but Eliza was silent, stirring her tea. "It's not worth the risk."

"And who knows what she wants out of it, anyway? I've seen these fine ladies before: they get these ideas into their heads about helping the *deserving poor*." Sarah snorted loudly: Eliza's eyes flickered to her, disgusted. "In no time she'll have moved on to someone else, mark my words."

"I went to Mr. Lethbridge today—" Rebecca started to say, but Eliza interrupted, her eyes still on Sarah.

"You're wrong. Mrs. Besant isn't like those other fine ladies. I know 'cause she used to come to Grosvenor Square when I worked there."

"You never said." Rebecca turned to her sister, surprised.

"She's a friend of Mr. Browning's. And she would sometimes come down to talk to us in the servants' hall." Eliza lifted her chin. "Most of those folks, they don't look at you, not really. But Mrs. Besant did. I *liked* her."

"Well, it costs nothing to be nice," Sarah said. "Fact is, she wants something from us, and it doesn't matter to her if we risk our livelihoods, as long as she looks like she's doing some good." She raised a finger, pointing it at Eliza. "Working in a factory is different to working in a big house. You put a foot wrong, they get someone to replace you, just like that. That's something you've to learn, love."

"If you're talking about what happened with the cutting machine, it's not *my* fault the cord broke," Eliza snapped back. "What was I supposed to do?"

Sarah sighed. "They shouldn't have put you on cutting in the first place. There's a knack to it, when the cord comes loose. All you have to do..."

"Let's talk about something else. Please." In the light of the oil lamp, Rebecca looked weary: the shadows under her eyes turned purple, and tendrils of hair had escaped from her wild mane in the short time they had been sitting down, sticking to her face. But the other two ignored her.

"I could have *lost my hand*," Eliza snapped.

"No, you *couldn't*."

"How do you know?"

"Because I've been working in Pillar and Perkins since I was twelve, and all you've done is skivvy for some fine folk…"

"I was *not* a skivvy! I—"

"Enough, Eliza." Rebecca's face was stern and uncompromising as she looked at her sister. "Sarah's just trying to help."

"Help?" Eliza felt her chest swell with anger, and she chewed and swallowed the last of her bread furiously before pushing to her feet. "I don't need help from any of you." She took her shawl from the hook on the wall, fixed a cap on her head, and rushed for the door.

Outside in the passage, she heard Sarah say, hesitant— "Should we—"

"Let the child do what she wants," was Rebecca's response. "I'm too tired."

Eliza squared her shoulders. This was the *last* time her sister would call her a child. And, she swore, as she came out onto the darkening streets of East London, she would *not* be back.

∽

The sun had just set, and above the elegant white houses of Grosvenor Square, the clear blue sky was tinged with yellow. The Brownings' young coachman had got down to open the door of the carriage house when one of the horses reared her head in alarm. Peter Albright turned with a flap of his cape, and reached up a black-gloved hand to pat her muzzle. "Here, girl, what's the matter?"

Then he heard them too: footsteps, loud on the pavement. Peter stared when he saw who it was, and let go of his horse's bridle, striding up to meet her. "Eliza! What are you doing here?"

"I wanted to see you." Eliza Moss was out of breath, wisps of red hair coming loose from under her cap, but she was smiling. The sight distracted Peter from his worries for a moment. He took her hands and pulled her close to him. That smile was what he had fallen in love with a year before, when he had first caught a glimpse of the Brownings' scullery maid. Her face was sharp and angular, but when she gave one of her wide, toothy smiles, it became all softness, and her blue-green eyes were warm and bright.

"You shouldn't have come," Peter told her, trying to sound stern. "You don't work here anymore. And the Brownings have guests over." He glanced up at the windows of the house. "Come inside, quickly."

Once the horses had been put in the stables and rubbed down, Peter took off his cape and gloves, and brought Eliza into the carriage house. She had been quietly watching him at his work, a thoughtful expression on her face. Now she came forward, at a quick step, and threw her arms around him. Peter hugged her back, glancing over her shoulder at the door, which stood ajar so that a sliver of daylight showed through. "Now, then, what's the matter?"

"Peter, let's run away." Eliza's voice was muffled in his shoulder.

Not sure if he had heard her right, Peter pulled back, holding Eliza at arm's length. She met his gaze with a pleading look. He glanced at the door again—he thought he had heard the crunch of gravel. But in another instant, all was quiet again. He squeezed his eyes shut for a moment. "Eliza, it's not a good time. I said we'd meet at the weekend—let's talk about it then."

"I can't wait any longer." Eliza stepped closer to him, and he looked at her again, warily. "I can't stand that place anymore, I *can't*." She grabbed his hands. "Let's run away, and—and—"

"And what?" Peter said, gently, squeezing her hands. Eliza was only a few years his junior, but she had never seemed younger to him than now. "What do you expect me to do? I've got no money. I can't just wave a magic wand and get you the life you want…"

"Don't talk to me like that." Eliza let go of him again and crossed her arms over her chest. "I'm not a child. I know things cost money. But if I stay any longer in the factory, I know something bad's going to happen. Mum never wanted me to work there in the first place. And I've got a little saved up now—I know *you* do, too—"

"Not enough. Not nearly enough to get us away. *Eliza.*" Peter reached for her, but she backed away. "You worry too much. Nothing bad's going to happen at the factory. You have your sister there to protect you. I'm only asking you to work there for a little while longer. And then, you and I…"

"I can see now," Eliza interrupted. Her eyes were cold and piercing. "You don't want to marry me."

Peter shook his head, gathering his patience. "Eliza, you know I do."

"That's why you didn't want me to tell Rebecca about us." She spat out her words, furious and spiteful. "That's why you didn't stop me getting the job at Pillar and Perkins. You wanted to get away from me."

"I'm going to talk to you like you're a child now, because you're acting like one." Peter came forward and seized her shoulders, looking down into her face. "And you're going to listen. Eliza, like you said, things cost money. And you'll make much more as a piece worker than as a scullery maid. That's why I want you to stick it out in the factory a little longer. Once we've saved up enough, then we can tell your sister, and leave this place behind. Maybe we can even bring her with us, go somewhere in the country, where there's farms and fresh air." He gave her a little shake, and saw the tears winding down her face. "Eliza, I love you. But you know I can't give you much. I told you that when I promised to marry you."

As he let go of Eliza's shoulders, she stepped back, and swallowed. She was shaking as she said, "And now I'm setting you free. I don't want to see you again, Peter. Not ever."

"*Eliza—*" Peter turned, reaching out a hand as she ran out of the carriage house. Slowly, he let it drop to his side. There was no use calling her back when she was in a mood like that. He only hoped she hadn't meant it.

5
IN HIS SIGHTS

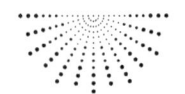

Edward Pillar had stumbled upon the lovers' tête-à-tête by chance, and it had highly amused him. All right, perhaps it hadn't been by *absolute* chance. From listening to them talk, he knew now that the girl—Eliza—used to work in the house as a servant, not so long ago. But all the same, it was not often that he accompanied his father to the Brownings—and more rarely still did he stay for dinner. Of course, the whole evening had been about as riveting as watching paint dry. Henry Browning, who gave such impassioned speeches on labour laws in the House of Commons, couldn't seem to put two words together at his own dinner table without making someone yawn. It was always a pity, Edward reflected, when a man's private life made such an unfavourable contrast to his public one.

The wife and daughter were even worse—neither of them much to look at, and when the men joined them in the drawing room after dinner, they insisted on boring everyone at the piano. One piece might have been charming—two, acceptable—but they just kept *going*, their courage renewed with every word of compliment they received. They even played a duet together. Father kept shooting pointed looks at Edward, the significance of which he understood well enough. He didn't care. As soon as tea was over, he made his escape. Let his father take the carriage home; he would rather walk than stay another minute and feel his soul evaporate with boredom.

A grey dusk had fallen over the square as he stepped out of No. 6, and it looked like rain. Remembering the umbrella that he had left in the carriage, Edward crossed down the alley that led to the quiet service street behind the houses. He was coming over the gravel approach to the mews when he heard the raised voices within and stopped to listen.

The girl was Rebecca's sister. He suspected it as soon as she mentioned the factory, and his suspicions were confirmed when she came running out of the carriage house a few minutes later. He could see right away that it must be the same Eliza, and that she was young, and pretty, and crying—and, from the look of her, most certainly *not* a child. Edward stepped back in case she should see him, but she went running the other way, her long red hair tumbling down her back. He ran a hand over his burnsides and smiled as his imagination caught fire.

It would be something to have the love of a girl like that. A fool like that coachman couldn't appreciate it: it took a more worldly eye, like Edward's, to see the possibilities. Peering through the gap in the door, he had seen the way she threw herself at the boy: he had heard the way her voice trembled with emotion as she begged him to run away with her. And then her anger, her cold, righteous anger, when he refused her. Yes, she would be quite something; Edward could feel it.

6
A GRISLY OPPORTUNITY

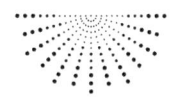

It had been another bad night. In the grey dawn, Eliza woke up sweating, afraid to move, convinced that beside the door stood a figure who would rush forward to claim her if she stretched one hand out from beneath the bedclothes. When she worked up the courage to light the oil lamp, she saw that it was just Rebecca's coat.

After that, she overslept, and had to walk to work alone. It was only fifteen minutes from their lodgings to the factory; they were luckier than the girls who lived further out, in Bromley and Whitechapel and such places. But then again, Eliza reminded herself, those girls had other people around them: parents, sweethearts, friends. Now that Peter was lost to her, all *she* had was Rebecca, and even they weren't speaking at the moment.

She got into work just as the bell rang, and the foreman—not Wilson today, thankfully—assigned her to a bench toward the back of the boxing room. It was a relief to see that she was on filling duty. Her mood did sour somewhat, though, when she saw Sarah straight ahead, sitting in the place she had occupied the day before. And the girl even had the nerve to turn around and give her a smug smile. Grimacing, Eliza turned her attention to her work.

While filling the matchboxes was certainly less frightening than cutting, it was much easier to fire up the matches by accident as you were taking them out of the frames. To Eliza's embarrassment, it happened to her that morning twice in quick succession. The first time, she was quick enough in sweeping away the burnts that the foreman didn't see, though a few of the girls at the end of the row—including Rebecca—glanced at her. The second time, he let her off with a warning. But she felt Rebecca's eyes on her again, and was glad once she had to run downstairs to get another frame.

When she came back into the boxing room, out of breath and hot from the running, she did her best to avoid the other girls' gaze. There was Sarah again, though: as she passed her at the cutting machine, Eliza held her breath, certain that the other girl going to make some snide remark and then she wouldn't be able to control herself, she would lose her temper and snap back and then the foreman would fine her for fighting and Rebecca would be even angrier with her and—

A loud *crack*. It stopped Eliza right in her tracks. She turned and everything was slow, as though in some nightmare. Down at the end of the row, the cord had come loose from the cutting machine and Sarah's hand was caught; it spun tighter and tighter, and then she screamed and reared back in her chair. Eliza pushed forward, but stopped again when she saw the blood, and that Sarah was missing a finger, and that her face was contorted in agony as she sobbed and cried out for help.

People were shouting: a foreman nudged Eliza out of the way and went to help Sarah, winding an arm around her shoulders. She dipped as he tried to lift her, and Eliza ran forward again, this time to help. Together they got her out of the boxing room and down the stairs, and all the while Sarah was whimpering and sobbing and Eliza said whatever came into her head, spoke absolute nonsense just to keep Sarah from screaming outright or looking at what remained of her hand.

Outside in the courtyard, the foreman shouted at one of the pale-faced women who came up to them to get help. Then it was an agonising wait, and someone else came to tie a handkerchief around Sarah's hand to stay the bloodflow, and Eliza kept a hold of her and kept talking—talking, and watching the shaft of sunlight creep across the stone. Pale faces peered out at them through the windows. Then—at last—a cart drew up, and they carried Sarah away.

Someone told Eliza to get back to work—she wasn't sure who. At any rate, when she got back inside, she could only make it up a few steps before she stopped on the stairs, her legs too weak to hold her. The fumes filled her nostrils and the roar of steam engines filled her ears, and then an arm went around her waist and a refined voice spoke in her ear. "Pardon me, but I think you're about to faint. You'd better hold onto me."

∾

It was better than anything he could have planned.

Of course, of *course*, he felt sorry for the girl, Sarah, who had lost her finger. A sad thing for her; after all, what kind of work could one get after that? Of course, he would not have wished such a fate upon anyone.

But here Eliza Moss was now because of it all, stretched out on the sofa in his father's office and sleeping like an angel. He had carried her there after he found her on the stairs, and no one had paid him much mind: they were in too much of a frenzy about the accident. Father was elsewhere, discussing the question of compensation with Mr. Lethbridge. And Edward had done *his* duty, too. He had rescued a girl from collapsing. She had been in a state of absolute shock when he came upon her: white as a sheet and shaking like a leaf. Perhaps another accident might have occurred if not for his quick attention.

And, through the second such manifestation of his good fortune in two days, the girl whom he had rescued just happened to be pretty Eliza. Kneeling by the sofa, Edward gazed down at her sleeping face, and was reaching out to touch one of those pale cheeks when her eyelashes began to flutter open. Quickly he withdrew his hand and watched as she raised herself up on her elbows, taking in the scene around her.

"Where am I?" she said then, in some distress. She tried to sit up, and Edward put a hand to her shoulder. Her eyes landed on him and widened in awe. And then, by degrees, she grew even prettier as a rosy flush came over her cheeks.

"Don't move quite yet," he told her, gently. "You have to drink something for the shock." He rose, straightening, and walked to where his father's crystal decanter of whisky had been placed on one of the shelves. He got a glass and poured in a little of the amber liquid.

"I have to get back to work," Eliza said: she was sitting up properly now. Edward passed her the glass.

"You can stay a little longer. I'll vouch for you."

She looked at him again, the glass in her hand. "Are you— the son?"

Edward nodded, unable to help a little smile. "Yes, my dear. Now drink."

Eliza did as he said, her round eyes still watching him over the glass. She took a mouthful and made a face. Edward laughed, and took the glass back. "Feeling better?"

"Yes, sir." Eliza got to her feet. He reached out to steady her: an unnecessary movement, but one for which he was rewarded by the sound of her quick intake of breath. "I must—thank you, sir, for being so kind to me."

"No thanks are necessary," Edward replied, and as she moved toward the door, he added, "You must allow me to rescue you again."

Eliza turned to stare back at him, a question on her parted lips. Edward smiled to show her that he was in jest. "I enjoy rescuing pretty girls."

The flush in her cheeks deepened: she smiled, a little uncertainly, and murmured something indistinct before she left. The door swung closed behind her, and Edward walked back to his father's desk. He collapsed into the leather chair with a satisfied sigh and reached for a cigarette.

7
TIME TO CRY

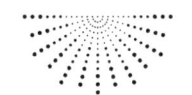

Rebecca knew she would never forget the sound of her friend's screams, even if she lived for a hundred years. Feral, bloodcurdling, made up of pure panic and agony, they reached into a place deep inside her and shook, and rattled, until everything was upside down. She had seen accidents happen at the factory before, but never to someone she knew as well as Sarah—and *never* to someone who took such care with their work.

She and her sister clung tight to each other on that terrible evening, their argument forgotten. Eliza had come back to the boxing room around an hour after Sarah's accident, and no one had reprimanded her, which was curious in itself—but what concerned Rebecca more was the dazed look on her sister's face, which was still there now as they walked home from work. The night air was cold on their faces, the greasy light of the gas lamps making little splashes on the dark pavement ahead, and neither of them spoke.

By the time they got home, Rebecca knew what she had to do. As Eliza went to light the lamp, *she* went straight to the basket in the corner of the room. She picked up dirty dresses and aprons, rummaging through the pockets, her movements clumsy and feverish. After a few minutes, her sister asked from behind her,

"Becca? What are you looking for?" Her voice was hoarse from crying.

In answer, Rebecca drew out the card. Without turning, she said, "If Sarah wasn't safe at work, then none of us are."

With a sniff, Eliza said, "I could have—told someone that machine wasn't working right. I could have said something."

"You did." Rebecca turned, in a whirl of black skirt. "They didn't listen." She swallowed and put a hand to her chest as she attempted to slow her own breath. "You know, I've been working in Pillar and Perkins since I was fifteen. Seven years. And I've seen this happen too many times. I *can't* keep doing nothing."

Eliza wiped her nose on her sleeve, and curled her hands around her back, hugging herself in the cold as she sat down on their bed. "So what are you going to do?"

"I'm going to write to Mrs. Besant," Rebecca said, slowly, as though she could hardly believe the words coming out of her mouth. "Because it's time someone came and helped us."

8
GENTLEMEN AND FACTORY GIRLS

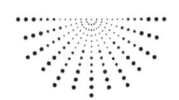

The house on North Audley Street was finer than any Rebecca Moss had ever visited before, and as she was shown into the drawing room, she could not help gazing around at the pretty wallpaper, the piano, and the writing desk.

"Mrs. Besant is busy at the moment," the maid told her, taking her coat. "You may wait for her here."

"Thank you." Rebecca gingerly sat on the edge of an armchair and pretended not to notice the way the maid was eyeing her attire. It was a cold evening, so she had put on a red wool petticoat and two linsey skirts. She was wearing her mother's blue jacket on top, and the undersleeves that she had washed last night showed through snowy white. Her black bonnet had also belonged to Mum, and she was careful as she took it off, tying the strings around her neck.

The maid shut the door behind her with a disapproving sniff, and then the room was silent for a time. Every now and then, Rebecca fancied she could hear raised voices from upstairs; she wondered if the servants were arguing about something. *So much for maids being more dignified than factory girls.* She smiled at the thought of how much that would annoy Eliza if she said it to her.

But it was nice to sit still for a while, especially after such a long day of sweat and noise, at the end of which she had hurried home to change and then set out for the long march to Mayfair. It was Friday, and more than two weeks had passed since Sarah's accident. Rebecca had not been to see her yet: she was dreading the prospect, even as she felt herself torn up with concern. It would be hard to see her friend suffering and know that she could do nothing to help; but maybe, after all, Mrs. Besant could change that.

When she had been waiting for about a quarter of an hour, she heard a door opening and closing, and the maid came in again with a young man in tow. "You may wait here, sir," she told him, just as she had told Rebecca. He sat down on the sofa with a sigh. Beyond a nod in Rebecca's general direction, he did not acknowledge her presence or look at her. She wondered who he was. Might he be Mrs. Besant's son? But then why would the maid have sent him here to wait? And he wasn't really dressed like other gentlemen she had seen: he was wearing a faded brown waistcoat and old-fashioned trousers in a checked pattern.

As the minutes ticked by, the voices from upstairs rising and falling, Rebecca tried not to stare at the other guest too much, but that proved impossible as he started to fidget more and more. He would take a notebook out and scribble in it, his blond fringe flopping over his forehead; a moment later he would cast it aside again with a sigh. He did this several times, until she finally asked,

"What are you doing?"

The young man looked up with a start. He had pale grey eyes behind his glasses. Rebecca had not been sure how to address him, but at his look of surprise, she saw that he was a gentleman, and felt embarrassed for her directness. "I'm sorry, sir."

With a flap of his hand, he dismissed both question and apology, and returned his attention to his work. "I hope she doesn't take much longer." He had an Irish accent, which Rebecca noticed was slightly more refined than Sarah's. "We have a meeting in half an hour."

"Are you in the Fabian Society too?"

He nodded and pointed with his pen to the ceiling above as the sound of another shout came echoing down. "That's her husband."

Rebecca stared up. "You mean Mrs. Besant's husband? Making all that noise?"

"Wasting her time, as he always does. They're separated, you see. He's a clergyman, has a parish in Lincolnshire. But she has to put up with his visits if she wants to see her son and daughter."

"And does he…" Rebecca stopped herself in time. "It's none of my business, I'm sure."

The gentleman just laughed at that and returned to his notebook. A moment later, thunderous footsteps came down the stairs outside the drawing room. One door slammed, and then another, and Rebecca, unable to resist the urge, turned her head to look through the window. Outside, she saw a short man, fitting his arms into a long black coat as he stormed down the pavement and out of sight.

"Rebecca, isn't it?" Mrs. Besant had come into the drawing room. She looked weary but stern, her shoulders squared in her black gown and her small, deep-set eyes glittering with something like determination. "Thank you for your note. I am sorry to have kept you waiting so long. And—oh. Thomas."

"I've brought the figures on the shareholders of Pillar and Perkins," the gentleman said, brandishing his notebook. Mrs. Besant stared, then put a hand to her forehead.

"The meeting. I forgot. Rebecca, I am giving a lecture at Essex Hall tonight, so I'm afraid we'll have to keep this interview brief. Come with me, come with me. I am sure you had a long walk here and I don't want it to have been in vain..."

In some confusion, Rebecca rose with a rustling of skirts and followed the lady out of the drawing room. She glanced at the gentleman before leaving, but he was writing something down and did not look back at her.

9
FALLING FOUL

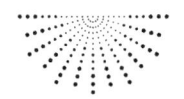

As the carriage set off from North Audley Street at a slow trot, Thomas Barnwall began to tap his foot on the floor. After a minute or two, Mrs. Besant looked across at him, and shook her head.

"Really, Thomas. That's not going to make us go any faster."

"I'm sorry," he said, ceasing the motion. "I just don't want to be late."

"Well, we're *going* to be late." Mrs. Besant glanced out the window at the passing Georgian houses. It was starting to rain. More quietly, she said, "That is something I could not help."

"What did he want?" Thomas asked, after a moment. "Your husband?"

"Frank?" She sighed heavily. "He wants me to stop speaking publicly about Pillar and Perkins. When I told him that was quite impossible, as I have already pledged my assistance to many of these girls, and as there is no way to give them assistance without bringing attention to the question in the first place... well, naturally, he was quite upset."

"I can't say I really blame him in this case," Thomas said, and as she turned to stare at him, he held up his hands. "What I mean to say is that Richard Pillar is a powerful man. Once he hears of your involvement, he is bound to make things difficult for you."

"I'm not afraid of him. In any case, those girls… If you'd heard them speak about the conditions there, Thomas, you would know what I mean. The girl who came today…" Mrs Besant shook her head. "I only wish I had been able to talk to her for longer."

Thomas thought of the factory girl in her garish clothes, sitting demurely in the drawing room and watching him when she thought he couldn't see. Despite himself, he smiled. "You ought to have brought her along to the meeting. Perhaps she could have given the lecture in your place."

"It's no laughing matter, Thomas." Mrs. Besant leaned forward, then reached for the support of her armrest as the carriage ran over a pothole. "This girl, Rebecca, lives with her sister in one room. She earns eight shillings in a week, and her sister earns four—that is, if they are lucky enough not to be fined, which is something none of the girls whom I have spoken to seem able to avoid. Their father was a docker, and he died in an accident some years ago. Their *mother* died more recently from 'phossy jaw', as the poor child called it, and the company has done nothing to help them since."

"That *is* unfortunate," said Thomas quietly.

"And what is more, her friend lost a finger in an accident at the factory two weeks ago, and *again*, the company seems to have done nothing to support her." Mrs. Besant fell back against her seat again, shaking her head. "It is not unfortunate, Thomas, it is *inhuman*. I wish I could speak to her, too—the girl who had the accident, I mean. Rebecca gave me her address. But I have interviews tomorrow with several others, and I must meet Mr. Browning…" She stopped short and looked at Thomas pointedly. Seeing where her mind was heading, he began to protest.

"No. Impossible. Quite impossible."

"Impossible, for you to go to Bromley and interview a few of these girls in my stead?"

"I shall be working on my book," Thomas said, weakly.

"But your book is about this very thing, is it not? How do you expect to learn about workers in the East End without speaking to them yourself?"

Thomas shifted in his seat uncomfortably. "I would prefer to steer clear of anyone in the employ of Richard Pillar."

"You fear his retaliation?" Mrs. Besant's stern eyes were fixed on his. "If I write something about these girls, Thomas, it will be my name upon the document, not yours. I am simply asking for a little help in conducting the interviews..."

"Is that supposed to make me feel better?" he snapped, and she blinked, startled. "I don't want you falling foul of that man, either. What am *I* supposed to do if something happens to you?"

Her expression had softened, but she moved to put more distance between them as he leaned forward in his seat. "I am more fortunate than them. And with your help, I *know* that I can change things for these girls without threatening my own safety. *Thomas.* If you're afraid, think of how much more afraid they must be."

He raised his grey eyes to look at her again, his expression abashed. Mrs. Besant slowly began to nod, as though in response to someone he could not hear, and when next she spoke, her voice had taken on that sonorous quality that she usually reserved for her speeches. "'The people are silent. I will be the advocate of this silence. I will speak for the dumb. I will speak of the small to the great and of the feeble to the strong. I will interpret the complaints ill-pronounced, that through ignorance and suffering, man is forced to utter.'"

There was a pause. And it was infuriating, because Thomas knew exactly what she had done, but still he felt stirred, deep in his soul. It was just the same feeling as when he had first seen her speak to a crowd, five years before, not long after he had arrived in London. He smiled wryly, as the carriage pulled to a stop outside Essex Hall.

"Very well. When you quote Victor Hugo, I cannot argue with you." As the coachman opened the door, Thomas stepped out first, and then handed Mrs. Besant onto the dark, wet pavement. "Come, we'd better hurry. Here's your speech."

"What would I do without you, Thomas?" She smiled at him, and he took her arm, a full head taller than her, as they made their way into the hall.

10
WHAT PEOPLE SAY ABOUT FACTORY GIRLS

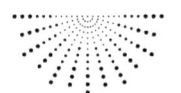

It started raining not long after Rebecca left Mayfair, and by the time she got onto Fleet Street, St. Paul's dome was no more than a dim shape, blotted out by washes of grey that ran down the evening sky like tears. Her lovely clothes were soaked through, and she knew it would take hours for them to dry in front of the range.

Eliza walked out as far as the Old Ford Road to meet her. The rain had stopped by then. When Rebecca saw her waiting on Bow Bridge, she stopped for a moment and smiled. Then she ran forward to seize her sister's hands. "You shouldn't have come out. I hope you didn't get wet."

"I missed you," Eliza replied, and passed her dry shawl around Rebecca's shoulders.

They passed over the footbridge toward the old china works. The match factory was somewhere behind, in a great tangle of buildings, and below them was the River Lea. There was a boat

moored on its far bank, its long mast stretching up as though it would pierce right into the sky. Rebecca could hear the water slapping against it. When she looked down at the water, she could see the dark mud swirling and churning. It made her feel funny.

"Eliza," she said, without looking up at her sister. "Don't come out here alone anymore."

"*You're* alone," Eliza pointed out.

"It's different. I'm careful."

"*I'm* careful, too. How did it go with Mrs. Besant, anyway?"

Rebecca considered for a moment. They had come off the bridge now, and onto a narrow street. Beside them stretched a row of drab, dark houses. Shadows moved to and fro behind the windows. She hurried her sister on, toward their own street. "I wish you'd been there with me. I felt… silly."

"Silly?" Eliza repeated.

"Well, it's like what you said about working in the Brownings… it's a different world. Everyone looked at me funny."

"I *told* you not to wear all those colours."

Rebecca rolled her eyes, and continued, "Even Mrs. Besant, who was so kind… She looked like she felt sorry for me all the time we were talking. And I'd barely sat down before she was hurrying me out again."

"I'm glad I didn't go," said Eliza, with a vengeance.

"Anyway, she wants to meet me again." They got inside their building and made their way up the narrow, creaky stairs. "At Sarah's, when I go to see her tomorrow." Rebecca turned to Eliza. "Come with me this time."

Her sister avoided her gaze. "I couldn't, Becca. What if she recognised me?"

"So what?"

"I'd be too *ashamed*." Eliza's voice rang out a little too loudly, just as they were passing one of the neighbours' doors, and she clapped her hands over her mouth.

"Ashamed?" Rebecca repeated. "What's there to be ashamed about? We do honest work, we go to church every Sunday. Our parents were good and decent, hard-working in their way."

Eliza was shaking her head. "You know what people say about factory girls."

"'Course I do. None of it's true, though, is it?"

Her sister was silent. Rebecca studied her for a moment more, then sighed. "Fine. I'll go on my own." She pushed open the door to their room. Musty air rose up to greet them, and with a sigh, she began to peel off her soaking layers. Eliza went to light the lamp, and the evening drew in around them, warm and cosy after the cold, wet streets, and they did not speak of the matter again.

11
BONNER'S GATE

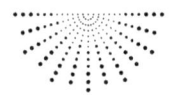

For many of the workers in Bow, Victoria Park was the closest thing to a back garden that they had. It was bounded by two canals, and on a Saturday afternoon, there were always several different groups preaching on the central lawn: Calvinists, socialists, anarchists—even Mormons.

Edward Pillar steered clear of them all, and found a bench near the drinking fountain, where he sat casually and took out a book. From here, he had a clear view of Bonner's Gate, and every now and then he would glance up from the print to see who was coming in. He kept close track on his pocket watch. For the last two Saturdays, he had seen Eliza come through that gate at midday. She would wander around the park for about an hour, sometimes longer. The only problem was her sister, who never seemed to leave her side. Edward knew better than to approach the girl when Rebecca Moss was standing guard.

He had been interested in Rebecca for a time, after all, and the stubborn little thing had never budged.

Every girl was different. That was a lesson Edward had learned over the past few years. He remembered, at first, that he had been more eager and impatient in his pursuits of the fairer sex; now, at the more dignified age of thirty, he liked to take his time. It was important to observe the girl first for a while and refine his technique. For instance, last Saturday, he had noticed that when the Moss sisters sat down together for a while, Eliza had taken out a book to read. *That* had been surprising, certainly, but he had also seen an opportunity in it, and so today he had brought one along with him.

Of course, it was important to remember, as well, that even *his* patience had limits. He knew a lost cause when he saw one: Rebecca was a good example. And so, when he checked his pocket watch and found that it was half past twelve, with still no sign of Eliza, he made up his mind to leave.

And then—he lifted his head again to check one last time, just to make sure, and there she was, walking through the gate. Edward's heart began to beat faster. *Why were you so late, you silly thing?* But it could not have been more perfect. She was alone: no sister in sight. She was even prettier out of her factory clothes, too: she had on a shawl, but it had slipped down from her shoulders, and in the warm weather, she did not seem too concerned about adjusting it. And the sunlight lit up the fairer strands in her red hair—Edward had to remind himself to look down at his book before she sensed his gaze.

She disappeared for a few minutes as she was walking around the perimeter of the park, but it was not long before she came upon his path—as he had known she would. Edward glimpsed her red shawl out of the corner of his eye, and slowly turned a page in his book. He had been reading the same sentence over and over for some time.

Her footsteps crunched over the gravel path as they came toward him. She was walking slowly, as though she wanted to take in everything. She passed him by, making for the drinking fountain—and then, just as Edward turned another page in his book, she doubled back and came up to his bench.

"Mr.—Pillar?" Her voice was shy and unsure. He looked up, and feigned surprise.

"How do you do?"

"My name's Eliza," she told him, as though he could have forgotten. "I—didn't know that you came here, sir."

Edward shrugged lightly, and gave her a little smile. "I like this place. It's—peaceful." And of course, just as he had uttered that last word, the booming voice of a new speaker echoed across the park. He winced inwardly.

But Eliza, oblivious to the irony, burst forth in agreement. "I think so too." Her smile was dazzling—so wide and innocent. "I love coming here. Normally Rebecca comes, too, but today she's visiting our friend..." The smile dimmed. "The girl who had the accident."

"Ah. Of course." He made his voice quiet and sombre. "What a terrible thing that was."

"Yes, it *was* terrible. I wanted to—to thank you, sir, for being so kind to me, when it happened. But I think..." Eliza stopped, looking embarrassed.

"What is it?" Edward said kindly. "You may speak frankly with me, you know." As she continued to hesitate, he put a hand on the space beside him. "Come, why don't you sit a moment."

"I—really oughtn't..." Eliza was blushing now, glancing around to see that no one was watching: but the crowds were centred around the main lawn, and most of the path was deserted. "All right, just for a moment."

She sat, as far from him as the bench would allow, and as Edward closed his book, spoke up again. "I think… they could do more for her. She hasn't got anything since the accident."

"By *they*, do you mean my father?" Edward said bluntly, and as she began to protest, he held up a hand. "It's quite all right. I agree that his response has been unfortunate. But, between you and me…" He leaned in, just a fraction, and noticed that she did not flinch away. "I don't see how he could have done otherwise. The company, you see, has run into a bit of trouble."

"Trouble?"

"Oh, your jobs are safe enough for the moment, I should think. But it is difficult to afford to compensate workers in times like this. And the girl—Sarah, is it? The girl, I am told, has a father who works."

"Well—yes." Eliza was evidently mulling his words over. "I didn't think of that." She glanced at him, and then at the book in his hands. "May I ask, sir, what you're reading?"

Edward held up the book so she could see the title. "*Bleak House*," she exclaimed. "I've heard that's very long—and difficult."

"I have read it many times," he said, with a smile. "Would you like to borrow it?"

"I…" In this light, her eyes looked very blue, with only a hint of green. They met his, and lingered, and her lip trembled a little. "Sir, you're very kind, but I couldn't…"

Edward passed the book into her hands. There was a moment of brief contact, before he withdrew his own hands. "Try it. See what you think. And you may return it to me whenever you like." He rose from his bench and took up his hat. She was still staring at him. "Good day, Eliza."

There was no need to wait for her response. He knew that she would come again. He had seen it in her eyes. She would follow him down this path, if he played his cards right—and if her sister didn't do anything to interfere. It was the same with all of them, Edward reflected as he strolled away through the greenery of the park. Whether they were ladies or factory girls, whether they were innocent or wise in the ways of the world, deep down, they all wanted the same thing. Deep down, they were all bad.

12
THE O'BRIENS

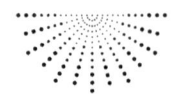

The O'Briens' house was on a squalid street in a dark corner of Bromley. It was a sunny afternoon when Rebecca arrived, but the rooftops overhead leaned close to one another, and the few rays of sunlight that dripped down between them were cold and dirty.

A tiny boy opened the door when she knocked and gazed up at her with blue eyes round as saucers. He did not seem to know what to do, until Sarah came up and gently eased him out of the way. "Go back and help Dad with the fire, Simon." She looked up at Rebecca, who had tears in her eyes. "Oh, come on in, and don't be looking at me like that. There's plenty to do before her Ladyship comes."

The place was not much bigger than the space Rebecca and Eliza shared, considering how many there were in the family. There was a narrow passage, then a kitchen and a bedroom, and then, a series of stone steps up to an attic where the children, including Sarah, all slept. The girls started by sweeping up these steps. Sarah's injured hand was bandaged, and though she took more breaks than Rebecca, she seemed determined to help.

"At least it wasn't my right hand," she told Rebecca, as they worked. "I can manage all right with just one. Lily—Lily! Bring the stuff."

Sarah's younger sister came running with a bucket. In it was a mixture of boiled glue, whiting, and pipeclay in two quarts of water. First the three of them rinsed the steps, then they laid the mixture on with a flannel and left it to dry. They did the same with the kitchen floor and the hearthstone, cleaning around Sarah's father Pat, who had finished stoking the fire and was reading the newspaper. Two of Sarah's brothers, including the little Simon, helped them carry more coals from the back of the house.

"Be sure and keep it good and warm," said Pat O'Brien, lowering his paper for a moment to address them. He was mostly bald, with deep ridged lines on his forehead, and dark eyes that were just like his daughter's. "I don't want our guest thinking we can't afford a coal fire."

By the time they had finished sweeping up the passage and scrubbing the entrance step with sand, it was nearly two o'clock, the time that Mrs. Besant had said she would drop over. Rebecca wiped her forehead, which was damp with sweat. She was wearing an old print dress under one of her work aprons, since her nice clothes were still drying at home. Sarah had loaned her a scrap of blue cloth to wrap around her hair as they cleaned. Her friend was sitting now at the kitchen table, her head down. "Someone put on a kettle," she said without looking up. "Our guest will want tea. Lily..."

"You need to rest," Rebecca said, coming to crouch beside her friend. She swallowed as she saw how pale her face was. "I'll tell Mrs. Besant you're not well."

"I'm all right," Sarah said, with a sigh. Her bad hand was cradled against her chest. "It always hurts for a bit after I change the dressing."

Rebecca sighed, and put a hand to her friend's shoulder. They both started at the sound of a knock on the front door. Simon, who had been playing with a bit of string, dropped what he was doing and went running.

"Simon—" Sarah dropped her head, weary. "You go after him, Becca, will you."

Rebecca did as her friend said, following Simon into the passage. "Wait a minute, love, and we'll answer it together," she told him, and picked him up, resting him on her hip as she went to open the door. She blinked as she saw who it was. "Oh."

"You were expecting Mrs. Besant, no doubt," said the Irish gentleman from the day before. "Since she is busy with interviews today, I have come in her place. I don't believe

I have introduced myself yet: my name is Thomas Barnwall."

∼

The fire was unbearably hot, and Thomas didn't know whether they needed it for the girl, Sarah, or whether it was just the way they lived all the time. Either way, it was the first thing he noticed when he came into the dingy kitchen, and he had barely been sitting down five minutes before his forehead was dripping with sweat. He took out his handkerchief as discreetly as he could but caught the eye of the girl's father as he was dabbing his forehead with it.

"Er… and how long did you work in Pillar and Perkins?" he asked Sarah, turning back to the table. He could still feel Mr. O'Brien's eyes on him.

"Ten years. I started when I was twelve."

"I see." Thomas scribbled this down in his notebook. He was using shorthand, and it was a good thing, too, as he had noticed more than once the girls craning their necks to try and see what he was writing. "And your parents…?"

"I work in the lumber mill on Bow Common," said O'Brien from behind Thomas. "That's where we make the splints that go to Fairfield for the matches."

"Ah. Thank you." Another scribble. "And your mother—"

"Gone back home to Cork." O'Brien spoke for his daughter again, forcing Thomas to turn around and meet his gaze. "She used to make matches, too, when she was here."

"I see," Thomas repeated. He could feel a drop of sweat winding its way down his temple but didn't dare wipe it away with that man staring him down. "And, er —Sarah— do any of your brothers or sisters work in Pillar and Perkins?" He had noticed a few children around the place, though they had all disappeared when the interview started. The girl he had met in Mrs. Besant's house— Rebecca—had been carrying one of them when she answered the door and seemed annoyed when Thomas had asked if it was her brother.

There was a rustle of newspaper as O'Brien—mercifully— returned to his reading, allowing Sarah to answer the question. "No, thank the Lord. Lily was going to start next year—she's the second oldest—but we won't let her now. Not after what happened to me."

"Yes, and that was one of the things that I wanted to ask about," said Thomas. "Is it true that you've received no support from the management since your accident?"

"Nothing," Sarah said. She lifted her bandaged hand onto the table, turned it palm upwards so that he could see the stump where her index finger should have been. Thomas swallowed. "This is what they did to me. They paid for the doctor that kept me from bleeding out. Nothing else. I've been there ten years, like I said, never made a mistake with my work before. There was something wrong with that machine, and they knew, and did nothing to fix it."

It was a horrible sight, and yet Thomas felt he could not look away. "I am... sorry that this happened to you."

"You don't have to be sorry, son." Out of the corner of his eye, Thomas saw O'Brien fold up his paper and put it down on his lap. "You can help stop it happening to someone else." He braced his hands on his knees and leaned forward. "You're Irish, too, is that right?"

"I'm from Dublin, yes," said Thomas, stiffly. Sarah was shaking her head at her father, but he ignored her.

"And I take it you care about helping your fellow countrymen and women? There's around two thousand people working in the match factory, most of 'em Irish or with Irish parents. Did you know *that*?"

"I didn't." Thomas took up his pen again, and with an air of decision, turned to Rebecca. She had not spoken yet in the course of the interview, though he had sensed her watching him for much of it. He did not mind her gaze as much as he minded O'Brien's. "Mrs. Besant mentioned that your sister is also working in Fairfield: is that correct?"

She nodded; she looked almost pleased. But as her lips were moving to respond, O'Brien—who had evidently not finished his interrogation—spoke up again.

"Do *you* work, son, if you don't mind my asking?"

"Dad..." Sarah started to say.

"No, I *don't* mind, sir." Thomas finished writing and stubbed his pen with such force that the nib broke, blotting the page. He put it away quickly and turned his chair around with a scrape to face O'Brien. The heat of the fire blazed at his face. "At the moment, I am doing clerical work for the Edison Telephone Company. I am also writing a book about the long Depression, with particular focus on workers here in the East End."

"And would you say you're an expert, then? Seems to me you don't talk to the likes of us very often."

"Dad, he's only trying to help," said Sarah, who looked pained.

"Is it *helping* to write some book no one's ever going to read?" O'Brien folded up his paper and used it to point to Thomas as he addressed his daughter. "I've told you before and I'll tell you again, Sarah, talking to folk like this is a waste of time. Men like Richard Pillar are tight with their purse-strings, and losing some of his cash is the only thing that'll scare him enough to change his mind."

"I think I had better take my leave, since it is clear I am not welcome here." Thomas rose to his feet and gathered up his things as calmly as he could. No one attempted to stop him, but as he was moving for the threshold, he turned back to face the trio. From here, the firelight made all of their faces look crude and badly drawn, like unfinished sculptures. He fixed his eyes on O'Brien. "But if you're talking of a strike, sir, that is the *very* thing we want to avoid. With Richard Pillar, it is not just money at stake, as you suggest. The bad publicity arising from our investigation *will* force him into making changes. He is a Liberal, after all, and has his reputation to uphold. A strike should be a last resort for all of you." With a bow, "Thank you for your time."

Out in the passage, it took a moment for his eyes to adjust to the dimness. Even when they had, he found he could not locate his coat and hat. In the court outside, he could hear children playing. Their voices drifted in toward Thomas, setting him even more on edge, and with a start he realised that he was trembling with anger. It had been a long time since he had met someone from his own country—though, the way O'Brien had looked at him, he might as well have been from Timbuktu.

Catching his breath, Thomas leaned a hand against the wall. As the door opened, he quickly took it away again.

"I've got your things, sir," said Rebecca, closing the door with her free hand. "I put them away for safekeeping. In case the children…"

"Thank you," said Thomas, exhaling heavily as he took his coat from her. She watched him as he put his arms through the black sleeves, and then handed him his hat. Today she was not so much the gaudy bird she had appeared to be before, or perhaps it was simply that her colours looked less garish outside of Mrs. Besant's drawing room. She still had the bit of blue cloth wrapped around her hair. That had been the first thing Thomas noticed when she answered the door; it made him think of something, a painting he had once seen, perhaps.

"You were very quiet today," he said to her, fixing his hat. "Didn't you have anything to say?"

She tilted her head, considering. "I'm still not sure."

"You mean about speaking to us? I confess I wasn't sure about the idea at first, either." Thomas paused, adjusting his hat. "But you can trust her: Mrs. Besant. She is always true to her word. If she says she can help you, then help you she will."

"And what about you, sir?" Rebecca asked his back, as he was opening the door. He held it with one hand, looking back into the dim passage where she stood. "Are *you* going to help us?"

"Of course," Thomas said, after a moment. "I will help Mrs. Besant in whatever way I can—interview as many of you as she needs me to, so that we can make a thorough investigation of Pillar and Perkins and collect our findings."

"Then you'll want to talk to my sister, too. You did ask about her after all, didn't you?" Rebecca stepped forward and held out a hand. "Give me paper and pen, sir, so I can write our address."

A little bewildered, Thomas did as she said, and watched as she scrawled with the broken nib, frowning at the blotted ink. Finally she looked up, handing the paper back, and he saw the challenge in her eyes, daring him to say no. "If it suits you to come next Saturday at the same time, we will be at home."

"Very well," Thomas heard himself say, though later he would wonder what exactly he had agreed to. "I will see you then."

"Goodbye, Mr. Barnwall."

13
BLEAK HOUSE

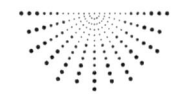

It was starting to get dark, and there was still no sign of Rebecca. Eliza was reading *Bleak House* when the oil lamp started to flicker. She looked up, saw the wicked shadows it threw across the ceiling, and her breath caught in her throat. Queen Victoria was glaring down at her from the picture above the table. "No," she whispered, and then she heard them—footsteps stomping through the passage outside their room, a heavy sigh, a *thump thump*—

"Sorry, I'm late." Rebecca came in, breathless, and untied the strings of her bonnet as she kicked the door closed. "We can have jam with our tea today! Sarah gave me some. Well—what's wrong with you?"

"You scared me," Eliza murmured.

"Come on, help me lay the table."

It was not until later, when they were getting ready for bed, that her older sister spotted *Bleak House*. Rebecca was going to close the window when she saw it on the chair where Eliza had left it. She stopped and picked up the book, running her hand over the binding. Quietly, reverently, "Eliza, where did you get this? It's beautiful."

Eliza was sitting on the bed, brushing her hair. The oil lamp was burning low, and it was so cold that she had not yet worked up the courage to undress, though her legs were tucked under the bedclothes for warmth. "One of my friends from the Brownings gave it to me."

"That's very kind," Rebecca said, and did not question her sister further as she put down the book. "Sarah was asking for you today. You know they still haven't given her anything?"

"I'm sure they will." Eliza's voice was confident. "It's probably just difficult at the moment."

"Difficult?" Rebecca was unable to help the edge that crept into her voice. With fingers trembling from the cold, she began to unlace her stays.

"Because the company's in trouble. Didn't you know?"

"Who told you that?"

"I can't remember." Eliza lowered her hairbrush and ran a hand over the worn bristles. "One of the girls. Everyone's been talking about it."

"Have they?" Rebecca folded up her stays and wrapped her arms around herself, shivering in her shift. "Because Mrs. Besant told me they got a dividend of twenty per cent from their shareholders this year."

"I don't know what that means."

"It means Mr. Pillar and his managers are making a lot of money." Rebecca hurried across to the bed and took a portion of the covers. "Hurry up and undress, won't you, before I freeze to death."

"Maybe you shouldn't believe everything Mrs. Besant says," Eliza said, ignoring the last part of her sister's response.

"I thought you liked her." Rebecca turned to stare at her sister. "Whose side are you on, anyway? Don't you hate working at Fairfield?"

"I've got used to it," Eliza said neutrally. "Like you said I would."

The hairs on the back of Rebecca's neck prickled. She felt odd, in the grip of some fear she could not identify. "What are you not telling me? *Look* at me, Eliza."

But her sister just moved out of her reach and began to undress, in utter silence. Once the oil lamp had been extinguished, Rebecca listened to Eliza tossing and turning for what seemed like hours, before sleep finally came to claim her weary limbs.

14

HEARTS OF STONE

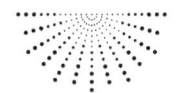

Outside Bow Church, a statue of the former Prime Minister had been erected some years before and paid for by Richard Pillar. William Gladstone stood on a marble plinth, with one hand clutching a roll of parchment and the other extended toward those below him. This hand, outstretched magnanimously towards the masses, had been painted red not long after the unveiling of the statue. No one knew who had done it, but the story went that after Mr. Pillar decided to stop a shilling out of the girls' wages every week for the upkeep of the statue, some of them had retaliated by cutting themselves and letting their blood drip onto the marble.

Rebecca wasn't sure if she believed it. She certainly knew *she* had never done anything like that. Up until a few weeks ago, the thought of even speaking to someone outside the factory about the conditions there would have seemed the height of rebellion. Work had always just been work for her. Before Pillar and Perkins, it had been the packing warehouse on Mile End Road. Before the warehouse, it had been school and learning her letters.

But on that Sunday, as she passed under the red right hand of William Gladstone, she couldn't help looking up and smiling. Sarah noticed—the O'Briens had caught up with Rebecca and Eliza after service—and hung back to speak to her. "*You* look happy."

"It's a nice day," Rebecca replied casually.

"Oh, it's more than that. You're thinking about that Mr. Barnwall, aren't you?" Sarah nudged her. "I saw the way you were looking at him yesterday."

"Don't be silly." Rebecca rolled her eyes. "It isn't as if a gentleman like that would think of me, anyway."

"So, you *do* like him!" Sarah was grinning from ear to ear now. Partly because it made her glad to see her friend happy again—and partly because hearing the words spoken aloud sent a warm thrill through her—Rebecca did not contradict her.

"I've arranged for him to come see us next week. So he can interview Eliza, of course," she added, hastily.

At this, Sarah burst into delighted laughter, that echoed around the churchyard. It was so loud that Eliza turned back to look at them reprovingly. She was walking a little way ahead on the path, hand-in-hand with one of Sarah's little sisters.

"What's so funny?" Rebecca demanded. "Like I said, I know better than to expect anything from a gentleman like him."

"Of course," Sarah said, regaining control of herself, and her tone grew almost sombre as she turned to look at her. "But you should be careful, Becca. *He* might expect something from you."

Rebecca raised her eyebrows at her friend. "You met him too, Sarah. Did he look like a ladies' man to you?"

"No," Sarah said, and they both started laughing again.

"Do you have to be so loud?" Eliza stopped on the path to let them catch up with her, while the children ran ahead to their father. "I'm ashamed to be seen with you."

"Oh, come on, Eliza," said Sarah, slinging an arm around the younger girl's shoulders. "Let us have our fun. Why don't you…"

"Eliza."

The girls turned around at the sound of the unfamiliar voice. They had come to the entrance of the churchyard, and by the iron-wrought gates, a fellow in a dark cape and top hat was standing. He looked like a servant—a groom or coachman, perhaps. As they stared at him, he took off his hat, ran a hand over black, curly hair, and again said,

"Eliza." His eyes flicked between the three of them. "I have to talk to you."

"Go on ahead," said Eliza to the girls, so sharply that they obeyed without protest. When they had gone a little way, Rebecca looked back at the gates, but her sister was already running to catch up with them, one hand on her cap to keep it from blowing away. The young man had vanished.

"Who was *that?*" Rebecca asked, with a glance at Sarah.

Eliza shrugged. "No one important."

15

OUT OF THE FRYING PAN

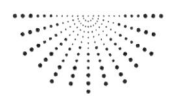

It had been a month since Thomas Barnwall had had the chance to work on his book. He did not think he had ever been so busy in all his life. He buzzed through his days with boundless energy: in the mornings he worked at a desk in the Edison Telephone Company; the afternoons he spent with Annie Besant at her house, poring over dozens of documents about Pillar and Perkins that dated back as far as twenty years, and the evenings were often taken up with interviews, when the matchwomen had finished their shifts.

Sometimes he and Annie would go together, but more often than not, they would split up for expediency: they visited lodging-houses and tenements all over the East End, in Whitechapel, Hackney and Bromley. Thomas interviewed the Moss sisters in Bow two more times after Rebecca had given him their address, and though he found that he could not get much information out of the younger one, Eliza—she was quiet and sullen, often suspicious—her sister proved surprisingly useful in drawing her fellow workers into the project.

The sun began to smile down upon London more and more as the days sped into spring, and the cherry-blossom trees in the city parks were blooming when an unexpected blow struck their investigation. A widow named Emma Elizabeth Smith was brutally attacked and murdered one night in Whitechapel. At their kindest, the newspapers described her as a woman of loose character, but this did not make much difference to the girls of Pillar and Perkins. Some of them lived only a few streets away from where the attack had happened; a few had known the victim, and one or two even entertained the superstition that the same violent fate might be visited upon them if they continued to go against their employers. Overnight, they stopped nodding to Mrs. Besant and Mr. Barnwall in the street and would shut the door on them if they came to visit their houses. They began to travel in larger groups to and from work, women young and old lumped together, until it was almost impossible to approach them at all.

Thomas was disappointed. He might have been unwillingly dragged into the whole affair at the start, but now he was a part of it, and there was so much more that he wanted to know. More frustratingly still, the Fabian

Society appeared now to have other concerns besides the matchgirls. His frustrations burst forth one evening, on the way home from a meeting that had been dominated by Miss Black's lecture on the Consumers' League.

"This is why they despise us."

Annie Besant, squinting over a copy of her halfpenny magazine, *The Link*, said without looking up, "What do you mean, Thomas?"

Thomas stared out the carriage window. There were large pools of darkness on the pavement in between the streetlamps, and indistinguishable shapes moved within them. "I mean all of the people whom we try to help. They always end up despising us because *we* always end up forgetting them."

"We have not *forgotten* about the matchgirls, Tom, and they know that."

"But what have we done for them, exactly? Hardly anyone outside the Society knows about our boycott."

"That will change," said Mrs. Besant calmly, turning a page in her magazine, and tutting at the smudged print. "Once we rouse the clubs and hold a few public meetings, the word will spread. And I intend on writing an article in this very magazine." She held it up, as though he had not noticed it before.

"And the interviews?"

"I think we tried our best. We have all the information we require: lists of wages, and fines... In any case, the girls are frightened now, and won't speak to us again."

"Rebecca Moss will speak to *me*," he said without thinking, and Mrs. Besant looked up at him, eyebrows raised. "I'm sure of it."

"I shan't ask *why* you are so sure, but I would advise you not to seek her out again, Thomas. The time has come now for us to keep our distance. Once I have published the article…"

"Why wait?" Thomas interrupted. "Why not publish it now, if you say we have all the information we require?"

Mrs. Besant closed her magazine and put it away, with an air of annoyance. She folded her hands in her lap before meeting Thomas's gaze again. "Because, as I said, we must spread the word first. And…" She hesitated. "Because I want to speak to Richard Pillar first."

"What? Why?"

"After the article is written, he is likely to threaten me with a libel suit. He has done so with others before. I want to be able to say that I gave him the chance to defend himself." Mrs. Besant glanced out the window as the carriage came to a halt on Fleet Street. "Even if I don't believe him worthy of it. This weekend, there is to be a party for Henry Browning's birthday. Richard Pillar will be there, and I intend to ask him a few questions." As Thomas opened his mouth, "He will know nothing of the girls' involvement with us, naturally."

Thomas was silent for a moment. He had not thought much of Richard Pillar in the frenzy of the last few weeks; the man had become a kind of abstract of greed and malevolence, lurking at the edges of their investigation. Now he felt his old fears creep back again. "You must be careful." The injunction sounded feeble to his own ears, and after a moment he added, "Let me go with you."

"To Mr. Browning's party?" Mrs. Besant was staring at him.

"You said before that it will be your name, and your name alone that appears when the article is published. Well... perhaps I'd like Richard Pillar to know mine, too."

~

The London residence of the Pillars was a townhouse in Marylebone, though over the years, the success of the match factory had allowed them to purchase, in addition, a house in the country and a cottage by the sea. Since his coming of age, Edward Pillar had spent a lot of time flitting between these various residences—rather *too* much time for his father's liking. It wasn't that the boy couldn't be clever and industrious, when he applied himself to the task at hand. Richard had no fears in that quarter; he knew that upon his death, he could rely on Edward to carry on the business. But until that happened, it seemed that his son was content to remain as he was, drifting and unencumbered by responsibility.

On Friday morning, Richard caught his son at breakfast. "Where are you off to today, then?"

Edward calmly turned a page in his novel, swigged from his coffee and informed his father of a hunting party in Norbury Park which apparently required his attendance. "I shall be back by tomorrow lunchtime."

"I should certainly hope so," thundered Richard, and he reached across the table and plucked the novel out of his son's hand. "What's this? *Bleak House?*"

"Yes," said Edward, with a shrug as he wiped his hands on a napkin. "It's not as good as I remember."

With a sigh, Richard handed the novel to one of the maids who had come to pour some more tea and waved his hand in dismissal. "Put it away, please. *Edward…*"

"Yes, Father?"

"You will come with me to Henry Browning's party tomorrow."

"I'm afraid that will be quite impossible," Edward said, rising from the table. "I have engaged to meet a friend tomorrow when I return."

"Oh, and I can guess what sort of *friend* that may be." Richard rose, too, and walked around the table until he was standing opposite Edward. His son was a head taller than him, and Richard attempted to look stern as he looked into Edward's icy blue eyes—the boy had his mother's eyes. "Listen to me, Edward. You know I have always thought a young man should have his indulgences. However, there is a time and place for such things. And when you are married…"

Edward sighed and turned, making for the door. His father followed him, out of the breakfast room and into the hall, while the footmen scrambled to clear the way for them. "When you are married, you will have to choose these indulgences more carefully. Do you understand me, boy?"

"Perfectly," said Edward, coolly, turning to face his father again as they stopped opposite the main staircase. A maid who had been dusting the banister scuttled out of sight. "You wish me to marry Olivia Browning, and die of boredom."

"You know my reasons, Edward," Richard snapped, losing his temper again. "I have my reputation as a Liberal to think of. You know the accusations that have been levelled against my politics in recent years. To have Henry Browning in our family will dispel some of that doubt."

"I know your reasons." Edward sounded almost bored; he had not so much as flinched at his father's raised voice.

"And you *will* be there tomorrow." Richard Pillar could hear the desperation in his own voice as he called after his son, who had begun to ascend the stairs. "You will be courteous with Olivia. You will not embarrass me again, boy."

Edward did not reply as he reached the top of the staircase, turned and disappeared.

16

THE DIPPING ROOM

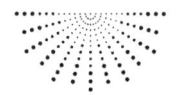

"She's been meeting someone. I know it."

"The lad we saw in the churchyard that time?" Sarah turned to Rebecca. They were sitting on the front step of the O'Briens' house in Bromley, enjoying the last rays of evening sun on their faces. In the court, Simon and the other children were playing, drawing chalk on the cobblestones.

"Must be," Rebecca said, with a defeated air. "And he's been lending her books. She goes out every Saturday afternoon, and comes back with something else."

"Well," said Sarah, after a moment's pause, during which they could hear church bells on the air, "That doesn't sound so bad."

"It's not, I know, but…" Rebecca fidgeted with her skirts, crossing her ankles and then uncrossing them. "It's that she won't tell me anything. I've tried to talk to her, so many times. I've told her I don't want her going out alone, not after what happened to that woman in Whitechapel. But she just—doesn't listen. She seems to be in her own world most of the time."

"Is this since they moved her downstairs?"

The question made Rebecca pause. About two weeks ago, the foremen in the factory had assigned Eliza to the dipping room, where most of the men worked—where the vapours were at their worst—where their mother had worked until she died. She winced, and admitted, "Since before then. Since... the interviews started."

"Simon, watch!" Sarah called out, as they heard the approaching wheels of a carriage. Along with the other children, her brother came running back to the house. Sarah took hold of Simon and put an arm around his shoulders as the others went inside. He looked at Rebecca with wide blue eyes as Sarah continued, "So Eliza doesn't like Mr. Barnwall as much as you do?"

"Stop," Rebecca laughed, nudging her friend. After a moment, her smile faded again. "She... well, she promised to keep quiet about the interviews. But she all but told me she disagrees with doing them."

"I don't understand that girl," Sarah muttered, with a shake of her head. "After seeing what happened to me..." She glanced at Rebecca, and seeing her friend's stricken expression, stopped short. "Tell you what."

"What?" Simon said, making them both laugh.

"Let's all go to the Paragon tomorrow night."

"I can't afford it," Rebecca said at once.

"My treat," Sarah said, and as her friend looked at her doubtfully, she relented. "Fine. Dad's treat. He'll be going, too. Loves to see the acrobats. Oh, come *on*, Rebecca. It's been so long since we went together. And a bit of fun might be just what your sister needs."

17
ONE BRIGHT SPOT

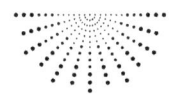

Even as the weather grew warmer, Eliza's days had grown all the more miserable. The one bright spot in her week came on Saturday afternoons, when she would go to meet Edward in Victoria Park. They would sit on a bench in some far corner, away from prying eyes, and talk about books. She loved feeling his eyes on her when she spoke. Peter had never looked at her like that—as though she were something astounding and exciting.

After *Bleak House*, Edward had lent her *David Copperfield* and *Hard Times*. She never got far with any of them. The illustrations were pretty, and the pages smelled clean and expensive, but she was always too tired to stick with the crowded narratives and numerous characters. Still, it was thrilling to flick through the pages and know that *he* had read the same words she was reading now. Sometimes, when she was feeling discouraged, she would hold up her own battered copy of *Oliver Twist* and compare it to whatever beautiful book Edward had lent her.

Her nightmares were full of daytime horrors now, too, all mixed up with the memories of her mother. She dreamed of glowing jaws, of matches setting her world alight and burning away everything she knew. Last night had been no different, and when she set out in the early afternoon to meet Edward, the bright sun hurt her eyes. Victoria Park was too green, and the voices of the speakers on their soapboxes too loud.

Eliza sat and waited, but Edward never came. Grey clouds swirled to fill the sky above her, the air grew colder, and when spits of rain began to slide down her face, she got up and left. The walk home to Greengoose Lane she barely remembered. All she could feel and see was her whole life stretched out before her, an unending grey road, full of smoke and dirt and rain.

∽

"Is this about *him?*" Rebecca asked, as she hung the dripping stockings in front of the range. "Is it the servant, from the Brownings? The one who's been lending you those books?"

Eliza had got home soaking wet a few minutes before and seemed intent on getting into bed just as she was until Rebecca stopped her. Then she just stood, shivering and hugging herself, as Rebecca helped her off with her things and into her shift. She did not speak at all, and there were tear tracks on her cheeks that had mingled with the mud of the rain. Now her face was clean, and she was wrapped up in blankets.

"Eliza." Rebecca came up, sat on the bed, and put a hand to her sister's shoulder. "*Please* tell me. What has he done to make you so upset?"

Eliza did not reply, just pulled the blankets up to her chin and stared at the queen's portrait on the opposite wall. Rebecca tilted her head so as to better see her sister's expression, and then felt it strike into her heart with unexpected force: the memory of that winter's day, after their mother had died, when her sister had lain in bed just like this.

She had not come to the funeral. Getting home in the evening, with her arms full of tributes from neighbours and her heart full of tears, Rebecca had laid it all down and got into bed with Eliza, and she remembered holding her sister close, feeling her icy cold to the touch. It had been weeks before they spoke again.

"Eliza," she said now, stroking her sister's hair. Her voice broke. "Eliza, please don't do this again."

"I can't help it," Eliza mumbled then, and Rebecca went on stroking her hair for another minute before she said,

"Fine." Rising to her feet, "If you won't tell me any more, then I'll go and speak to him myself."

Her sister voiced no protest as Rebecca got ready, pulling on her ulster coat and bringing her sister's shawl. She took one last look at Eliza in the bed, and then stepped out and locked the door carefully.

Outside, it was only raining lightly now, and specks of sunlight gleamed in puddles on pavements, rooftops and cobbled streets. Rebecca set off at a brisk pace and did not slow down until she had reached Grosvenor Square.

18

RED AND WHITE

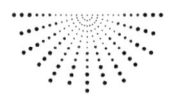

Thomas felt out of place at Henry Browning's party, but then again, he was used to feeling out of place. Since he first arrived in London five years before, he could not fail to notice the way people regarded him differently here. His accent, his cheap clothes—all conspired to keep him out of the best circles of London society. But he had found better company: he had found Annie, and others who were willing to accept him as their equal.

She was astounding today, Mrs. Besant. Dressed up for the occasion, in a new white silk blouse, she had kept quiet at first, but then, as all the guests began to circulate in the drawing room following luncheon, she left Thomas's side and went right up to Richard Pillar. Miss Browning was playing the piano, and the sound of the concerto drowned out the words of their conversation at first. But Thomas watched as the pleasant smile faded off Mr. Pillar's face, as his posture grew stiff and his hands began to fidget with his pocket square.

The piano went silent at just the right moment: just as Mrs. Besant was saying, in cordial but carrying tones, "Is it true, sir, that it would be possible to replace white phosphorus with red phosphorus in the match-making process, as some other factories around the country have done in the last few years?"

"You are correct, madam; it would be possible, but not prudent. White phosphorus is easier to transport and far less costly to supply—"

"And far more toxic than red phosphorus, if I understand correctly," Mrs. Besant finished. Other conversations were dying away now as people turned to listen. By the piano, where he had been watching Miss Browning play, the younger Mr. Pillar was staring at his father. Sensing Thomas's gaze, he shifted to look at him instead, and Thomas quickly looked away. There was something in that young man's eyes that unnerved him.

"If you are suggesting, madam," Richard Pillar continued, through clenched teeth, "that I do not value the safety of my own workers, then I would advise you not to make rash assumptions—particularly as you are not in the business yourself…"

"Of course, I am not in the business of manufacturing matches: that is true," Mrs. Besant conceded. "But I am in the business of improving the lives of those less fortunate than ours. And I—"

"With respect, madam, our company has done more for those less fortunate than you or any of your colleagues. You talk and write about rights for workers, yes, but what do you do for them in the end? Do you pay them wages? Do you take them off the streets, put clothes on their back and food on their tables?" Richard Pillar had gone red in the face, but he had puffed out his chest and looked down on the lady proudly, as though convinced of his triumph.

Mrs. Besant regarded him thoughtfully for a long moment. And then, in a voice that was lethal in its calm, she said, "Your actions will be judged, sir. I would advise you to remember that. You *will* be held accountable, by powers higher than myself: by powers higher than law or parliament or queen. The world is watching, Mr. Pillar."

"You were wonderful," exclaimed Thomas, when they had escaped the drawing room, where a heated debate was now taking place between Mr. Browning, Mr. Pillar and several others. "Truly wonderful. He looked as though he had seen a ghost."

"It is no victory, Thomas; not even a small one. Not compared to what awaits us. I will not celebrate until I have seen justice done for every one of those girls." But still Mrs. Besant could not seem to help sharing in his smiles, as they stepped into the garden together, and out of the stuffy air of the party.

19

PETER

Rebecca unwound the shawl from around her head and knocked at the door of the servants' entrance. As she was waiting on the steps, she patted down her damp hair and stifled a sneeze. Across the green of Grosvenor Square, trees were dripping and bowed down with the wind.

"What is it?" A maid opened the door: she looked flushed and harried. "What do you want?"

"I'm looking for... someone." Rebecca paused, frowning. "He works here—a coachman or groom, I'm not sure."

The maid sighed, then examined her more closely. "Are you Eliza's sister?"

"Yes," Rebecca said, relieved. "Yes, how did you—"

"You look like her," the maid said, as she led her inside.

"That's funny, people always say we look nothing alike, except for our hair—"

"Wait here, stay out of the way." As a shout echoed down the passage from the kitchen, the maid pointed to a chair pushed up to the wall. "We're run off our feet today, as you can see. I'll see if Peter's around."

"Peter," Rebecca repeated to herself, slightly puzzled, as the maid ran away. She sat, sighing as the weight came off her feet, and wound her hands together in her lap. A couple of footmen passed at a quick pace, stepping out the entrance she had just come through. They were gone about a quarter of an hour, and when they came back smelling of smoke, Rebecca, who was still waiting, called out,

"Sorry—do you know where—"

"We're in a hurry, love," said one of the footmen over his shoulder, and then they were swallowed up into the noisy kitchen.

Rebecca sighed. She was starting to wonder why Eliza had seemed to enjoy working with these people so much. But of course, she knew the answer to that now. It was this boy, Peter: *he* was the reason why Eliza used to come home from work glowing with happiness. He was the reason why she had shed so many tears when Rebecca had made her hand in her notice with the Brownings. And *he* must be the reason Eliza was inconsolable now.

Gritting her teeth, Rebecca got to her feet, leaving her damp shawl on the chair. She walked down the passage and into the kitchen. Servants shouldered past her, some halting to admonish or question her; Rebecca ignored them and continued on through, into the servants' hall next door. There was a fire burning in the hearth, and she spread her hands towards the heat before catching a flash of movement in the corner of her eye.

At one end of the small hall, rain-spattered windows looked out onto a garden. But the rain itself had evidently stopped, for two figures were walking on the path that wound around the perimeter. Rebecca stepped closer to the window to make them out and saw that they were guests from the party: the gentleman turned his head slightly and a smile spread across Rebecca's face, unbidden. It was Mr. Barnwall—Mr. Barnwall, here? She was too delighted to question it, and there was Mrs. Besant beside him. They were talking together, laughing, and—Embracing? The smile dropped from Rebecca's face. She blinked, thinking she must have misunderstood something: but there was nothing to misunderstand, Mr. Barnwall had his arms around Mrs. Besant, his head leaning on her shoulder. They looked intimate, and happy. Suddenly it had all clicked together in Rebecca's mind.

This was why Mr. Barnwall had been helping in the interviews. This was why he had often seemed reluctant, and yet at the same time so eager to do right by the girls:

to do right by *Mrs. Besant.* This was why he had often spoken of his colleague with such admiration. It was more than admiration, Rebecca could see that now, and she was unprepared for the cold wave that swept through her body at the realisation. She had known there was no chance Mr. Barnwall would think of her. So why should she feel so disappointed?

"You were looking for me?"

Rebecca turned from the window, flushing as though she had been caught doing something untoward. The young man from the churchyard was here, the one with black, curly hair and a round, honest face. His cape was wet, and he was still wearing gloves.

"I'm Peter. You're Eliza's sister, aren't you? Is something wrong?" He spoke very quickly, as though he were nervous. "Has something happened to her?"

"Nothing," Rebecca said. Her tongue felt heavy in her mouth: her mind did not seem to be moving fast enough to keep up with him. "She's... fine."

"Well, then you must have a message from her. Has she agreed to meet me?" His eyes were wide and hopeful. Rebecca could not summon the anger she wanted to feel: the anger she had felt only a few moments ago at the thought of her sister's tears.

"I haven't got a message. I—nothing. I shouldn't have come."

"Wait, please!" Peter called, but Rebecca was running away, out of the kitchen, out of the house and the square and away from that part of the city, that never failed to make her feel foolish and cheap and insignificant.

20
UNEASY ALLIANCES

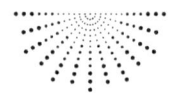

The sky had darkened over the fine houses of Grosvenor Square, and inside the Brownings' drawing room, the gas lamps had been lit. Edward Pillar, who had been forced to stay by Olivia's side as a page-turner, was watching the card game at the other table with wistful eyes when his father came up to his side, and said in a low voice,

"Come, we are leaving."

Edward did not question it; he simply made his excuses and followed Richard out of the room. For the last hour, he had been contemplating some means of escape from the dull party, but his father was the last person he would have expected to provide him with it.

"The carriage is waiting outside," Richard said as they reached the hall, and were handed their coats by a servant. Then, meeting Edward's gaze as he pushed an arm through his sleeve, he sighed sharply and added in explanation, "I do *not* intend on being harassed by that woman a moment longer."

"Mrs. Besant?" Edward could not help but feel a little amused as he followed his father down the steps to the carriage. The door was thrown open for them, and they climbed in one by one. "What did she do, Father? Beat you at cards?"

"You know very well what she did," Richard replied shortly. "She has been interrogating me since the moment she arrived in that house. Herself and her colleague, the Irish fellow with the bowler hat..."

"Thomas Barnwall," Edward supplied. "I was stuck beside him at dinner. Barely seems to know how to use a knife and fork. But then, Annie Besant likes her charity cases, doesn't she?"

"Well, they seem to have made me their villain. They..." Richard broke off, and his chest heaved for a moment as he looked out the window of the carriage. Edward's eyes narrowed.

"You're not *afraid* of them, Father?"

"Don't be foolish," Richard snapped. "But—they do seem to know a great deal about our practices. So much that it makes me uneasy."

"Their boycott will never work." Edward leaned back against the carriage seat, crossing his hands behind his head. "Bell and Black is the only other match factory in London that uses red phosphorus instead of white, and it doesn't make both lucifers and safety matches as we do. We meet a demand, Father. You have told me so yourself."

"Yes, that is true. But I fear…" Richard trailed off and did not finish his thought. Edward, who had already grown bored with the conversation, turned his attention to the window. He watched a group of factory girls on the pavement as they passed, and his mind drifted to Eliza, as it had done frequently throughout the day.

He wondered how long the faithful little thing had waited for him. There had been no way to get any word to her that he would not be in the park, for he did not know her address. Perhaps, after all, Edward thought, he *had* been moving too slowly with her. It was clear to him now how business got in the way of pleasure, and how that situation would only worsen in the next few weeks. What with paying his attentions to Olivia Browning, and joining his friends' hunting parties at the weekends, he did not see how he would have time to set aside for Eliza. And yet he could not give her up. He was too curious, too excited. Her smile, her adoring eyes—they must be his and his only. He would find a way.

Lost in his pleasant reverie, Edward did not notice that the carriage was taking much longer than usual to reach Marylebone until the familiar surrounds of Mile End Road were going by outside the window. "Father? Where are we going?"

"Where do you think, boy? To the factory."

"But it's Saturday," Edward said, bewildered.

"There is something I must check." His father was drumming his fingers on his knee, jumping at every jolt in the carriage as though he thought it would upend them onto the street. *He has truly lost his mind*, Edward thought, watching him. That was when he heard the music, drifting toward them on the night air. And for the third time in the course of weeks, fortune smiled upon him and his plan.

21
THE MUSIC HALL

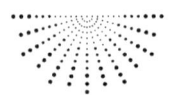

Rebecca had not expected to enjoy herself as much as she did when Sarah dragged them to the Paragon Music Hall that evening. She had come home from the Brownings inclined to slump into dejection just as Eliza had, and it was only with a great effort that she had managed to rouse herself and feign high spirits for the both of them. But soon after the band started playing the overture, she found that she did not have to pretend anymore: it was impossible not to smile in the Paragon. Well—unless you were Eliza.

While one of the comedians came on stage, Sarah's father slipped away through the crowds and came back bearing lemonades for all of them. Rebecca closed her eyes as she took her first sip. It was so sweet and delicious that she didn't want to swallow it. She opened her eyes again and saw her sister drinking deeply. "Say thank you," she mouthed.

"Thank you, Mr. O'Brien," said Eliza, in a voice so flat and low that it was almost drowned out by the cheers that broke out around them as the comedian finished his routine. Sarah's father just grinned and ruffled Eliza's hair. She reached up to smooth it again when he had turned his back.

"What's wrong with you?" Rebecca muttered into her sister's ear.

"I told you I didn't want to come," Eliza replied, and there were actually tears in her eyes as she spoke. Rebecca looked at her in disbelief.

"Don't you know how lucky we are? Look at this place." She gestured to the shining brass gaseliers, the domed ceiling, the side pillars with carved elephant heads. "We didn't have to pay a farthing to come here tonight. Sarah did all this to cheer you up. So don't—"

"Come on, come on, settle down everyone," called the chairman as he came out onto the stage to announce the next item of the programme. As the audience's chatter died down, Rebecca closed her mouth and turned from her sister. Sarah was looking at her questioningly: she gave a shrug in response.

The acrobats swung onto stage in a flash of colour, and Mr. O'Brien cheered and lifted Simon up so that he could see better. Distracted, Rebecca glanced at Eliza again, and then at the audience around them. Here in the pit, it was mainly tradesmen, clerks and factory workers like themselves. Rebecca's gaze drifted up—up, toward the private boxes. And for a moment, she was sure that she had seen him in one of them: Edward Pillar, watching not the stage but the audience below. She was still staring when Sarah tapped her shoulder.

"Isn't that your Mr. Barnwall?"

Startled, Rebecca looked where her friend had indicated, and spotted a blond head toward the front of the crowd. Thomas Barnwall—if indeed it was him—was cheering and clapping with a couple of other young men.

"He's not *my* Mr. Barnwall," she replied, after a moment, and took a sip of lemonade. Then, unable to help herself, "He's Mrs. Besant's."

"Mrs. Besant's?" Sarah rounded on her with a laugh. "That can't be true! How much older than him is she? And isn't she married?"

"Trust me," Rebecca said darkly. "I know what I'm talking about."

Before Sarah could reply, her father turned around and handed Simon into her arms. "He needs to go out."

"And can't you—" Sarah started to protest.

"Miss Lundberg's about to come on," he replied, matter-of-factly. Sarah rolled her eyes, adjusting her grip on Simon, and then Eliza said,

"I can take him."

They all looked at her. She was flushed from the heat of the theatre, and had a pleading look in her eyes. With a shrug, Sarah let her little brother down onto the ground. "Thanks, Eliza."

Eliza did not respond. She just took Simon's little hand in hers and led him off into the crowd.

22
A DARK LIGHT

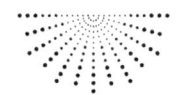

Richard Pillar stepped inside the deserted factory, jangling his keys in his hand. With his free hand, he held up his handkerchief to his mouth as he passed the dipping chambers, and walked on, his footsteps echoing in the silence. He passed windows that faced onto a dark courtyard and climbed creaking stairs to his office.

The smell of smoke still lingered in the air when he entered; no doubt it was thanks to Edward. Richard shook his head as he lit the oil lamp. In the long mirror above the fireplace, his reflection flared into being. *That* gave him a start: Richard stared, and ran a hand over his jowls, his balding head. It felt like only the other day that he had been Edward's age himself, handsome and eager, full of possibility. How could it be, then, that now he looked so—ghoulish? It was just the light.

Edward had insisted on getting out of the carriage at the Paragon. Richard had not possessed the energy to protest. He was sure his son had appointments to keep, and at any rate, his mind was still full of Mrs. Besant and the Fabian Society. It was difficult to be spoken to as a monster, to be seen as a Scrooge—when one was only human; when one was trying one's best. Richard Pillar glanced at his reflection again and blinked away.

Then he walked, slowly, to his desk. He searched through each drawer, pulling out various employee records that he had requested from the secretary, all of which detailed the compensation (or lack thereof) to workers struck down with phossy jaw. When he had got through the last of them, Richard carried the papers to the fireplace. Off the mantelpiece, he took a box of Pillar and Perkins' safety matches and struck the first one.

As the records began to burn with a great line of greedy flame, Richard noticed a piece of paper that had fluttered to the floor. It was yellowed with age, the handwriting faded.

April 1871

Dear friend,

I cannot go on in this way. You told me once that everything we have done has been to honour the legacy of our fathers, but I cannot believe that anymore. Is it possible to lose sight of—

Richard Pillar wrenched his eyes from the paper. For a moment, he felt a chill in the air: a raising of the hairs on the back of his neck: a murmur of wind. Someone was in the room with him. But he did not turn.

"You always were a sentimental fool, Perkins," he said instead, and then he dropped the letter in the fire and watched until the words faded away into flame, and he was left alone once more.

23
BACK AT THE PARAGON

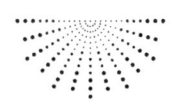

The foyer of the Paragon Music Hall was splendid, with marble bars and Oriental doors draped with rich velvet curtains, that led to the auditorium and upper gallery. The band was playing "God Save the Queen" as Eliza came back through with Simon in tow, and she halted for a moment to listen. From here, the music was distant enough to be slightly distorted, and the voices of those singing along with it were drowned out. As she stood with Simon tugging on her hand, a curtain twitched, and one of the doors opened to give way to Edward Pillar. Eliza's breath caught in her throat as she saw him. His blue eyes burned across the floor and devoured her.

"Simon," she said, crouching down so that her face was level with the little boy's, "Go back inside to the others. You know where to find them?"

Simon nodded, and obeyed. Eliza straightened again and met Edward's gaze.

Outside, the night air was cold and crisp, and the terrace that wound around the building was empty of people. With a quick step forward, Edward had clasped Eliza tightly to his breast. His eau de cologne overpowered her. "I thought you might be here."

"I wasn't going to come," she said into his shoulder, her voice slightly muffled. He had never held her like this before.

"Your sister saw me too. She might be out any minute." Edward drew back, holding her at arm's length. The band was still playing. "We must—why are you crying, silly thing?"

Eliza raised her eyes to him. Her heart was swelling—it was impossible to feel this much happiness at once. "I think—I must be dreaming."

"You're not dreaming. Now, come here and let me kiss you. I've been waiting for *so* long to kiss you, Eliza."

"I—I shouldn't." She glanced towards the door, where a lighted square spilled out from under the doorway.

"Now, don't play a lady's games with me. I know you're not like that, Eliza." As she looked back at him, uncertainly, Edward softened his expression. His eyes reflected the lighted windows of the theatre and gleamed like blue jewels. "I *am* sorry I didn't come to meet you today. My father made me go to a stupid party, and there was no way I could tell you, you know. But Eliza..." His hands drifted down from her shoulders to her arms, took her hands in his. "I thought of you the whole time."

She gazed at him, without speaking. A drop struck her cheek, and she thought about how it was going to rain, and how wonderful that was. Edward stepped closer. "Come with me, Eliza."

Eliza's lips parted. "Do you mean..."

"Of course, I'll do what's right."

"Then you'll marry me?"

"Of course, I will, you foolish girl. Now come here."

"But I couldn't leave her. My sister."

"Your sister will survive without you." His voice was still playful, affectionate as he stepped even closer. "But *I* can't." He took her in his arms, huffed a breath into her hair. "Please don't make me, Eliza."

The singing voices were gone. The band had stopped. And Eliza tipped her head back and looked into Edward's face. "Foolish girl," he said again. He smiled into her eyes and bent to kiss her.

Sarah said that Eliza had probably gone home early. That was after Simon had come back to them alone—after they had searched the Paragon from top to bottom and asked strange faces in the dispersing crowd if they had seen Eliza. So, Rebecca chose to believe her friend, because it kept her from thinking of Edward Pillar's face in the shadows of a private box—or of a dark figure stalking the streets of Whitechapel...

She believed it all the way home, long after she and the O'Briens had parted ways. She believed it as she ascended the creaky stairs to their room, believed it even when she discerned no light under their door. But when she opened it and breathed in the musty air of their room; when she lit the lamp and saw Queen Victoria's face frowning down at an empty bed, she could not believe it anymore. Rebecca fell to her knees and shed her first tears since Mum's death.

24
AGAINST THE RULES

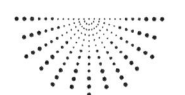

Eliza slept well these days, now that she was away from that room of ghosts and night terrors. When she did have a bad dream, Edward was always there to comfort her. It was getting warmer now, as spring turned to summer, and the small apartment off Fleet Street would get hot and airless during the day. When Edward was gone, Eliza would throw open the window and lean out, looking down at the alleyway below. She was not supposed to do that. There were many things that she was not supposed to do, and the list only grew and grew the longer she lived with Edward.

But she did not have to work anymore. A woman came and cooked their meals for them in the evenings, left food in the larder and did their washing once a week. Edward bought Eliza clothes and other pretty things. She began to sleep in later and later in the mornings, until often she would not wake until midday, stretching her arms and watching her soft sleeves trailing down her wrists, while outside carriage wheels rolled and voices shouted.

Edward had said that he would marry her, on that faraway night in the Paragon when her life had changed. But very quickly, Eliza saw that he had no plans to do that, and she learned not to ask him about it anymore. It did nag at her sometimes, the fact that he had won her by a lie. Maybe she might have acted differently if she had known—or maybe not. There was no way of knowing.

All she knew was that she was happy just to *be* with him, most of the time. His touch, his smile, his eyes: she learned to love these things even more than she had before. She had loved him since the day he had rescued her after Sarah's accident, but now she breathed the same air as him, shared the same space, and there was something different about that. She could watch him when he was sleeping, when all of his defences had melted away and he looked just like a boy. She could trace a finger along his cheek and tell herself, "He is mine."

It helped to keep that picture of Edward in her mind, during those times when he was awake and not acting like himself. He could get angry or upset if Eliza asked about something he did not want to talk about, or if she broke one of his rules. For instance, he didn't like her going outside when he was gone from the house during the day, because he was afraid of what might happen to her. He didn't like her to eat too much, either, and often, before leaving in the morning, he would write out a list of what she was allowed to have. Sometimes, he would even tell her she could not eat at all until he was back. It was her punishment, he would say, for being bad.

On one of these occasions, Eliza was lying dizzy and weak on the bed. The window was open, and a couple of flies had come in and were chasing circles around each other on the ceiling. It was sometime in the afternoon—there was no clock in the apartment—and somewhere near midsummer—there was no calendar, either. Eliza was not sure what she had done this time to deserve her punishment, but Edward had left angry that morning.

The sound of a knock on the door startled her, and without moving, she turned her head to look. The door to the narrow, dark hall stood open, and it was the door beyond that which began to shake from pressure on the other side. The handle turned—Eliza's terrified eyes watched it—but the door was locked, and it did not give away.

Then, a voice instead of a knock, which made her go still all over. "Eliza? Are you there?"

She did not dare breathe.

"It's me. It's Rebecca. If you're there…" A sound like a sigh, and a soft thump as though someone were leaning against the door on the other side. "If you're there, don't be afraid. I'm not angry. I just want to see you."

Eliza blinked a few times. She had to remind herself that this was not real. Rebecca had come here many times before. Sometimes, when Eliza was with Edward at night, she would appear in the corner of the room. Sometimes it was Mum who came and just looked at her daughter, with a sad smile and one hand on her lumpy jaw—she just *looked*.

"Eliza, please." The pain in Rebecca's voice wrenched her heart as she lay there. "I just want to see you for a minute. I need to know you're all right."

One of the flies landed on Eliza's cheek, and as she batted it away, she suddenly realised that this *was* real. Her sister was really here, talking to her through the door. But if she answered or opened the door, it would be breaking his rules.

"You've been gone two months," Rebecca went on. "I miss you, Eliza. I'm not angry, I just miss you."

What did the rules matter? She had broken them before, and anyway, Edward was already angry at her. With a shifting of sheets, Eliza sat up. Her head spun for a moment, black spots dancing across her vision, and then she had gathered herself once more.

"Are you there?" Rebecca's voice was quieter now. Eliza turned toward the door. Her mouth opened, and then closed again, as she looked down at herself. The trailing lace sleeves, the exposed part of her chest, her hair loose around her shoulders. Slowly, she shook her head.

With one more sigh, she heard Rebecca give up and go away, her footsteps echoing into silence. Eliza fell back against the bed and turned her thoughts to her own rumbling stomach. She hoped Edward would not be back too late.

～

Tears blinded Rebecca as she made her way up Fleet Street, and she kept her gaze lowered to the pavement, turning and weaving around the shoes that went by. Her heart was still thumping. Standing outside that door, she had felt sure, *so* sure that her sister was there. But then, she had felt the same thing with every place she had visited over the last few months. For as it turned out, Edward Pillar had been pursuing girls from the factory for years. Some of them could recall certain spots around the city where he had brought them, which was how she found out about the Fleet Street address. But as in every one before it, Rebecca had been met with only silence. Silence could not tell her anything.

No more, she thought, with a shake of the head. She could take no more of this, the quick, hopeful dash, the thumping of her heart as she came close to finding her sister, and then the silence.

A quick glance up ascertained that the path ahead was blocked by men rolling kegs into a tavern, and Rebecca turned to cross the street. Her right foot had only just left the pavement when someone grabbed her and tugged her back. She watched as a carriage passed the space where she would have been, splashing droplets of mud on the hem of her skirt. The coachman shouted at her to watch where she was going, and she just stared.

"Rebecca?" She looked up to meet the gaze of her rescuer, and instantly regretted it. Thomas Barnwall's eyes narrowed as he saw the tears in her own. She could see her reflection in his glasses, pale and frightened looking. Rebecca looked away.

"Is everything all right?" He had taken off his hat, a gesture which barely registered with her as it should have. A light touch to her elbow guided her a little way down the path, until they had skirted around the delivery men. Rebecca shook her head in an attempt to clear it.

"Yes, sir. Thank you." Vaguely, she wondered what he was doing here, but could not summon the energy to ask.

"I haven't seen you since our last interview, I don't think."

Rebecca did not contradict him, though looming in her memory was that April night in the Paragon: the brass band playing, and a faraway feeling of disappointment as she watched Mr Barnwall with his friends.

"You know Mrs. Besant's article is to be published tomorrow."

"Yes," Rebecca said again, mechanically. "We're having a meeting about it."

"A meeting?" He sounded confused. Somewhere in Rebecca's mind was the nagging sense that she ought not to have said anything, but she shook it away.

"Yes, so I must get home. Good day, sir." Turning, without meeting his gaze, Rebecca gave Mr. Barnwall a parting nod and hurried across the street, checking this time to make sure she would not need rescuing again.

25
MATCHWOMEN

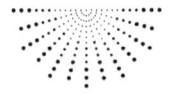

Over the past few months, since the interviews had started them thinking and talking, the matchwomen of Pillar and Perkins had taken to meeting in various places, including Victoria Park, Mile End Waste, and, most often, Rebecca's lodgings on Greengoose Lane. She sometimes thought her willingness to host these meetings had less to do with a thirst for revolution on her part, and more to do with a need to fill the space that had been left empty by Eliza.

She had never understood before why her sister hated living in that room so much, but now that she was gone and the evenings were beginning to stretch out, dark and lonely, it started to make more sense. When Rebecca woke one morning to find that her father's daguerreotype had fallen from the chimney-piece during the night and its glass cracked down the middle, that did it for her. She determined that she would not be alone in that place for longer than she had to, and so the meetings started.

Some of them were just girls, with wide, curious eyes and hair so fine it looked like a baby's. Some were older, like the Chapman sisters, who were in their thirties and had never married. Then there were those with the beginning signs of phossy jaw, who always carried themselves a little differently: a difference that came, perhaps, from the perpetual pain that racked their bodies. But every single one always wore her best hat and Sunday dress when coming over to Rebecca's, and brought a piece of tribute with her, whether it was a penny loaf or a bottle of brandy.

When they were all assembled as they were today, with their chatter filling her cramped room from floor to ceiling, Rebecca would look around at the colourful dresses and cheerful faces and feel a swelling of pride in her breast. How much Eliza would hate it, she would think, and that inevitably brought a tear to her eye. She had never been one to cry before her sister had run away.

"Any luck?" said Sarah, and Rebecca turned to find that her friend had been watching her. They were sitting together on the only chairs in the room; most of the other girls had settled on the bed or the floor.

"I went there this afternoon," Rebecca said, scuffing her shoe on the carpet. "To the place you told me about, on Fleet Street. *Someone* was there—I saw the open window when I was outside. I talked through the door, but whoever it was didn't make a sound."

"Maybe Pillar's got her somewhere else," Sarah said darkly. "I only know that he *used* to bring girls there."

"Girls," Rebecca repeated, lowering her voice as she looked around at the other matchwomen. "You mean, maybe even some of the ones here?"

"Maybe," Sarah responded. As Rebecca turned to stare at her, she shrugged her shoulders. "He's a busy man."

"Why didn't you tell me this before?" Rebecca said, but her voice was soft and unaccusing.

"I thought you knew. He was after you, too, for a while, wasn't he?"

"I saw him." Rebecca spoke in an undertone now, so low that Sarah had to lean in to hear her. "I saw him there at the Paragon that night. He must've been meeting Eliza for weeks, and I never knew till it was too late. I could *kill* him."

"If you killed him, the rest of you would all lose your jobs," said Sarah, with a grin. "And then we'd be in a bigger mess than we are now." With that, she cleared her throat and whistled until the room had quieted down. "Right, are we all here? Anyone missing? Let's get started."

26
KEEPING SECRETS

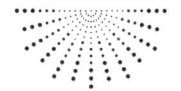

"And what do they talk about, in these meetings?"

"I'm not entirely sure. Rebecca didn't say." Thomas Barnwall put his hands in his pockets as he walked side by side with Mrs. Besant. It was a hot, hazy evening. Since Mrs. Besant's husband was on the rampage back home, they were going to Thomas's lodgings on Fleet Street to put some finishing touches to the article. "But I don't think it's such a bad thing."

"I don't think it's a bad thing either. Not necessarily." Mrs. Besant grimaced, adjusting the brim of her hat to shield her eyes from a flash of sun. "Those girls ought to have a union, and their meeting together is the first step towards that. However…"

"You are afraid of what else they might do?"

"I'm afraid they are too close to the situation. Change can only come from above. It is our duty to promote that. Otherwise, if the matchgirls insist on taking matters into their own hands, we might be facing into something worse."

"A strike," Thomas supplied, grimly. "I've feared from the start that it might come to that."

"With any luck, it won't," Mrs. Besant replied. "Those girls have lost enough without losing their livelihoods, too. And what if—"

Thomas held out a hand, forcing them both to halt on the pavement. Mrs. Besant stared at him. "What—"

"There's Edward Pillar," Thomas said in an undertone, pointing across the street. "What's *he* doing here?"

Mrs. Besant followed his gaze, towards where the factory owner's son had just stepped out of a carriage. He straightened his coat, glanced around—they shrank back on instinct, but his gaze did not land on them. Then he lifted out of the carriage a girl with red hair and a dark cloak, who leaned on his arm as they disappeared down a side street.

"That's Rebecca's sister," Thomas hissed, though Pillar was far enough away that he would not hear him. "Eliza—I'm sure of it. But—"

"Let's go on," Mrs. Besant said, and slid her arm through Thomas's as they continued down the street. As he looked at her questioningly, she sighed, and flicked her gaze towards him. "Edward Pillar has a... reputation. I am not surprised."

"But she's a matchgirl, too. I interviewed her myself, and—and—" Thomas shook his head as he tried to articulate his thoughts. "Well, doesn't this harm our investigation?"

"It does not harm our investigation if no one knows of it," Mrs Besant said, calmly. "The girls' testimony has all been cited anonymously. And as I think it is as much in Edward Pillar's interests to keep this a secret as it is in ours…" She glanced at Thomas, "I don't think we have anything to fear from him. A gentleman's business is, after all, his own. Let us forget what we have seen."

Slowly, Thomas nodded, fully intending to do as she said. But when they were inside his poky lodgings, with Mrs. Besant settled at his desk with the article in front of her, asking his opinion on this and that phrase, he found Rebecca Moss's tear-streaked visage kept coming up in his mind. It wasn't as though it was any of his business, of course, how she might be mixed up with Edward Pillar. But that didn't stop him from scribbling a hasty note when Mrs. Besant had left the room and placing it in his pocket to post later.

27
WHITE SLAVERY

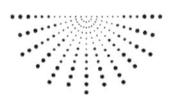

On Monday morning, the management of Pillar and Perkins gathered in the large meeting room on the office wing of the factory. Richard Pillar sat at the head of the table, with his son to his right, and Mr. Lethbridge, the secretary, opened the meeting by putting a copy of *The Link* in the centre of the table.

"'White Slavery in London'. That is what they have called this preposterous article—and by *they*, I am referring to Mrs. Annie Besant and Mr. Thomas Barnwall." The thin man quivered and took up the copy again. "With your leave, sir, I shall read an extract of what they have written about our company."

Richard Pillar gave a slow nod, his jaw clenched tightly. Beside him, Edward was drumming his long fingers on the table. Mr. Lethbridge cleared his throat and held up the magazine.

"'With chattel slaves Mr. Pillar could not have made his huge fortune, for he could not have fed, clothed and housed them for four shillings a week each, and they would have had a definite money value which would have served as a protection. But who cares for the fate of these white wage slaves, provided only that the Pillar and Perkins shareholders get their twenty-three per cent, and Mr. Richard Pillar can erect statues and buy parks?'"

Mr. Lethbridge stopped reading, adjusting his glasses as he looked up. Richard Pillar had held up a hand. He was a little flushed, but his tone was even as he said, "We need not concern ourselves overmuch with the *facts,* if one can even call them that, which Annie Besant has set down in this article. I do see the necessity for this meeting, of course, but I would advise you all to read the article for yourselves and see with your own eyes the conjecture and outright falsehoods on which this woman bases her argument."

"Father," Edward interjected, with a cough, and several pairs of eyes at the table wheeled around to regard him, "I have read it in full, and I must say that it gives me a little concern. Mrs. Besant makes some serious accusations against our company, and she seems to have a very thorough understanding of our wages and practices. She and her colleague must have interviewed a great number of the girls who work here. I could find out—"

"Thank you, Edward," said his father, "For illustrating my point so well." He turned his gaze to the other managers at the table as Edward fell silent. "Mrs. Besant may have an accurate knowledge of the wages our girls receive: that much is true. She points out that a less experienced girl may receive four shillings for piece work, while our dayworkers receive as much as thirteen shillings a week. The correlation between wage and the worker's competence is shown very clearly, so much so that I wonder if Mrs. Besant herself even knew what argument she was attempting to make."

There was a ripple of laughter from around the table. Richard Pillar reached for the magazine himself and thumbed through the pages until he had reached the article. "Ah! Yes. She then goes on to make the ludicrous claim that I stopped one shilling out of our girls' wages to fund the erection of Mr. Gladstone's statue, six years ago. Now, this is demonstrably false. But not only that, it gives us a good idea of which girls she and her colleague must have spoken with. If many of them told this colourful tale, then we may take it that any girl who has worked at our factory for a period of six years or longer is under suspicion of having consented to one of these interviews."

Comprehension had begun to dawn on Edward's face, though he was not smiling as some of the other managers were.

"And what of the meetings that have been reported between these girls, sir?" said Mr. Lethbridge.

"Well, we cannot stop them from congregating outside of work, of course. But we *can* keep a closer eye than before. Any gathering of significant number within the factory walls will be noted: any girl complaining about her work will incur a fine." Richard considered for a moment, and then continued, "We will not punish them indiscriminately, of course. Any girls who wish to refute the claims made in this article ought to be given a chance to do so."

"Very good, sir," said Mr. Lethbridge. "If anyone else has other concerns or questions which they may wish to raise with Mr. Pillar…"

After the meeting was over, Edward rose from his chair in a languid movement, but his arm was stopped by his father and he was held back as the managers filed out. Dryly, "Have I done something to offend you, Father?"

"I'll have none of your jokes now, boy." Richard looked closely into his son's face, and it seemed to Edward as though some hard defence had fallen away from his expression: his eyes had an almost wild look to them. "You are to stay in town for the next few weeks, until this matter is resolved."

"But Father—"

"Wherever you spend your nights is no concern of mine, but I will need you on hand, Edward."

His son swallowed, hard. He had gone a little pale. "Father, I thought I mentioned to you that I was planning to go to the Worthingtons—"

"And I am telling you, now: you are *not* to leave London until we are in safe waters again. Is that understood?"

"Yes, Father," said Edward, tightly.

"Good boy." Richard clapped him on the shoulder and passed him out. "It is not always pleasant, to do our duty." His voice floated back as he left the meeting room. "But I trust you will not disappoint me in this."

Edward waited until his father was out of earshot before seizing up the magazine, tearing it in half and throwing it to the floor. When that did not satisfy him, he kicked over a chair and nearly struck his own foot. His breath came in short, sharp gasps as he raised his hands to his head and ran them through his hair. Finally, he cried out, when he was sure that no one would hear him.

28
THE READING ROOM

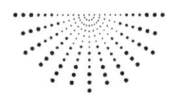

Thomas Barnwall had obtained a reader's pass to the British Museum two years after arriving in London, and on Wednesdays, he always spent a few hours in the Reading Room. He sat at a desk under the great dome and went through court documents, essays and articles on female labour. Around him was a deep well of silence as others worked at their own projects. Thomas read until the clock struck six, at which point he gathered up his notes, put on his coat and hat, and departed that shrine of knowledge and learning.

Outside, the sun had set. There was a chill in the air from when it had rained earlier. Thomas went to the bottom of the steps and waited, while gentlemen and ladies passed. Pigeons pecked about nearby, sometimes flapping so close to his face that he jerked back. A slight headache began to throb between his temples, and he had just taken off his glasses when Rebecca arrived.

"Sorry to keep you waiting, sir. I came straight from work."

"So, you got my note," Thomas said, pinching the bridge of his nose.

"I got your note," she repeated.

"Come, let's sit down." He took her arm, steering her over to one of the stone benches in front of the museum. When he had put on his glasses again, he looked at Rebecca more closely. Her colours were more subdued than he was accustomed to seeing: she was wearing a heavy ulster coat over her work apron, and a black bonnet that covered her red hair. There were shadows under her eyes, and she had a soft, sad look to her mouth.

Thomas cleared his throat as he tried to think of the best way to begin. "Ah—when I met you on Fleet Street the other day…"

"I'm sorry if I was rude," she said at once. Her bonnet was a bit too loose, so that she had to tip her chin up to look at him. "I wasn't expecting to see you."

"No, I quite understand. That is—I feel I should warn you." Thomas turned toward her on the bench, and Rebecca looked startled—not so much by the movement, it seemed, as by his words. What little colour there was left in her cheeks leached out.

"Warn me, sir?"

"Yes." He measured his next words carefully. "Edward Pillar is not the sort of man you ought to be mixed up with."

"Edward Pillar?"

"Yes." It was a little disconcerting, how she kept simply repeating everything he said. Thomas forced himself to meet her gaze. He made his voice as gentle as he could. "I don't want to pry, of course. But you looked so unhappy the other day when I met you, I felt it my duty to warn you. Mr. Edward Pillar has a reputation, you see."

Rebecca reached up and tied the bonnet strings more securely under her chin. She did not say anything, but her movements were short and sharp, as though she were angry. Thomas's throat felt a little dry. This next part would be the most difficult. "I also feel I should tell you, I saw him with your sister later that same day."

Her eyes flew up to meet his, and when she spoke again, she seemed to be in intense agitation. "Eliza? You've seen Eliza?"

He nodded. "Of course, I would not have said anything had I not felt it my duty—"

"Where?"

"On Fleet Street, around the same place where I met you. My lodgings are not far, you see. I…" Thomas broke off, bewildered, as Rebecca pressed her hands to her face, lowering her head until it was almost level with her lap. "I don't wish to distress you, truly. I simply thought…"

"You're sure?" she interrupted again, lowering her hands and turning to look at him. She was still hunched over, as though she did not have the strength to sit up. "You saw Eliza, and she looked all right? And Mr. Pillar: you're sure it was him?"

"Well—yes." Now Thomas was truly at sea. Why were people so much more baffling than books? His eyes followed her as she dragged her hands down her face again and breathed in sharply. She looked half-mad. "I was under the impression that when I met you the other day, you had just been to see… well, Mr. Pillar."

Rebecca turned to stare at him. "*No,*" she said, after a long moment. "No, sir, you're mistaken." She sounded weak, and when she spoke next, it seemed more to herself than to him. "I'm just glad she's all right."

After a long, uncomfortable silence, Thomas cleared his throat and straightened on the bench. "So—are you telling me that it is your sister who is involved with Edward Pillar, and not—you?"

Rebecca stiffened. In a low voice, without looking at him. "Does that make a difference, sir?"

"I suppose it doesn't," he replied, crisply. "But as both of you have given testimony to myself and Mrs. Besant, which we have included in our article, I should think that any—ah, intimacy with Edward Pillar would rather complicate the question, if it became known."

Another silence. A lady passed with a dog and glanced curiously at the pair on the bench: the gentleman and the factory girl, sitting as far apart as the bench would allow them. As the bells of St. Paul's began to chime, the sound distant on the evening air, Rebecca spoke. "My sister disappeared two months ago. I've suspected for a long time that she is with Edward Pillar, and what you've told me, sir, confirms it. But she is a child." She glanced at Thomas, and he did not meet her gaze. "I don't think she would have chosen this for herself, if… things were different."

"Nevertheless, it seems that she *did* choose it," he said, shortly. "And were people to find out—"

"I've been trying my best to get her back home, these past few months. I've kept it a secret as best I can—"

"And yet *I* found it out." Thomas shrugged his shoulders. Then, turning towards her again, "And as for yourself, Rebecca, if you have had any involvement with him in the past, you may be sure *that* will be found out easily, too. I really wish—" With a bit-back sigh, "I wish you had disclosed this in our interviews. It changes everything."

Slowly, Rebecca shook her head. "I don't have to explain myself to you." Steadily, she met his gaze. "I've been nothing but honest with you and Mrs. Besant." She rose from the bench, and he could see that her hands were

139

trembling a little. "And I didn't walk all the way here from Bow just to defend my virtue to you, sir."

Thomas was too taken aback to reply. He just watched as the matchgirl turned and strode away, sending pigeons scattering at her approach. By the time he called after her, she was too far off to hear.

∼

Rebecca didn't know whether she was relieved or angry, now that she knew that Eliza was, indeed, alive, and by all appearances, well. To have her suspicions confirmed, when a corner of her mind had been whispering darker possibilities to her, ought to have taken a weight off her shoulders. But instead she just felt wound up, tight as a coiled spring. It might have had something to do with the way Mr. Barnwall had looked at her—or with the long walk home which awaited her.

As it got dark, Rebecca took a shortcut through Bethnal Green and came around by the gates of Victoria Park. Inside, dark trees and black space loomed, as though it would reach out and drag her inside. She had been walking on an empty path for some minutes when she began to hear footsteps behind her, advancing quickly.

Rebecca sped up too, as fast as her weary legs would allow. She could hardly breathe, her skin prickling with suspense. Quicker and quicker, the footsteps followed.

Past the canal, there was a lit stretch of street leading up to the church: if she could reach it on time—

With the dark, stagnant waters of the Union Canal to her left, Rebecca swung away as a hand touched her arm and screamed out. Her flailing fists struck her pursuer and would have sent him headlong into the canal had he not grasped the railing at the last minute, hoisting himself up and gasping. "I'm sorry—I'm sorry! I didn't mean to frighten you!"

"Then why are you following me?" she replied, trying to sound strong and fearless, but her voice cracked.

"*You* shouldn't be alone," the young man retorted, as he lifted his head, and then Rebecca recognised him: the round, honest face and black curls. He was the Brownings' coachman, though he was not wearing his livery now, but a ragged coat and cap. "I'm sorry. I wanted to talk to you. I'm Peter—"

"I remember," Rebecca said, warily. "And I suppose you remember my name, too."

"Yes." He ducked his head for a moment. "You're Rebecca, Eliza's sister. You came to the Brownings the day of the master's birthday. I've been wanting to talk to you since. I heard that Eliza…"

"Eliza," Rebecca cut in, as she began to stride on again, "is with our aunt in Sunderland."

"But you see, I know that's not true." He hurried to keep pace with her. "Because I know you don't *have* an aunt in Sunderland." As she began to interrupt, turning towards him, he went on, "I know everything about your family, Rebecca. Me and Eliza, you see: we had an understanding between us."

"Impossible," Rebecca said, shaking her head. "She would have told me."

"But I wouldn't let her, you see." They had come to a halt again, and Peter spread his hands, giving her a pleading look. "Just—hear me out, Rebecca."

"I must get home."

"Let me walk you. *Please.*"

Rebecca shrugged her shoulders, and as they set off again, Peter started talking. "The engagement was Eliza's idea. I thought she was too young, that she might change her mind. I—didn't want to rush things." He glanced across at her and shook his own head. "She wanted to tell you. She wanted to tell everyone—but I made her keep it a secret. And when she came to me a few months ago, asking if we could get married sooner, I said no. I didn't have enough money saved up, but I didn't think—your mother had just died, and maybe Eliza was… maybe she needed something I couldn't give her."

"Do you love her?" Rebecca said, unable to help the harshness that creeped into her tone. His words were too familiar to her.

"Yes," Peter burst out. "Of course, I do. You have to believe me. I just—didn't think. Like I said, I thought she was—too young."

"When Eliza loves," Rebecca said slowly, "She loves with all her heart. She can't help it."

"I know that. I know that *now*. And I shouldn't have—I should have given her more hope."

"I wouldn't say you're the only one to blame." Shaking her head, Rebecca said, "I am, too. And Eliza—at least a little."

"What has happened to her?" Peter asked, his voice desperate.

Rebecca thought for a moment. She could still see Mr. Barnwall's expression, pained and disgusted. And so she heard herself say, "I don't know. She just—disappeared."

"Have you been to the police station?"

They were coming up the Old Ford Road now, where splashes of light illuminated the pavement every hundred yards. Slowly, Rebecca shook her head. Peter stared at her. "But why not? If she just disappeared? You think they wouldn't bother about her, because she's a factory girl? There *are* people who care about her—I know if I told the master, he would see to it that something is done—"

143

"*No*," Rebecca said firmly, and, with an effort, met his gaze. "We will not involve anyone."

"But—"

"I have a pretty good idea of what has happened to her."

"Well, tell me then!"

Rebecca swallowed. "I know she's safe."

"*How* do you know that?"

There was a pause. As they came to the bend in the road which led to Greengoose Lane, Rebecca turned to Peter. It suddenly occurred to her that he was quite young—certainly younger than her. She put a hand to his shoulder, gently. "Listen to me, Peter. There are lots of other girls out there besides Eliza. You should forget about her."

He was shaking his head. "I can't—I couldn't."

"You should forget her." Rebecca held his gaze for as long as she could. "You should trust what I'm telling you: trust that she is all right." And then she dropped it, not before she saw the glint of tears in the young man's eyes and let go of his shoulder. "I'm sorry."

29
AN INCONVENIENT TRUTH

Edward did not know what had possessed him. Once he found out what was the matter with Eliza, the game ought to have been up. It had happened plenty of times before, after all, and he had never had any difficulty in sending the girl away with a bit of money and moving on with things. What was fun at first inevitably ended up tired and worn out: he knew that. He ought to have let it go, but when it came to the point, he found that he couldn't.

He had come back to Fleet Street last Saturday, furious at Eliza for something he couldn't quite remember, only to find her lying pale on the floor, with the maidservant at her side, and for one frightening moment, he thought that he must have killed her. She was weak as a kitten and dizzy as a top, even when they got her to eat something, and through the night she got up more than once to get sick. Then, the next morning, Edward brought her to be examined by the doctor, and it became clear that though she was not dying of starvation, he now had another problem on his hands.

The thing was, he had grown so used to her that the decision was not as simple as it ought to have been. Edward spent all Sunday evening thinking it out, and finally settled on bringing Eliza to the cottage in Devon, installing her with one of the servants there until her confinement—and then on Monday, there was the business with Mrs. Besant's article, and finally Father told him he would have to stay in town, at least until it all blew over. Who knew when that would be?

Edward Pillar came back to Fleet Street that evening furious—this time at himself instead of at Eliza. There was no way he could have stayed angry at her, in any case, not when she came running into the hall to meet him, jumping into his arms and smiling like a child at Christmas. He buried his face in her neck and forgot for a moment about meetings and articles and interviews. "I'm sorry I've been a brute," he murmured, and forgot, too, what he had been going to ask her about her sister, Rebecca.

Later, he said, "I wanted to take you to the country." The evening air was drifting in the open window, and they were standing in its breeze. It was still light outside, and a pink haze shimmered over the rooftops and chimneystacks. Edward knotted his hands around Eliza's waist, and thought about how content he was. "But it's not possible yet, my dear."

"It's all right," she replied, her voice faint.

"But you can't stay here, either. You understand, my dear, don't you?"

In reply, Eliza kissed his cheek. Edward fell silent then, just staring out at the city, but his mind was busy, turning over itself with plan after plan. Just a little longer, he thought. He could have this indulgence for just a little longer. But there was no eternity in his mind: he was his father's son, after all.

30
TRUE OR FALSE

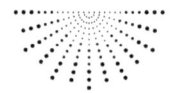

It was rare for Mr. Richard Pillar to tour his own factory during working hours, and Rebecca Moss had only seen it happen a handful of times in the seven years that she had been working at Pillar and Perkins. As such, when he strolled into the boxing room a few days after Mrs. Besant's article had been published and stood for a long moment surveying the workers before him, she felt her heart sink. It was one thing to meet with the other girls and talk about Mr. Pillar's tyranny, and quite another to see him in the flesh, and feel the waves of displeasure emanating from his person.

His eyes were small, dark and cold. His mouth was a long, hard line, and as, at the foreman's hasty orders all the machines in the room were shut off, a dreadful silence fell upon the room. The smell of burnt matches lingered in the air. Mr. Pillar opened his mouth and gave a little speech.

It was similar to ones Rebecca had heard before; at the unveiling of Mr. Gladstone's statue some years before, and at the ceremony celebrating the fortieth anniversary of the company, when they had all been let out of work early and not paid for the hours they had lost. She found out later that Mr. Pillar had given the same speech to the girls working downstairs in the dipping room, where the phosphorus fumes clung heavy to the air, and to the girls working in the drying chamber, where great fans churning overhead had almost drowned out his words.

Mr. Pillar spoke of the company's small beginnings in Plymouth. He spoke of his deceased partner, Mr. Arthur Perkins, and of how he and Mr. Perkins, and their fathers before them, had endeavoured to expand the business of matchmaking while remaining true to their religious ideals. He spoke for some time about lucifers, and safety matches, expounding on the difference between them. He spoke of the government's attempt to introduce a tax on matches seventeen years before, a measure which the queen herself had opposed, and of how the matchgirls had united with their employers to stop it happening. And finally, Mr. Pillar spoke about how grateful he was to have such loyal workers in his factory, and of how he sometimes thought of himself as their father, providing for them and guiding their behaviour when necessary.

When it was all done, and silence had fallen once more, Mr. Pillar turned to Mr. Lethbridge, who had been standing at his side throughout the speech. He nodded.

Mr. Lethbridge walked forward, handed a piece of paper to the foreman, and pressed a pen into his hand. The foreman rested the paper on one of the workbenches of the girls at the front, scribbled something, and then passed pen and paper to its occupant: Sally Chapman, who was the oldest of all the girls present, at thirty-five. She frowned down at the paper.

"All that is required of you," Mr. Lethbridge said, while Mr. Pillar stood silent beside him, "is to sign your name on the document. For those of you who cannot write your name, you may put down initials instead."

A ripple spread throughout the room. Girls elbowed each other and whispered. Rebecca looked around: she knew there were some among them who could not read or write and would not be able to understand what the document said when it came their way. A drop of dread wound its way down her spine, and she coughed and said, as all eyes in the room turned to her, "Begging your pardon, Mr. Pillar, sir, but can't you tell us what—"

"They want us to say that the things in Mrs. Besant's article weren't true," Sally Chapman interrupted, turning in her bench so that she could meet Rebecca's gaze. Her eyes shifted to the other girls around her, and then, in a deliberate motion, she passed the pen and paper, unsigned, to her sister Judy. Judy, without even looking at the document, passed it to her neighbour, and on and on it went, the whispers growing louder and into a chant,

Don't sign don't sign don't sign, until Mr. Pillar shouted, "Enough! *Silence!*"

He got his wish. But it was not the silence of before. It was a heavy silence, that shifted and crackled and promised all sorts of things that should have been impossible. A flush overspread Mr. Richard Pillar's features, and his mouth sagged in disbelief as he looked around him. When the document had made its rounds, he yanked it out of Mr. Lethbridge's hands, looked it over, and then strode out of the room without another glance.

"Back to work!" the foreman shouted, and as the machines started up again, Rebecca had to stop herself from smiling.

31
TROUBLE

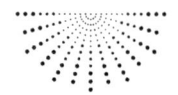

His father was in a black mood that evening, and so Edward absented himself as soon as he could. He went straight to Fleet Street, where Eliza was waiting. She looked better than she had for some time, with two spots of colour in her cheeks and a shy, dreamy smile. Every few minutes, her hand drifted to the curve of her stomach, then quickly flitted away again, as though she were ashamed of her own happiness. Edward watched her as they ate dinner, and finally, after the servant had poured them wine, he took up his glass and said,

"Your sister has been causing a bit of trouble."

"My sister?" Eliza's eyes flew up to meet his across the table: the smile faded from her face. They did not speak of Rebecca very often.

Edward sipped his wine and waited until the servant had left before he continued, languidly, "The girls at the factory seemed to have rallied around her. There was some business with an article that was published a few days ago, a pack of lies about the factory. The Fabians are boycotting us, you see. Hardly surprising, considering that organising boycotts is all they seem to do with their time. At any rate, when the matchgirls were asked to sign today that the article was false, they refused. And your sister, from what I hear, was the first among them to speak up."

Edward put his glass down. Throughout his speech, a mixture of emotions had passed over Eliza's face, and now she had her eyes trained on the table in an expression of studied blankness. He watched her for a moment more before saying, "You wouldn't know anything about that, would you, Eliza?"

"What?" she said, too quickly, and when she met his gaze again it was as though she were forcing herself to look at him.

"The article. It seems many of the matchgirls were interviewed for it. Your sister was likely among them, given her reaction today. But you would have noticed someone coming to your house to interview you, would you not?"

"I never saw anyone." Eliza's voice was quiet, and she was looking away again. "Maybe it happened after I left."

153

"Yes, of course," Edward said, easily. "That is the most likely explanation." He dropped the subject, and soon Eliza was smiling again, as their talk turned to other, more pleasant things.

It was later, much later, when the city was shrouded in darkness and the bells of St. Paul's had just chimed for midnight, that he shook her awake from her slumber and whispered in her ear, "Come, get dressed. We're going."

"What…" Eliza sat up in bed, bleary-eyed, as Edward lit a candle. She squinted up at him. "Where…"

"Somewhere safe," he replied, and seizing hold of her arms, he lifted her until she was in an upright position. "It's like I told you, my dear. You can't stay here, not in your condition. You will need a servant watching over you."

"But I thought you said we can't go to the country…" She followed after him across the room, stumbling in the semi-darkness. Edward opened the armoire where her new clothes were hanging, and then turned.

"We cannot. But I have arranged something else." As she opened her mouth, he leaned in closer to her. "*Eliza.* No more questions. You must trust me, as *I* trust *you*." His emphasis on the last part of his sentence was not lost on her: he watched her jaw go slack, and her eyes dart away. It was all he could do not to smile. "Now, you'd better pack your things, my dear. I shall help you."

32

MILE END WASTE

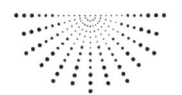

Thomas Barnwall had only come to the meeting in Mile End Waste because Mrs. Besant had insisted on bringing him along. It wasn't as though he was speaking, after all, and now that the article was published, he really had fulfilled his commitment to the project. Besides that, there was a heavy, driving rain which ought to have kept everyone away from the place. Instead, they had come in droves, gathering under the dripping trees in the park.

The matchgirls were toward the front of the crowd, distinguishable by their hairnets and white aprons. As soon as he saw them, Thomas knew that he wanted to wash his hands of this whole business once and for all. He told himself that was his only reason for going to speak to Rebecca, wincing as he was jabbed by an elbow here or tripped up there by someone's long coat. Mr. Browning was at the podium, talking about the sweating system of

Pillar and Perkins. To his right stood Mrs. Besant, and as her questioning eyes found Thomas pushing through the crowd, he shrugged his shoulders.

Rebecca was talking to the Irish girl, Sarah, when Thomas drew up to her side, and she did not look at him straight away. A couple of the other girls looked around at him, whispering among themselves, and he took off his hat. As applause rang out, signalling the end of Mr. Browning's speech, he turned to Rebecca, and with the glance she swept over him, he found the first words out of his mouth were, "I believe I owe you an apology."

"You believe?" she repeated. She had no bonnet today, but a knitted shawl had been wrapped around her head to protect against the wet, and raindrops flecked her face, clung to her eyelashes.

"Fine," he said, in a low voice, with a glance at the podium. "I'm sorry for offending you. My questions the other day were impertinent."

Rebecca appeared to consider this for a moment. She glanced at Sarah, who pointedly looked away, as though she were not listening in like everyone else around them. Finally, Rebecca gave a jerk of the head, and moved a little away from the crowd, until they were out of earshot. Their shoes squelched over the muddy grass, and the steady *drip drip drip* of a leaf overhead was striking Thomas's face when Rebecca put a hand to his arm. He looked down, mildly surprised by a sudden inclination to cover it with his own.

As though she had sensed his thoughts, Rebecca coloured and dropped her hand quickly. "We can stop here." She met his gaze again and raised her eyebrows. "So, do you still think I've been telling all our secrets to Edward Pillar?"

"No," Thomas said, shutting his eyes for a moment. "Of course, I don't. It was ungentlemanly of me to assume—that is, it is your sister who has been... unfortunate. And not you."

"I thought you said that Eliza chose her own fate," Rebecca said, quietly.

"I was wrong to say that, too."

Rebecca suddenly seemed distracted, looking off toward the crowd again as the sound of Mrs. Besant's voice drifted toward them. A moment later, she asked, "Don't you want to go back and listen to her?"

"To Mrs. Besant?" Thomas frowned. "I've heard her speak a hundred times. Rebecca..." As she turned around again to look at him, he took off his glasses, dried them on his coat, and put them back on. She still had her eyebrows raised, but there was a softness to her expression that had not been there before. "I heard what you all did at the factory, yesterday. I wanted to congratulate you."

"Well, what else did you expect us to do?" she said, crossly. "We weren't going to say it was all lies just to save our own skins. Undo all the hard work you've done for us..." But he caught the smile twitching at her lips and couldn't help answering it with one of his own.

"Excuse me." They both turned from their conversation, to see a young, dark-haired man who had just emerged from the crowd. He was in a coachman's livery and seemed to have eyes only for Rebecca as he said, "I have to talk to you."

Thomas's gaze flickered between the two of them. Rebecca's eyes were wide, and she gave a little nod before walking off with the young man. He watched them go, and Rebecca looked back at him over her companion's shoulder, a little uncertainly.

Later, when the crowd was beginning to disperse and the meeting was officially called to an end, Thomas was talking with Mrs. Besant and some of the other Fabians when he glimpsed the pair again. The rain had eased off, and they were walking slowly around the perimeter of the park. The young man had his head bowed, and Rebecca's hand was on his shoulder.

"Thomas?" said Mrs. Besant, and there was an unmistakable edge to her voice. He wrenched his eyes away. "Miss Black just asked about your book."

"Forgive me," he said quickly and thought it best not to interrogate the sinking feeling within him as he rejoined the conversation.

∽

The grey world outside Mile End Waste grew a little brighter as the rain eased off, and people began to pour in and out of the shabby shopfronts and taverns again. Rebecca watched them through the gates of the park.

"Is it true you're all going to strike?" Peter asked as they walked along. He was moving stiffly, his head jerking around every few minutes to check the group of Fabians that stood around the podium.

"We're not sure if it will come to that yet," Rebecca said automatically, though inside her heart was thumping the answer: *Yes, yes, yes*! That had been the only answer from the moment Mr. Pillar tried to get them to sign away their own truths.

"My master's for it," said Peter, glancing again at Mr. Browning, among the group of Fabians. Jerking back to Rebecca, "I can't stay here long. I shouldn't be talking with you: I ought to be getting ready to drive him back."

"Well, why *are* you, then?" Rebecca said, gently. "I've told you to try to forget about Eliza. I know it won't be easy, but…"

Peter shook his head once, twice, until she had stopped speaking. She saw him bite his lip. "I should have listened to her. She hated the match factory." He looked to Rebecca, desperate for her agreement. "She should never have been sent to work there. She should never have left the Brownings."

"We had no choice," Rebecca said sharply. Over the past few months, she had had many of those same thoughts herself, but it was different hearing them voiced by someone else. "After our mother died…"

"I could have helped you. I could have married Eliza and asked my master for a pay rise…" Peter heaved out a breath.

"It's no good thinking like that now. How could you have known?"

"How can *you* be so calm about it all?" Rebecca flinched back as Peter rounded on her. "She is your sister. Do you know where she is?"

"I…"

"Have you seen her? Do you really know if she's all right? Do you really know what has happened to her?"

It was Rebecca's turn to shake her head. She felt a dangerous stinging in her eyes. Angry at Peter for making her cry here, of all places—where Mrs. Besant and Mr. Barnwall and all the girls who looked up to her might see

—she did not hold back the words that came rushing, boiling, out of her sore heart.

"I know *exactly* what has happened to her. She has run away with a man well above her station and brought shame on herself and me. She has made her bed, and now she must lie in it." Rebecca gave a bitter laugh at the appropriateness of that saying in this case. But then her eyes drifted to Peter's, and she saw how the colour had drained from her face: how his eyes bulged wide in his sockets.

"Run away?" he gasped—more like mouthed. "You mean, eloped?"

Slowly, Rebecca shook her head. "No, Peter. She's his mistress."

He stopped dead on the path at that, one hand clutching at his chest. Rebecca put a hand to his shoulder as his head drooped. Her own harsh words were still echoing in her head. "I'm sorry," she began to say, but he interrupted,

"Who?" She could hear the breath whistling through his teeth.

"Edward Pillar." Peter's head drooped further toward his chest at the name, until Rebecca began to worry that he might lose his balance altogether. She tightened her grip, looping her arm through his.

"Now you know why I wanted you to forget about her." Her voice was no louder than a hiss. "I've tried to look for her these past few months more times than I can count. She doesn't want to be found. She—it looks like she doesn't want to leave him."

"Yes," said Peter, in a strange, faraway voice. "I—yes." The *clip-clop* of hooves from a passing carriage seemed to rouse him, and he snapped his head up, turning to squeeze Rebecca's hand once. "I must go."

"I'm sorry," she said again, helplessly, as he began to hurry away, and it struck her that the words might not just be for him alone. Somewhere in London—wherever she was, Rebecca wished that her sister could sit up and hear them, too. Now that it was too late, she could not help thinking of all the words that had gone unsaid between them.

33
A GREAT CHOKING WEED

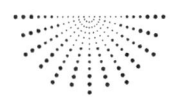

Mrs. Annie Besant's study was small and cramped in comparison to the other rooms in the house. It had originally been her husband's, and many of his things remained on the bookshelves. She wasn't exactly afraid of moving them; it was more that she liked to keep a token of him here. Though not a sentimental woman, she still remembered a time when she and Frank had been very happy: when their views had perfectly aligned.

An unfortunate consequence of keeping his things, however, was that the mess of papers on her desk had spread out and joined with the mess of books on the bookshelves, until the whole space was as cluttered and overwhelmed as her mind had become over the past few months. Had she known that Pillar and Perkins would invade her life in this way, choking other causes like a great weed, she might not have set out to interview the matchgirls on that first day. And yet they reached for her in her dreams: their pale, tear-streaked faces told her that she could not give up now; she had to finish the business.

Thomas was usually the only person who could make her feel calm, but even he seemed agitated today. Annie watched him as he stood by the window. With his profile lit by the setting sun, the expression on his face ought to have looked grim and forbidding. Yet the light seemed to flow through him, gleaming in his glasses and turning his hair gold. It reminded her of how he had looked on the first day they met, after she had given a speech on Home Rule. She had spoken humbly, cautiously, under the shadow of Nelson's Column and the National Gallery. After she was done, and applause rang out all across Trafalgar Square, she had seen only one person in the crowd: the young man who gazed up at her with hope and adoration in his eyes.

"Mr. Browning has pledged a pound," she said, partly to break the gloomy silence, and partly to return her mind from the sunny meadow into which it had wandered. Looking down at the pile of envelopes before her, she took out another and opened it. "We have also received ten shillings from another MP, and twelve shillings from Mr. Tomlin of the Merchant Tailors' Company." Her gaze strayed to the telegram from Richard Pillar, which had arrived a day after her article was published, and which she had turned over to stop herself from reading its threats again and again. "This should help us keep our word to the girls. If any of them are dismissed in consequence of our interviews, we can help pay their wages, at least for a time. But we shall need more subscriptions…"

She looked up again at Thomas, and sighed. "What is the matter with you?"

He turned quickly, as though he had just noticed she was there. "Nothing." A hand rose up to rake through his hair. "How do you… suppose we shall get more of these subscriptions?"

"No need to pretend you've been listening to me," Annie said crisply. With her attention returned to the notes, she went on, "Five shillings from Mr. Williams. You've been quiet since we got back from the meeting. Did Rebecca Moss say something to injure you?"

"Why should you think that?" he said at once, and his forced laugh was enough to twist a knife into her heart. Not a sharp one; after all, she was not a sentimental woman. But she felt it all the same. "As though *she* could injure me. No; I am thinking of her sister and Edward Pillar, and that whole business."

"There is nothing you can do about it," Mrs. Besant recited: it was not the first time, after all, that he had broached the subject since the day in Fleet Street.

"But I have been thinking…"

She squeezed her eyes shut for a moment and prayed for patience.

"I have been thinking that we might use it against him." Thomas came forward until he was standing by her chair. "You said before that Edward Pillar has a reputation. If, perhaps, he has seduced other girls in the factory—well, would that not strengthen our case against Pillar and Perkins rather than weaken it? These girls are abused, after all, in every other way, and we have shown that. Why not…"

"I know what you are trying to say." She met his gaze and spoke with a calm that she did not feel. "But those girls went with Edward Pillar of their own free will. Rebecca's sister went with him of her own free will—"

"We don't know that," Thomas interrupted. Spreading his hands, "That is… perhaps *she* did go with him willingly. But did he not use his position to his advantage? Is that not to be criticised, too?"

"Not by us," Mrs. Besant replied. As Thomas began to protest, she plucked the telegram off the table and held it up so that he could see. "Reflect for a moment, Thomas. I am already being threatened with libel. Our enemies cannot disprove these girls' testimonies, so instead they will try to cast doubt on their characters. It is our duty to stand in the way of that, not to add fuel to the fire."

Thomas's eyes flashed for a moment, but then his shoulders slumped in dejection. "You are right, of course. It... it is not my place."

"Go home," Annie told him, gently, as she laid a hand on his arm. "Rest. You did well today."

"I did *nothing* today." His response was so quiet that she barely heard it, but there it was: a sharper knife to her heart this time, and she watched him go out with his coat thrown over his arm, and his glasses askew. When he had left, she dropped her head into her hands and massaged her weary forehead.

After all, perhaps the sun had blinded her on that long-ago day in Trafalgar Square, and that look in his eyes had been nothing but the reflection of her own soul's longing.

34
HIDDEN

It was not an ideal solution, nor by any means a permanent one. But Mrs. McKinnon had always had a soft spot for Edward, and she was the only one of the servants who knew of the secret room. It had been put there by the previous owners of the house, used as servants' quarters until a new wall had been built, converting the storeroom to a library. Then Richard Pillar had bought the house, inherited its housekeeper, and the room was forgotten about, its door hidden behind a hefty bookshelf.

Eliza did not complain when Edward settled her there. After all, the room was about as large as the accommodations she had grown used to in Fleet Street. She got her meals brought to her by Mrs. McKinnon, who followed Edward's orders and kept a careful silence with her new charge. In the evenings, Edward came to her.

"It's not forever," he told her. In Fleet Street, she had been able to look out the window: here, that was absolutely forbidden, in case one of the servants saw her. "I am only asking you to wait a little longer, dearest."

All in all, the arrangement worked rather well for about a week, until his father stepped in, and with his extraordinary talent for disrupting Edward's plans, decided that the announcement of his engagement to Miss Browning should be moved up. What was more, the occasion was to be marked with a party at their house, of which Richard informed him the morning before.

Edward stared at his father across the breakfast table. "Now? You choose to have this party—*now*? While Mrs. Besant accuses us of avarice and indulgence?"

"Her lies cannot touch us," said Richard angrily, with a glare at his son as the maid leaned over to pour his coffee. "And Mr. Browning will honour the ties of our friendship."

"Ah. So this is about *Henry*." Edward leaned back in his chair, with a smile.

"Careful, boy. That is your future father-in-law you are speaking of." As the servants left them alone, Richard dropped his glare, his anger seeming to deflate. "Can you blame me, Edward, if I am in need of some good news? This woman wants to destroy me. And Mr. Browning and I may have… different views on the matter, but you have made a solemn promise to his daughter, and I intend on keeping it."

Edward nodded his head. He could see that the publicity would be a positive, if nothing else. It was something he ought to have predicted. But there were so many ways in which this might go wrong… with a quick, unconcerned smile to his father, he vacated the breakfast table and went downstairs. Chairs scraped as the servants rose to their feet at his approach. He ignored them all.

Mrs. McKinnon was in the wine cellar. She turned, keys jangling at her hip as Edward closed the door behind them. The folds of her face softened, as they always did when she saw him, and she said, in her lilting Scottish accent, "What is it, Master Edward?"

"You have heard of the party tonight," he said, out of breath. She nodded, still looking at him kindly. "It has come as—as rather a surprise to me. I would like to ensure that there are no… disturbances. Do you understand what I mean?"

Mrs. McKinnon nodded again. "Yes, sir. You needn't worry: I shall take care of it."

∼

Eliza trusted Edward: she really did. There were certain things she could not tell him, but that was only because she had chosen to forget them. Nothing about her old life

—not her engagement with Peter, nor Sarah's accident at the factory, nor the interviews with Mr. Barnwall and Mrs. Besant—occupied a space in her mind anymore. So naturally, she could not give him any of the information that he seemed to want. She trusted him, all the same.

But that night, she had her first vivid nightmare in what felt like months. She dreamt that she was lying on her workbench in the match factory. It was time to go home; all the other girls had already left, but Eliza couldn't move, her eyelids heavy with sleep. Every time they began to droop down, she would try to force them open again. The third time it happened, she saw Edward and her mother standing at the door of the boxing room, watching her. Edward was wearing tails and a white waistcoat and kept fiddling with his bow tie.

"It's not working," he said to Eliza's mother, who looked a little annoyed. "You didn't give her enough."

"I'm sorry," said Eliza, feeling obliged to interject at this moment, but her tongue felt heavy in her mouth. She tried to get herself into a sitting position—she really did. "I'll go home now, I swear..."

They looked as though they didn't understand her. Then, to her terror, she fell back, right off the bench, but instead of striking the hard floor, her head flopped on something soft, and at last she slept.

It was the prettiest room she had ever stayed in, and when Eliza woke up next, she was glad to find herself back in it.

Her bed had a feather mattress, the sheets crisp and clean to the touch. There was a porcelain ewer and bowl on the washstand beside her. There were lace doilies on the dresser. Her eyes took in all these details with relief, but then she realised that the light in the room had a blue tint to it, like that of twilight. Normally Edward was with her at this time.

Voices drifted toward her from somewhere, edged with laughter. Eliza sat up too quickly, and the world spun around her for a moment, then stilled again. She threw back her blankets, stared for an instant at a small brown stain on the top sheet. Mrs. McKinnon had brought her cocoa, and she had spilt a bit by accident: the memory popped up in her head like a green shoot, though she could not pinpoint the exact *when* of it. She let her feet dangle over the edge of her bed until they had struck the cold floor. She rose to her feet, straightened—stumbled—straightened again.

Laughter, louder, drifting in from outside. Eliza staggered to the door, catching a reflection of herself in the mirror as she went. She was white as porcelain, her red hair loose around her shoulders, her nightgown buttoned up to her throat. She turned the handle of the door and nearly wept when she found that it was locked.

Leaning her back against the door to ground herself, Eliza thought for a moment, as she looked around the room. She knew where she was—the Pillars' house, where Edward had brought her until they could go to the country—and yet she didn't know. For a moment, she wondered if the last few months had been some terrible dream. *Terrible?* That wasn't right... But still she wondered, if she tried hard enough now, could she open her eyes and find herself back on Greengoose Lane with Rebecca shaking her awake?

A rush of wind rattled the window of her room and fluttered the curtains that covered it. Eliza straightened, and moved toward it. She fumbled with the latch, which was stiff from disuse, until at last the window gave and she was looking out at a garden. Evening air caressed her face: reflected squares of light on the grass below told her that it was not too far away. She climbed out onto the ledge, the wind picking up the material of her nightgown and flapping it. She eased herself off, holding on with her hands until she was dangling, and let go.

The landing was hard, and pain shot through her left ankle. But Eliza found that after a minute or two she could still straighten and move again. The evening air seemed to be waking her up, and it was good to be outside again: out among the shifting trees and dark rooftops and soft, manicured grass.

A lighted window drew her forward, and Eliza limped along until she was standing outside the glass looking in. The darkness concealed her: no one saw her pale face. She saw Edward, in his finery as he had been in her dream, holding a champagne flute. She saw a young lady—but it couldn't be Miss Olivia, who played the piano so well and had always been so kind to Eliza and the other servants—come up and put her arm in his. And she saw Richard Pillar, smiling broadly as he spoke, and raising his glass. The party followed the movement: a group of faceless gentlemen and ladies who grinned into the dark.

Eliza did not feel her knees buckling beneath her, and this time when her head struck the ground, the surface was remarkably less soft. She stared up at the darkening sky for a moment, at the pale evening star, and smiled at her own foolishness.

35
THE SPARK

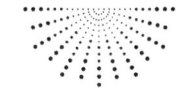

It was a cold morning, and there was even a hint of frost on the blades of grass beneath Peter Albright's feet as he came back from tending the horses. He went straight into the servants' hall, where they were all having breakfast, and stood warming his hands by the fire.

Snatches of conversation reached his ears. The lady's maid, Cooper, was talking about Miss Browning's trousseau to anyone who would listen. The footmen were talking about their night at the Paragon, and the housemaids were talking about… all at once, Peter stiffened and withdrew his hands, stuffing them in his pockets instead.

"I always knew there was something about her. She was always talking about wanting to be a lady. And making eyes at the young master and his friends—d'you remember?"

"I don't know," said the second housemaid. "She seemed quiet to me. Not the kind of girl who…"

"You talking about Eliza?" One of the footmen broke off his conversation to join the maids, leaning across the table. Peter sneaked a glance at him: he was grinning broadly. "She was a right goer, that one. Hardly a month working at Richard Pillar's factory before she went off with the son!"

"Stanley, quiet," said the first housemaid, with an anxious glance at Peter. "You don't even know if that's true."

"It's true enough that Harry saw them on Fleet Street one day," said the footman, nudging his colleague, who looked down, abashed. "What, you don't believe him?"

The second housemaid spoke next, after an uncomfortable pause. "She had *ideas*, Eliza did. Maybe she thought Mr. Pillar was going to marry her."

"Marry her! As if he would." Stanley laughed heartily. "As if he'd marry a—" and the word that he spoke next was so foul, it burned right into Peter's soul. It shrivelled up what had been pure and pulsing and alive in his heart, and turned it into something sordid.

He turned from the fire, strode to the table and pulled Stanley up from his chair by his white collar. The footman was taller than him, but Peter was stronger, his arms corded with muscle from working with horses all day. He landed two sharp blows before the butler came running in to seize his arms. Stanley's nose was bleeding, but he did not meet Peter's gaze as he was hauled away.

36
A FORGOTTEN DREAM

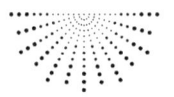

There was no point attempting to write something when one's mind kept wandering off in wild directions. Thomas Barnwall spent most of the night reading about the fall of the City of Glasgow Bank, but whenever he set pen to paper, he found that his thoughts were still tied up with the matchgirls, with Pillar and Perkins, and with a certain young couple he had seen walking around Mile End Waste the day before. As the grey dawn was creeping over Fleet Street, he finally gave up, extinguished his lamp, and curled up on his bed without getting undressed.

He woke a few hours later to blazing sunlight and numb fingers. The impression of a forgotten dream still pressed on his mind, like a handprint on a fogged-up window, and all at once Thomas knew what he wanted to do. He threw a coat on over his rumpled waistcoat and set out.

The road was bustling at this hour, and he made a few wrong turns before he found the side street down which he had seen Edward Pillar disappear the week before. There was a rag-and-bottle shop a few doors down which looked like the most likely place, and Thomas paused outside the house-door. It was locked, which did not really surprise him. His gaze swept over the assortment of objects in the shop window: blacking bottles, irons and books. Then he went inside.

The proprietor of the shop was polishing a piece of brass, and looked up under dark, bushy brows at Thomas. "What d'you want?"

"I'm a friend of Edward Pillar's," Thomas said quickly, making his voice sound as refined as he could. "I was told to—er—meet him here…"

The man's eyes narrowed and swept over Thomas, assessing. "A friend, hmm?" Then he gave a shrug and nodded to a door behind him. "Upstairs, first door on the left."

There was something in the man's expression—an unspoken assumption—that made Thomas flush as he pushed open the inner door and climbed the creaky stairs to where the man had directed him. He paused with his hand on the lock, turned the handle, and found—once again—that it was locked.

179

Yes, this had been a mistake. Thomas, in his half-asleep state, could still acknowledge that. Sighing heavily, he knocked on the door. *Nothing for it.* "Eliza?"

Silence.

"If you're there, my name is Thomas Barnwall. We met a few times before. I know you have no reason to trust me, but... I've come on behalf of your sister, Rebecca. I've come to warn you about this man, Edward Pillar. I don't think you are safe with him, Eliza. And..." Thomas paused, closing his eyes. He felt more foolish with each word. "My friend and I, we can help you. At least, I can promise you that we will try."

There was a dead silence. And then, just as Thomas was about to leave, he heard quick footsteps on the other side of the door. It scraped open, and he stared at the pale young woman with cropped hair and a dark, heavy fringe. "Sarah?" he stuttered. "Sarah O'Brien?"

37
LOST

Sleep was fitful but at least it was dreamless: shadows flickered past her eyelids, voices rose and fell, and hands moved her. Light flared and was extinguished. Finally, Eliza opened her eyes and turned her head to see Edward standing by the window with his back to her.

She did not speak, but he must have sensed the movement, for he quickly turned around. He was in his shirtsleeves, with his dark hair dishevelled and his full lips pressed so tightly together that they had almost disappeared. For a moment, they just stared at each other. And then he came forward to her side, knelt with a hasty, "Eliza, darling—"

She turned her head again so that she was looking away, and he broke off in his exclamation. At length he took up her hand instead, squeezed it in both of his even as she tried to struggle out of his grip. "Eliza. You lost the child."

The words drew a choked sound from her own throat. In answer, he bent his head over her hand, and an edge crept into his voice. "I am so sorry, my darling." But when Eliza turned again, and found herself looking at the top of his dark head, she felt strangely unmoved by his tears. "This is all my fault…"

"You're engaged," she told him, and a quaver went through his body. "To Miss Browning."

"I should have told you," Edward said, looking up at her. Eliza watched him, dully. "I know I should have—my father has arranged it all. If I had my way—"

"You'd marry me?"

He was silent.

"You love me?"

"Yes, of *course* I do. You know I do, Eliza, I have told you a thousand times. How can you—"

"You gave me something," she continued, still watching him. "The night you had the party here. You gave me something to make me sleep."

"No, that was Mrs. McKinnon. She thought it best, in case there were any disturbances. Of course, if I had known I would never have allowed it—"

"I *saw* you." Eliza's voice was hoarse. His grip on her hand had gone limp: she lifted it to point at the doorway. "You were right there, watching me go to sleep. I thought it must have been a dream—"

"It *was* a dream, Eliza—"

"Don't lie to me!" The force of her own voice seemed to startle him as much as it startled her. She struggled into a sitting position, bringing her face level with his. "You wanted me out of the way!"

Edward's beautiful blue eyes watched her, and something darkened within their depths. "Do you really wish to talk about who has lied to whom, Eliza? My father's business is on the verge of being *destroyed* by lies—lies you insist that you and your sister played no part in spreading."

"I'll tell you everything!" she cried. "I will, if that will make you honest with me, too! It was all Rebecca's idea: *she* made us do the interview with Mr. Barnwall, and I didn't even say anything to him—only about how old I was, and how long I'd been working in the factory, and how much I made a week. There, are you happy now?"

The slow smile spreading across Edward's face made a deep weight settle in her stomach. Eliza shook her head as she realised what she had just done. She threw back the covers knotted around her legs, and got out of her bed, her feet unsteady. "I want to leave."

"You can't," he said, from behind her back. "The doctor said you need rest. That fall you had could have given you a concussion, you know. You were very lucky it didn't. And your ankle—"

A white-hot rod of pain seized her left leg just as Edward was speaking, and Eliza reared back with a hiss. He grabbed her arms to support her, turning her around; she struggled in his grip. "Why did you do it, Eliza? Why did you jump out of the window?"

"I want to go home," she said, finally releasing herself and finding her own footing again. She limped towards the door. There were tears in her eyes, whether from the pain shooting through her leg or from the pain crushing her heart, she did not know.

Edward got to the door before her and stood in the way. He was not smiling now, but his voice was soft and gentle as he said, "This *is* home, Eliza."

"I want my sister." There was a lump in her throat now which made it difficult to speak.

"And do you really think she would take you back? After what you have done?"

Eliza looked down, swallowing.

"Well, do you?"

"Let me go." She lifted her head to stare at him, making her gaze pleading. "I want to go."

"You don't know how lucky you are." In one smooth movement, Edward had stepped forward and pressed her arms to her sides, his face inches from her own. "I could have you locked up for what you did. There's a place for girls like you, you know: *bad* girls who go jumping out of windows. And no one would miss you."

"You wouldn't do that." Her heartbeat was hammering loudly in her ears. "You love me."

"But do *you* love *me?*" As she nodded, he sighed, holding her at arm's length to study her face. "I don't believe you do, Eliza. Because I think that when you love someone, you obey them. You don't try to get them into trouble. Do you realise what kind of trouble I might be in right now if Mrs. McKinnon hadn't found you in the garden?"

Eliza was trembling all over. With a desperate yank, she freed herself from his grip one last time and threw herself at the door. Her hands caught the handle, and her weight landed on her left ankle and sent her sliding down with a cry of agony. Edward crouched by her side, brushed a lock of hair from her face, and pulled her up by her shoulders.

"I hate you," she spat at him, even as the tears slid down her cheeks.

"I don't believe that, either." Edward pulled her in until he had her clasped against his chest. He forced her chin up and pressed a kiss on her lips. "You're mine, Eliza. And you're not going anywhere."

38
NOT THE ONLY ONE

Sunshine streamed in through the window of the Fleet Street apartment and set the swirling dust motes alight. Thomas knew that it was still cold outside, but from here he could only see a perfect summer sky.

They sat opposite one another at the small table, neither of them looking at the bed in the corner of the room. The door to the hall stood open and swayed to and fro a little every now and then, stirred by some draught. Sarah had been white as a sheet when he first saw her; now she had flushed a dark red, her eyes avoiding his.

"You understand, I'm sure," Thomas said at last, "why I wouldn't have expected to find you here."

She made no sign of having heard him, saying instead in a low voice, "Did you mean it? When you said you could help?"

Thomas hesitated only a moment. "Of course, I did." As she lifted her eyes, watching him warily, he continued, "Mrs. Besant is collecting subscriptions from various parties who wish to help the cause. You are part of that cause: after all, your accident is proof of the factory's dangerous working conditions, and you gave us some very valuable information on the operations of Pillar and Perkins..."

Sarah was nodding, as though she knew all of this already. "But you were expecting Eliza to be here."

"Yes."

"You thought it was just her who got mixed up with Edward Pillar."

"Yes," Thomas said again, after a pause. "I was aware that he has a... reputation, but I didn't think..."

"I swear I didn't lie." Sarah leaned forward in her seat, clasping her hands in front of her. "Not to you, or Rebecca. I just didn't want to talk about it—me and him. It's been over and done with for years: I was so young when it happened, and he was so kind and handsome... he gave me compliments, he said he could help me..."

Thomas looked down. "I'm not here to judge you, Sarah."

"But you do judge me, all the same." Her words hung on the air: Thomas kept his gaze fixed on the table and tried not to let it drift toward her maimed hand. "I'm bad, I know I am. But I didn't know about Eliza and Edward until it was too late. I would've stopped it if I could. And I tried to help Rebecca find her, after."

Thomas nodded, slowly. This whole conversation was reminding him of a similarly uncomfortable one that he'd had not so long ago, in front of the British Museum. He remembered how *that* had ended. With an effort, he raised his eyes again, to meet Sarah's. He gave her a gentle smile. "It's all right. I believe you. And—I don't think you're bad."

She visibly relaxed, her shoulders slackening. "I've tried to be good, really I have. And falling in with him again was the last thing I wanted to do—but it's so hard to find a job, with my hand the way it is—and, well, I knew that Edward could help me. If I—helped him."

Thomas grimaced at that. "Have you met him often?"

"Just the once. And then… today." Sarah shook her head, a bitter smile twisting her mouth. "If he ever shows up."

"Let's go, before he does." Thomas pushed to his feet and held out a hand for her. As she hesitated, "Come, I promised to help you, didn't I?"

"Yes," she said slowly, looking up at him with a funny sort of smile, "But I know what gentlemen's promises mean."

"And you know that I'm not that sort of gentleman," he returned, gently.

Sarah considered for a moment more, and then took his hand, letting him help her up. "I suppose Dad would say we should all stick together."

Thomas snorted. "Your father would say that I'm not a true Irishman."

"He probably would." Sarah moved to stop him as he went for the door. "But, Mr. Barnwall, One more thing. I'm not the only one."

Thomas looked back at her, and he could not say why the expression in her dark eyes gave him such a chill. "What do you mean?"

"I mean, he's got girls all over town." Sarah's voice was quiet. "Some of them hidden away like Eliza. Some of them just wanting to help their families, like me."

Considering this, Thomas nodded, grimly. "Then this whole affair is much bigger than I thought."

39
SHORT

They had been kept short of work all week: Rebecca and the Chapman sisters, Sally and Judy, the first girls who had refused to sign the paper about Mrs. Besant's article. One day they would be sent home early, another they would be told to stay away until tomorrow.

The atmosphere in the match factory had never been without its tensions, but there was something about missing out on hours that made it positively unbearable to come back into the place. Every corner she turned, every step she took, Rebecca felt that people were looking at her: she felt sweat winding down the back of her neck, and a prickling in her spine and scalp. It was the sense that something was coming, and that something was taking its time: a blade hovering above her head, ready to come slicing down at some unexpected moment.

She survived her few hours on Friday, and after the bell for knocking off, went with Sally and Judy to the secretary's office to collect their wages. Sally went in first and came out with a face like thunder. "Two shillings six pence for the week," she said flatly. "What am I supposed to do with that?"

Judy went in next, her brow furrowed, and came out with the same amount. "And he says I'm not to come in till next Tuesday."

Then it was Rebecca's turn. She walked in with butterflies in her stomach. Mr. Lethbridge had his spectacles on and was looking at something on his desk. Without looking up at her, he began to read aloud. "'A typical case is that of a girl of seventeen, a piece-worker; she earns four shillings a week, and lives with a sister, employed by the same firm, who earns good money, as much as eight or nine shillings a week. Out of the earnings two shillings is paid for the rent of one room...' Now! That sounds familiar, doesn't it, Rebecca?"

He looked sly as a cat. The white hairs at the side of his head quivered as he chuckled. And Rebecca's heart sank as she realised that he was reading from Mrs. Besant's article.

"'The younger sister, poor child'," Mr. Lethbridge continued, as the tears welled in Rebecca's eyes, "... lives on only bread-and-butter and tea; now and then she goes to the Paragon, and that appears to be the solitary bit of colour in her life.' Well!" He put the article down with a flourish, and for the first time, met Rebecca's gaze through the lens of his glasses. "Your sister appears to be living a more colourful life now. Perhaps you would like to do the same?"

Rebecca wanted to scream, shout, throw something. But in the end, she did none of those things, just reached out a hand as Mr. Lethbridge handed over her wages in an envelope. It felt horribly light, but before she could even look inside, the secretary said, sounding bored, "One shilling eight pence. A fair wage for all your time off this week, I should think. And you needn't show your face here again, Rebecca Moss."

Silence, but for the scratching of a pen. Mr. Lethbridge had returned to his work. Rebecca's hand was shaking so hard that she could barely keep a grip on the envelope. And then, before she could think about it, she was kneeling on the hard floor.

"Please," she said. "Please don't do this."

Mr. Lethbridge glanced at her; he looked a bit discomfited by her position. "The decision has been made. There is nothing I can do."

"Please. This job is all I have. I've worked here seven years." Rebecca looked down, to see that her apron was bunched up around her knees. Her vision was blurring, tears sliding down from her eyes and nose, spasms building in her chest. "Please, sir. My sister is gone. My mother…"

"I know your situation." Then, as she let out a sob, "Well, it's no use crying over spilt milk, girl. You knew what you were doing when you spoke with those socialists. And it has caused us quite a bit of trouble. Oh, come now."

"Please…" She *had* known what she was doing; of course, she had. But that was all gone now, her righteous anger. Rebecca did not want to leave; she wanted to stay, begging from the bottom of her heart, until they changed their minds about her.

Later, she did not remember leaving the office, but somehow, she ended up out in the corridor, where she would have collapsed if not for the girls holding her up. They rubbed her back and patted her shoulder and said empty, comforting words, and Rebecca only stared and shook her head.

40
A LADY'S HONOUR

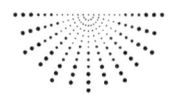

Mr. Johnson was the Pillars' venerable butler, and during the last few weeks, he and the housekeeper had had their work cut out for them. His usual reserve in speaking about his job had been broken down by sheer exhaustion, and so he told the young fellow all about it when he came in for his interview.

"It's all the trouble in the master's factory, you see. Annie Besant writes a few lines about some poor matchgirls, and suddenly everyone on my staff starts thinking they're hard done by, too. We've already lost two of our housemaids." They were sitting in the butler's pantry, breathing in the scents of fresh linen and wood polish. "Our coachman, James, handed in his notice last week."

"Yes, I saw your advertisement in the paper," said the young man. There was a blank expression in his dark eyes, making him look a little stunned. "I was working for Henry Browning before, in Grosvenor Square. But... I'm afraid I don't have a reference."

"Hmph," said Mr. Johnson. "Peter, isn't it?"

"Yes, sir. Peter Albright."

The butler examined him more closely, and pointed to his right eye, where the edges of a bruise had faded to yellow. "Got in a fight, did you? Is that why they dismissed you without a reference?"

"Yes, sir," said Peter, quietly, "But—if it helps to know—I stepped in to defend a lady's honour."

"A lady?"

"At least—she's a lady to me." Suddenly the young man looked impossibly sad.

Mr. Johnson could not help laughing a little, at the absurd situation he found himself in. A few weeks ago, he would have sent the boy on his way without question. But now... he sighed. "Well, we need a new coachman. And you've got experience. But you're out at the first sign of trouble, is that understood?"

Peter Albright nodded quickly and stretched out his hand as Mr. Johnson reached to shake it. "Yes, sir. Thank you."

41
CARPET BAG

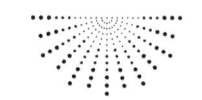

Rebecca was packing a carpet bag when she heard a knock on the door. She paused, looking up, as several different possibilities ran through her mind. Eliza, come back at last? Or someone from the factory to say that there had been a mistake, and they wanted her back?

"Rebecca, it's Thomas," came a voice through the door, and she sighed and went to answer it. He took off his bowler hat as he stepped inside. His hair was all flattened at one end, and his fringe was sticking up in several places.

"You look a sight," she said, too weary for politeness. "Like you haven't slept at all."

"*You* don't look much better," he accused. His eyes darted around the room, landing on the carpet bag, and he went still. When he spoke again, there was a funny quality to his voice. "You're leaving?"

Rebecca snorted, and returned to her packing, with her back to him. "And where do you think I'd go? I'm just taking some old things to the pawn shop." She did not look up, because she knew if she did, her gaze would land on the empty chimneypiece and she would regret it all over again. "It's about time I got rid of them."

Thomas drew up level with her, looking down at the bag. He picked up one of the pieces she had wrapped in newspaper. Rebecca's eyes followed him as he carefully unwrapped it to look at the porcelain shepherdess. "It's beautiful."

"It was my mother's." She took it back from him without meeting his gaze and replaced it after she had wrapped the paper.

"And are those your sister's clothes?"

Rebecca nodded, and clicked the clasps of the bag, closing it up. "She left a lot behind, when she went." After an embarrassed pause, "I'd offer you tea, but I've run out."

"No, I haven't come here for that. I just wanted to see if you were all right." Thomas turned as Rebecca passed him, the firelight flickering in his glasses. "I heard about what happened, at the factory. One of the girls told us—the younger Chapman sister."

"Judy should mind her own business," Rebecca muttered, pushing her arms through the sleeves of her long coat. She began to button it up, but her movements were clumsy, her mind distracted under his gaze.

"It's everyone's business, though," Thomas said, after a moment. "You see that, Rebecca, don't you? They dismissed you to make an example of you. They know that you gave us a lot of our information, and they want to pretend that they are still in a strong position. They—"

"Please," Rebecca interrupted. She freed her hair from under her collar and looked around for her bonnet. "It's all over with. I don't want to talk about it anymore."

Thomas came up, closing the distance between them. "You can't give up now." The earnestness in his voice surprised her. Then he took up the carpet bag. "And you don't have to sell your things. We can help—"

Rebecca reached for the bag, ignoring the brief contact of his hands on hers. "I might be poor, but I won't take your money, sir. I haven't come to that yet."

"But don't you see, it's our fault you're out of a job in the first place! It's our responsibility! You must..." Then, meeting her gaze, Thomas sighed and regulated his tone. "What I am trying to say is that you are not alone. You have friends, even if you will not take money from us."

"I've got no one." Rebecca didn't mean to be so honest, but his words had made her heart sink. "Only Sarah, and she's even worse off than I am these days. So I must do what I can."

Thomas shook his head, looking down so that she could not read his expression. "What about—the young man?"

"Who?" Rebecca frowned.

"The young man whom I saw you with, at the meeting in Mile End Waste last week." The lightness to his voice sounded rather forced. "And speaking of which, there was another one yesterday that you missed. A—a meeting that is. That is part of the reason why I was concerned about you... why I came here."

Rebecca was not proud of the fact that her heart had started racing at the change in his tone. "You mean Peter? Peter's not... he had an understanding with Eliza, before."

"Oh," was all Thomas said, but that "oh" spoke volumes. So when he reached for her a moment later, she was not really surprised. It was only a light touch, his fingers gently brushing her cheek, from the corner of her mouth to her hairline. Then he pulled his hand back as though it had been burnt. "I—I'm sorry."

Rebecca could feel that she had flushed, right to the roots of her hair. She gazed up at him foolishly and turned to watch as he fled.

42
WIMPOLE STREET

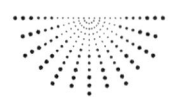

It was not his place to wonder about the strange goings-on at No. 12 Wimpole Street, and in any case, Peter Albright was not particularly interested in any of that. He had taken the job with Mr. Johnson out of pure necessity. That was what he told himself, at any rate.

Even if he *had* wanted to keep an eye on Edward Pillar's comings and goings—which he decidedly didn't—it would have been almost impossible. The man left early every day, and arrived back late in the evening, rarely making use of his father's carriage. When he was home, he spent most of his time in the library, where none of the servants were allowed except for the housekeeper, Mrs. McKinnon. And *this* was one of the strange goings-on of No. 12 Wimpole Street, which Peter began to notice despite himself.

The other was the ghost in the garden. He had dismissed that at first, too, as part of the servants' idle chatter. It was very likely, after all, that an excitable kitchen maid might glance out the window one night and see a sheet billowing in the garden and mistake it for a ghostly young woman. As Peter understood it, there had been an important party in the house that night, and the servants had probably finished off the wine themselves when it came back from upstairs, which did not help the maid's case. And the account that she had given of the apparition—flowing red hair, skin pale as death—might just as well have come from her own fancy of what a ghost should look like.

But then Peter started to hear noises, as he was lying awake at night. Distant cries and shouts, floating up from the floor below. He observed the plan of the house more closely and found that he slept right above the library. He saw that Mrs. McKinnon, the housekeeper, often yawned over her breakfast and snapped at the other servants, as though she had not slept well the night before. And he began to wonder…

It was unthinkable. And if it were true—well, the girl that he had loved was gone. In her place was a stranger, and Peter did not know what he might say to that stranger if they ever came face to face. But bit by bit, he began to feel some affection for the ghost of No. 12. And so, one July morning, when it seemed that Mr. Pillar's entire world was on the verge of falling apart, Peter took a newspaper from the pile that the footmen were ironing, tore out a section, stowed it in his pocket and waited.

At half past eight, as always, the mysterious breakfast tray was prepared in the corner of the kitchen, and the maidservant was shooed as the housekeeper said that *she* would take it up. But on this occasion, Mrs. McKinnon was called away by a commotion among the servants: someone had spilled a canister of sugar in the housekeeper's room, and it was all over the floor, and one of the maids was insisting it hadn't been her while the footman was saying it *had* to be—and in the confusion, Peter managed to get to the tray unnoticed, and slip the piece of newspaper under the linen covering before darting away again.

It was not his place, of course, to meddle in the strange goings-on of No. 12 Wimpole Street. But as soon as the breakfast tray had gone upstairs, Peter felt a gladness he could not explain, and tears in his eyes that he quickly blinked away.

43
BOYCOTT

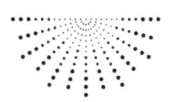

"With regard to our boycott of Pillar and Perkins, I have been asked whether this will not do an injury to the girls working there by decreasing the manufacture." Annie Besant paused for a moment, looking out at the crowd assembled in Goulston Street Hall. Amid a sea of caps and ragged coats, she saw Thomas standing near the front with a couple of other Fabians. He looked distracted, as though he were not fully attending to her speech. With a cough, she resumed, "My answer to such a question would be *no*. People must have matches, after all, and if they buy them from a firm which pays decent wages, thereby increasing the demand for their goods, the overall effect will be to drift the girls into the employment of these more respectable firms."

There was a smattering of applause at this. Leaning her hands on the podium, Annie looked in the crowd again, and saw that Thomas had disappeared. A moment later, she felt a touch to her elbow, and saw him at her side. "You'd better come outside."

She did not question him, knowing by the expression on his face that the matter was serious. With a few words of apology, she took her leave of her audience, and followed Thomas out a side entrance off the hall, onto Petticoat Lane where the evening air hung hot and heavy. Annie felt like she was wading through treacle as she followed Thomas: clad in her usual black, she felt beads of sweat begin to wind their way down her forehead.

She heard them before she saw them: a great clamour of female voices. Then she and Thomas had made the turn onto Goulston Street proper, where the stalls of the cloth market were being taken down after the day's business, and in between them, women and girls were marching, spilling from the pavement onto the cobbles. Some were carrying handwritten signs; some were still wearing their work aprons, while others had changed into their own clothes, splashes of colour on a canvas of white and black.

With darting eyes, Annie tried to count their numbers. She was conscious of a great weight settling in her stomach, and of a general feeling of confusion, as though she had set out to sea and lost sight of the shore. Her mind began to work furiously: how many subscriptions had they received so far, and how much, in total, had they now set aside for these girls? She knew the answer. *Not enough. Not nearly enough.*

But then she turned to Thomas, and saw that he was smiling, a full, delighted smile. "This is your doing," he said to her, voicing her own thoughts, but in such a way that made it sound like an achievement instead of a blunder. He was so young: she could see that now. He was just a boy. He had no idea of the fate that awaited these girls: the fate that Annie, with all her high ideals and impassioned speeches, had delivered right to their doorstep.

"They shall want you to say something," Thomas said next, and sure enough, Annie began to hear her own name called by the hordes: *Mrs. Besant, Mrs. Besant, Mrs. Besant*, over and over again. She looked around, a little frantic, to see if there was a place where she might stand and be seen by them. But before her thoughts could pursue that course any further, the doors of Goulston Street Hall were thrown open, and to the clamour of the matchgirls was joined the roar of the men and women who had attended the meeting, as they flowed down the steps and onto the street.

Caught between two streams of people, on a small island in the middle of Whitechapel, Annie Besant could feel that the trouble was only just beginning.

44
STRIKE

Eliza very nearly missed it. When Mrs. McKinnon brought her breakfast, she ate mechanically, for it all tasted the same to her. But as she was setting down the tray again, she heard a strange rustle, and looked under the linen to find that a piece of newspaper had been folded up there. With wide eyes, she flattened it out on her knee, and read:

Pillar and Perkins' Employees on Strike: *They Parade the Streets*

On Friday, it is asserted that Mrs. Besant, with Mr. T. Barnwall, was outside the works of Pillar and Perkins on Fairfield Road, urging the girls to go out on strike. On the same day, a girl employed in the box-filling department of the factory, understood to have supplied some of the information in Mrs. Besant's article 'White Slavery in London', was dismissed. That seemed to form the signal for the other girls, who, on the following Monday, marched out after sending in a deputation to the manager Mr. Carson. The other departments followed suit, and the eleven hundred employees paraded the streets in the neighbourhoods of Bow and Whitechapel.

Eliza hid the piece of newspaper under her mattress, but frequently took it out again during the day to run her fingers over the smudged print. Her throat, sore from crying, swelled with new emotion; her weary eyes filled with tears of awe.

45
INNOCENCE AND EXPERIENCE

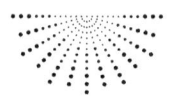

It was morning, and Edward Pillar was full of nervous energy: he kept dropping his cufflinks on the floor. At last, Eliza got out of bed and went to help him. Carefully avoiding his gaze as she fastened them on herself, she asked, "Is something wrong?"

"Something wrong? No, no. I just have an interview in an hour's time, that's all."

"An interview?" Eliza repeated, trying not to sound too interested. It had been a few days since she had read the news about the strike, and she had not heard anything about it since then. Whoever had hidden the newspaper clipping on her breakfast tray made no attempt to do so again. Edward, for his part, had not so much as mentioned it.

"Yes, just to answer a few questions about the factory." He waved a nonchalant hand, free now that Eliza had fixed on his cufflinks. Turning from her, he looked in the mirror and smoothed down his dark hair.

"And who's asking you these questions?" Eliza ventured, after a moment's pause. Edward met her gaze through the mirror, and she did her best to keep her expression blank.

"Someone from the *Pall Mall Gazette*, I think," he muttered after a moment, moving to smooth down his waistcoat. "Or the *East London Observer*. There's a couple of workers making a fuss over wages, you see, and naturally the papers are blowing it up into some grand affair."

Eleven hundred workers, Eliza thought, *if what I read was true*. "Is this to do with the article Mrs. Besant wrote?"

"Perhaps. Or perhaps it's about something else; it's difficult to keep up with what these socialists are doing these days. No doubt your sister is mixed up in it somehow."

"Do you know if—" Eliza began, impulsively, and stopped. She had been about to ask if he knew whether Rebecca was the girl who had been dismissed, but when she looked up to find Edward watching her, she realised that would betray what she knew. More quietly, "Do you know what time you'll be home?"

"I don't, dear one." Edward turned around and planted a kiss on her lips. Eliza shut her eyes and did not move until he was done. "But don't worry, I shall try not to overexert myself."

∽

The men of Pillar and Perkins had not struck, but since the women had done so, there was no work for them to do, and so on Fairfield Road, the gates had been shut on an empty yard and a smokeless factory. Inside his father's office, Edward Pillar sat ramrod straight, crossed his legs at the ankle under the desk, and looked calmly at the man from the *East London Observer* (it had been that one, after all).

"Yes, our growth has been gradual, as you say. The work of many years and three generations to get to where we are now."

"And, sir, if you care to comment on Mrs. Besant's statements—"

"They are false," Edward said at once. "The socialists are trying to create mischief for the girls who work in our factory, for their own personal motives." As a series of shouts drifted in through the open window from the road outside, he did not stir a hair. "Our business employs a large number of hands, and so we pay a large amount of wages every week. Of course, we want to see our workpeople well paid. And if one girl might earn the wages of three, we should be glad to see her do so. But we can only give the renumeration that our profits permit."

The reporter was nodding, writing rapidly in his notebook. Without looking up, he said, "And what do you think of the girls who have gone on strike, sir?"

"What do *I* think of them?" Edward repeated, incredulously, and as the reporter looked up at him, he quickly composed his features into a thoughtful expression. "I feel sorry for many of them. I know they must desire to return to work, but do not feel safe to do so." After a pause, "But I can assure you that when picketing starts, we will have the full assistance of the police, and any girls who *do* return will be well protected."

"And if they don't return, sir?"

"Well…" Edward gave a grimace. "Of course, we do not wish to deny our present hands of work, but if we desire, we can easily get plenty of girls from Scotland to take their places. We shall have to see how the situation develops."

"Very good, sir. Thank you for your time." The reporter put away his things, stood up and shook Edward's hand.

The instant he was alone again, Edward got a match and lit a cigarette. He blew out a skein of smoke just as the door opened again, admitting his father. "How many times have I told you not to smoke in here?"

With a long-suffering sigh, Edward stubbed out his cigarette in the ashtray and stood up to let his father take his place in the chair again. Richard Pillar looked terrible:

his skin stretched and waxy, the wrinkles on his forehead deeper than before.

"It went well, I think," he said after a moment, after his father had demonstrated no interest in anything but staring into space. "The interview."

"Wha—oh, yes." Richard looked back at Edward, with the ghost of a smile. "Very good. I knew I could rely on you."

Discomfited by the praise, Edward folded his arms over his shirt, and hovered by the desk. After another long moment of silence, his father seemed to come back to himself, clearing his throat. "I have just come from a meeting. With Carson and Lethbridge."

"Oh yes? And what have you decided?"

"They have told me..." Richard shut his eyes for a moment, so that the shadows beneath them looked more pronounced than before. "It seems this strike is gathering support all over the country. There was a demonstration in Glasgow this morning."

"In *Glasgow*?"

"By the Social Democratic Federation, to protest the importation of hands to our factory."

"But they—" Edward was floored. "How—"

"It is as if they know every move we are going to make. We must surprise them." Planting his hands on the desk,

Richard leaned forward, looking steadily at his son. "The girl you told us to dismiss."

"Rebecca Moss, yes. What about her?"

"We have decided to reinstate her." As Edward began to protest, "Listen to me for a moment, boy. I know that you acted with the company's best interests at heart. But her dismissal is what started this whole deluge. I have been in this business much longer than you, and I can tell you that sometimes one must make compromises."

Edward was shaking his head. "We will look weak, Father."

"We will take them by surprise. And in a few weeks' time, when all our girls are back at work, the socialists will find some other cause to champion. Mark my words, Edward. We are not going to let this little fiasco mar our legacy."

46
TO THE EDITOR

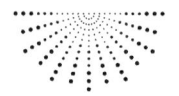

To the Editor of the East London Observer

Saturday July 7th, 1888

SIR—An interview appears in your issue of the 6th inst. in which Mr. E. Pillar accuses me and my colleagues of creating mischief for the girls for whom we advocate and acting out of personal motives. Since I can scarcely expect you to permit your columns to become a tilting ground between ourselves and Messrs. Pillar, I must content myself with saying that such an accusation exposes not only Mr. E. Pillar's error but also his hypocrisy. This gentleman's conduct towards the girls who are supposedly under the protection of his firm is well-known and may be attested to by a number of them. I would therefore encourage the public to be wary of Mr. E. Pillar's own personal motives, and judge for themselves on which side of this quarrel the right lies.

THOMAS BARNWALL

47
EXPLOITATION

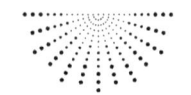

At the sound of a slamming door, Thomas jerked awake, raising his head from his desk, where he had fallen asleep a few hours before. He turned to see that Mrs. Besant had just marched into his apartment. "What…"

"I've been knocking for at least ten minutes," she snapped, and then brandished a newspaper at him. Thomas didn't need to look to see which one it was. "What is the meaning of this?"

Her edges were slightly blurred. Thomas cast about for his glasses, and when his hands came up empty, gave up with a sigh. "I had to do *something*. When I read his interview—I just had to. He had the gall to say that he felt sorry for the girls striking—that if they return to work, *he* will protect them? They need to be protected *from* him, not by him… and I thought that people should know…"

Mrs. Besant was nodding, pressing her lips together. "And what exactly are they to know?"

"That he has been exploiting the girls in his father's firm for years." Thomas finally located his glasses, fixed them on slightly askew, and began rummaging through the top drawer in his desk. With a glance at Mrs. Besant, he went on, "I have been investigating him. Ever since that day that we saw him in Fleet Street…"

"So this is about Rebecca Moss. I might have known."

"Not just her—not anymore. There are many more girls like her sister." Thomas drew out his notebook, thumbed through the pages to look at the notes he had taken. "I know you said before that these girls have gone with him willingly; that to expose his conduct would be to expose them, too, and undermine our cause. But I have spoken to a number of them over the past few weeks, and one was just fourteen at the time Pillar seduced her. This was only two years ago." He looked up to see what effect his words had produced in his companion: she had paled but was looking away. "And since the Stead Act of 1885, a girl under the age of sixteen—"

"I remember it quite well, Thomas," Mrs. Besant interrupted him. With a few steps forward, she brought her gaze back to his face, and seemed to soften a little. "But you are not William Stead. He had *The Pall Mall Gazette* behind him, he ran a thorough campaign—"

"I have been thorough, too, and some of these girls have told me they would be willing to testify against the man." Thomas turned another page in his notebook. "I cannot give out their names yet, but..."

"And that is just the problem," Mrs. Besant sighed. "Your letter is all insinuation, Thomas. And insinuation can be more dangerous than outright fact. You know how quickly these people act—my article hadn't been published a day when Richard Pillar's solicitors telegraphed to me. You may find that this story is snuffed out before you can get more evidence."

"I have all the evidence I need," Thomas said, but his voice was quiet. He turned back to his desk and pinched the bridge of his nose. He did not notice Mrs. Besant approaching until her hand fell on his shoulder.

"I have a daughter of my own, as you know," she said to him, quietly. "And if someone ever hurt Mabel the way that these girls have been hurt by Edward Pillar, I know that I would move heaven and earth to see justice done. Men like him ought to be punished. But—"

"Are you going to tell me again that it is not *my* place to do so?" Thomas's voice was flat.

Mrs. Besant squeezed his shoulder, so that he turned to look up at her. Her expression was not just kind: her eyes seemed to know everything and forgive everything. "I will just tell you, Thomas, that hateful as he may be, Edward

Pillar was right in one respect. You may have been too guided by your own personal motives in this."

Thomas had coloured: he opened his mouth to argue, but the fire went out of him a moment later. "I suppose… perhaps I have been. A little."

"Rebecca is not your equal, Thomas. And our duty is not just to her, but to all of those girls in Pillar and Perkins. We have promised them change. Think of *them*, when you write your article."

"My article?" He jerked around in surprise, staring up at her.

"Well, as you said yourself, *The Observer* cannot become a tilting ground between us and the Pillars. My own magazine will have to suffice." She gave him a half-smile. "After all, the damage is already done. Now you must see this to the end. And when they threaten you, you must say what I always do: that you intend to stand by your statements."

There was a long silence. Then Thomas returned her smile. "What would I do without you?"

"I hope you never find out. Now…" She let go of his shoulder and moved to look at his papers. "Show me what you have gathered so far."

48
NEVER COME DOWN

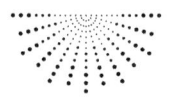

Rebecca had locked the door of her rented room, and though knocks came at all hours of the day, she never answered it. She knew what was going on. Sometimes she opened her window onto the smoky city air, and heard the distant shouts drifting from Mile End Road. She would look at the rooftops and chimneystacks, and wish that she could live up here forever, and never come down to earth again.

She had got a little money from pawning her mother's and Eliza's things, but it was already quickly running out, and she knew it would not be enough to pay next week's rent. She tried to make the food in her cupboard stretch for as long as possible. The tea was all gone, but there was a bottle of brandy left over from one of the meetings with the girls. Rebecca took it out sometimes, uncapped it and sniffed. Were it not for the fact that she could almost feel her mother's sigh of disappointment, tickling the hairs on the back of her neck, she might have started drinking it. There was nothing to lose anymore, after all.

And then came a knock on her door, accompanied by a voice that made her think she must be dreaming. "Rebecca? This is Mr. Lethbridge. I have come on behalf of Pillar and Perkins."

Rebecca sat up. Not having slept well the night before, she had been dozing in Mum's old armchair. There was a stale yellow light in the room, so that she could not tell what time of day it was. She passed a hand over her face and then rose, a little unsteadily, to her feet. As the knocking continued, she crossed to open the curtains, and saw seagulls wheeling away from the window against a bright, white sky. *Morning, then.*

There was a click as she unlocked the door and drew it open. "Sir."

Mr. Lethbridge, who had been turning to go, jerked back to look at her. He had on a long black coat, with a cane in one hand and a hat in the other. Standing face to face, Rebecca realised for the first time, with a funny start, that she was a head taller than him. She had never seen him away from his desk before.

"I am... sorry to disturb you." His eyes flicked over her, taking in her dishevelled appearance, and he frowned faintly. Rebecca just watched him. "You are not out in the streets, with the others?"

"Is there something you want, sir?" she responded.

He hesitated, patting the wisp of white hair at the side of his head, and then gestured to the door. "May I come in?"

Rebecca turned and led him inside, winding her shawl tighter around her shoulders, her face in a fixed expression of utter blankness. She drew out a chair at the table for him, looked up at the dark spot on the wall where the queen's portrait used to hang, and said, "I've got nothing to offer you, sir, except brandy."

"Then I shall take a little of that, thank you." Mr. Lethbridge leaned his cane against the back of the armchair and swept his coat underneath him as he sat. Rebecca rummaged in the cupboard, drawing out a glass and discreetly wiping it with her sleeve before she filled up a quarter.

"Thank you," the secretary said again as she handed over his brandy and settled in a chair opposite him. He drank a little, made a face, and put the glass down again. "Miss Moss, I'm sure you cannot be unaware of the events of the past week."

As he looked towards her expectantly, Rebecca made a noise of assent.

"And we, for our part, are aware that a certain action of ours may have incited the—the trouble. Therefore, we wish to offer you your job back."

Rebecca stared at Mr. Lethbridge, as a drowning man blinks at someone who has just thrown him a lifeline. He went on, "We were operating under the impression that you were the ringleader of this... this strike. However, as we now know that must be false, and that you must be as anxious to return to your work as many of the other girls who have been dragged into the streets, we wish to give you that opportunity."

"Thank you," Rebecca said, quickly, feeling that her mind could not catch up with his words. "I—I do want to come back, sir."

"Good." Mr. Lethbridge drank the last of his brandy, and when he looked at Rebecca next, his expression was actually kind. "I do not mind admitting that, when I was told to dismiss you, I had a lot of sorrow in doing so. You have always behaved remarkably well and done your work in a quiet and orderly manner, just as your mother did before you. Recent events notwithstanding... I think that those are qualities to be admired."

"Thank you, sir." Rebecca felt more confused than ever.

"If that is all settled, then, you may come to the factory tomorrow morning at nine." Mr. Lethbridge rose from the table and stretched out a hand for her to shake. "I look forward to seeing you."

As soon as he had left, Rebecca let out a long, heavy breath. But before she could think too hard about what had just happened, and begin to doubt herself, she focused her energies instead on finding a clean apron to wear tomorrow.

49
OUTSIDE THE GATES

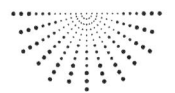

It had been a quiet day. The girls had gathered outside the match factory early that morning, and the police had shown up not long after to escort a small number of workers past the picket, amid catcalls and jeers. After that, Thomas had left his fellow socialists picketing to go to work. His employers at the Telephone Company, while aware of the strike going on, were growing less and less patient with his excuses about it.

He came back in the evening to find that not much had changed. The factory yard was quiet, there were a few police constables dotted around the place, and the girls were still outside the gates. The only difference he could notice was that a few of them were clutching collecting boxes, and that it looked like it might rain. Thomas's eyes were still roaming the crowd when he realised what—or rather, *who*—he had been searching for, and looked away, ashamed.

"The girls have been complaining," said Mrs. Besant in greeting, coming up to his side. She looked deeply weary. "I was gone for a little time—trouble with Frank, you know—and Mr. McDonald sent a few of the girls on a march to the West End. He tried to get them to collect money from the fellows at the Radical Club on Commercial Street, but most of the girls refused, as I knew they would. I tried to warn him about doing that."

Thomas nodded, slowly, and was about to inquire further when a girl burst free of the group and ran up to them. After a moment's confusion, he saw that it was Sarah, clutching an empty collecting box. She bobbed in hasty acknowledgement of Mrs. Besant before turning back to him. "Mr. Barnwall, have you heard?"

"I—that is, Mrs. Besant was telling me you were collecting in the West End—"

"Not about that," Sarah interrupted, and then, pushing her fringe off her forehead with a quick breath, "It's Rebecca. They want her to come back to work."

Thomas and Mrs. Besant exchanged uncertain glances. "How do you know—"

"My sister saw Mr. Lethbridge, the secretary, visiting Rebecca's lodgings."

"This is most surprising," Mrs. Besant said, after a moment's pause. "They have clearly designated Rebecca as the ringleader—but if they think that the mere act of reinstating her will satisfy these girls…" She glanced at the crowd around them, "Then they are more short-sighted than I thought."

"We have to stop her," said Sarah, who seemed to be barely listening. Her eyes were wide, fixed on Thomas in earnest appeal. "She hasn't been out with us, don't you see? She's not thinking straight, not since she lost her job. And if she said yes to Mr. Lethbridge—"

"Then that is *her* choice, my dear," Mrs. Besant said gently. "And there is nothing you can do to stop her."

But Sarah shook her head, still looking at Thomas. "Please come with me, sir. Just help me talk to her. If you come, I'm sure she'll see sense."

Thomas shifted from one foot to the other. He could feel his cheeks warm with embarrassment under Mrs. Besant's gaze. With a cough, "I'm sure that you, as your friend, could persuade her better than I—"

"Please, sir," said Sarah again, with a quick shake of the head that made him feel even more foolish than before. "We don't have time for this."

With a glance at Mrs. Besant, who was looking away, with her lips pressed so tightly together that they almost disappeared, Thomas sighed, and followed after Sarah.

CHAPTER FIFTY

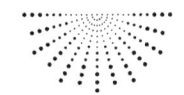

Edward Pillar stepped in from the rain, shrugged off his cape before the butler could get near him, and let it fall to the floor. He threw his hat on the hall table and climbed the stairs two at a time, his dark hair gathering into a point on his forehead and dripping down his face.

"Master Edward." Mr. Johnson caught up with him at the top of the stairs. "There has been a letter in the *Observer*—"

"I know it all," he growled. Without another word, he swept into the library, slamming the door behind him, and came to a dead halt. "F—Father."

Richard Pillar looked up from the newspaper he had been reading, and with a grim look, tossed it away. Frantic, Edward's eyes roamed past him, to the bookshelf that had been moved away from the wall, and then to the open door into Eliza's—into an *empty* room. He looked back at his father and swallowed.

"I see you were caught in the storm," said Richard, with an edge to his voice. He glanced at the bellrope. "Shall I ring for a hot drink? Some dry clothes?"

Edward shook his head, dumbly. He took one halting step forward, and then another, and finally summoned the will to speak. "Father—what's going on?"

"I might well ask you the same question," Richard said, quietly. "Or perhaps what I should ask is how you thought you could hide this from me?"

It was like being a boy again, caught skipping his lessons. Edward lowered his head and detested the tremble in his lip as he said, "I'm sorry, Father."

"I have warned you, so many times, to be discreet." His father rose from his seat and began to move around the table toward Edward. "You know the dangers. You know that with this strike, our friendship with the Brownings is already under strain. And *now*, with this—this letter…" He snatched up the newspaper again and brandished it at Edward. "Do you really think they will still want to be associated with us? You may say goodbye to your betrothal with Olivia. It's all ruined now."

Edward ought to have felt cheered by this—after all, he had never wanted that confounded engagement in the first place. But the expression of disgust on his father's face, combined with the shame that *Olivia* should have been the one to break off their engagement, and not he—all conspired to make Edward feel even worse than before. "I shall fix it, Father, I promise you. I can—"

"You will not do *anything*," Richard interrupted, his eyes blazing. "From now on, you will stay here, and stay out of sight. Stay out of trouble. No more interviews, no more statements. I have a mutiny on my hands as it is, and you will only make it worse."

Edward dropped his gaze to the floor again. "Yes, Father."

"And the girl…" His father stopped, just in front of him, and for a moment, his anger seemed to deflate. "Oh, Edward. Why could you not have disposed of her like all the others? Why bring her here?"

"I don't know," Edward said, so quietly that he was not sure if his father could hear him. "I was—I was weak, Father…"

Richard struck him across the face. As Edward reared back on his heels, he caught his shoulders again. "Look at me. *Look at me.* Because of your weakness, this girl is now costing us in more ways than one. I have sent her to the country house with Mrs. McKinnon, where she will stay for a time until this has all blown over. I will make sure to pay for her silence." His father paused, and then let go of Edward. "I… I understand there is some question of a child?"

"There was," Edward said hastily. "She lost it."

"Well, that does not mean we are safe from the possibility of another." Richard lowered his hand and looked up again to study his son's face. "A matchgirl," he mused quietly, after a moment. "You could not have chosen *anyone* else?"

"I could have," Edward admitted, a little pathetically, and when he spoke again, it was more to himself than to his father. "And I should have. She was more trouble than she was worth."

51
ESCAPE

With each new mile between herself and London, Eliza felt the tug on her heart grow more and more painful. Before, all she had wanted was to escape, but now, knowing what she did about the strike and Rebecca, the feeling that she was growing more and more distant from it all was almost unbearable.

She thought a few times of jumping out of the carriage and fleeing that way, but Mrs. McKinnon kept her beady eyes trained on her all the time, and Eliza was sure that the woman would wrestle her down before she could even get to the door. Later, when the housekeeper had begun to doze off, Eliza thought of pushing *her* out of the carriage, instead. She inched out of her seat more than once, arms outstretched towards her captor, but no matter how many times the savage voice within her insisted that the harridan would deserve it, it was something she could not bring herself to do.

She did not know where they were going, or why; she knew only that she had heard Richard Pillar's furious tones earlier that day, ordering her out of the house, and that then she had been told to pack up and bundled into the carriage, and that Mrs. McKinnon seemed to have gone along with the whole plan very reluctantly. Toward the beginning of the journey, Eliza had heard her more than once muttering under her breath, "Forgive me, Master Edward."

Now it was dark outside, and raining heavily, and Mrs. McKinnon was asleep, with her mouth drifting open and the great black coil of hair sinking further and further down on her head with each jolt of the carriage. And after running through various different plans in her mind with no success, Eliza could think of only one more thing she could do.

She knocked on the roof of the carriage and waited for the coachman to bring them to a halt. As its motion slowed, she watched Mrs. McKinnon anxiously, but the housekeeper only mumbled in her sleep, jerking around a little. Finally, when they had stopped, Eliza burst for the door, yanked it open, and stepped right into a puddle that splashed her up to her knees.

She gasped, stepped out of it, and turned to get her bearings. They were on the edge of a forested road, and up ahead were the lights of a town, blurry in the rain. Eliza drew a deep breath, and then splashed forward to the coachman's box, leaning up to talk to him. "Please, you've got to help me—I—"

He turned to look at her, and the rest of her words died in her throat. Eliza let go of the corners of her skirt and sank back down onto her heels. She blinked, and frowned, and felt tears begin to prick the corners of her eyes. Silently, her lips began to form his name...

"What are you doing? Get back inside." Mrs. McKinnon had got out, splashed into the same puddle Eliza had stepped into, and now looked very displeased. As she grabbed Eliza's arm with an iron grip, she glanced up at the coachman. "Are we nearly at Stony Stratford, Peter?"

"Nearly, ma'am," Peter Albright replied, and did not spare another glance for Eliza as she was dragged back into the carriage.

52
BLACKLEG

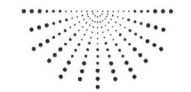

Rebecca answered the door after Sarah's fifth knock, but only drew it back a little as she peered out at them. "I'm not coming out."

"Aren't you going to invite us in?" Sarah said, pointedly. Rebecca glanced at Thomas and lowered her eyes again with a neutral expression. He coughed, and nudged Sarah, who sighed. "Fine. We'll just talk to you here, then, and never mind if your neighbours hear."

"I've got nothing to hide from them," said Rebecca, a little too quickly. "I've got nothing to be ashamed of."

"Are you sure?" Sarah said, coolly and then when Thomas nudged her again, closed her mouth, letting him take over.

"We have heard—ah, that is, we think that you might be…" Thomas stopped, abashed, as Rebecca raised her eyebrows at him. Of course, his mind chose that moment to remind him of their last encounter, and he was grateful for the dimness in the corridor as he blushed. "... that you might be going back to work."

Rebecca hesitated only a moment before nodding. "Word travels fast."

"You *can't!*" Sarah burst out, ignoring Thomas's warning glance. "Rebecca, you're the one who started all this. The girls all look up to you! You can't—"

"I haven't got a choice," Rebecca interrupted, adjusting her grip on the door. Her voice was flat, almost bored. "I've got to pay my rent. I've run out of things to pawn."

"Then you can come stay with me! And take some of the strike fund the socialists have been collecting instead of turning it down like a pig-headed fool!" Sarah glared at her friend as she caught her breath. "This is bigger than you now, Rebecca."

"Then what difference does it make if I go back?" Rebecca said, unperturbed by Sarah's raised voice. "If the strike will happen anyway—"

"It *will*," Sarah said, pushing forward until Rebecca shrank back a little, "But the minute those girls see you go over the picket line, you'll be a blackleg. They won't look up to you anymore: they'll hate you. And don't say you don't care what they think of you because I *know* you do."

There was a brief silence, and then Rebecca said, in a hard voice, "It's late. I've got to be well rested for tomorrow." She began to close the door.

"Rebecca, wait." Thomas put a restraining hand on Sarah's shoulder, and watched as Rebecca looked out through the gap again. "Listen to me. The very fact that Pillar and Perkins offered to reinstate you proves their weakness. It proves that we are already winning this battle."

"Or maybe they just want to take me back because I'm a good worker." She was regarding him with a kind of angry wonder. "Did you ever think of that, Mr. Barnwall?"

"Believe me, Rebecca, when I say that is not true. No matter what lies they might have told you to entice you back, these people do not value you."

"And you're saying that *you* do value me? That Mrs. Besant does, too? Then tell me, sir, what am I fit for, if not this?"

Rebecca stared at him, her eyes wide, breath coming fast. Sarah, caught in the middle of the argument, looked like she wanted the ground to swallow her up, and Thomas was too taken aback to reply straight away. At last, he said, lamely, "I don't know. Something… something better? There are better firms than Pillar and Perkins."

"Maybe there are." Rebecca looked grimly satisfied. "And maybe you should go back to Mrs. Besant now, where you belong. Sir."

There was something in her tone that made his temper rise up: it had been a long day, after all, and he had been so patient through it—but now—"Go back to Mrs. Besant?" he repeated, spluttering. "What on earth are you talking about?"

Rebecca was trying to close the door again: Sarah trapped it with her shoe and turned to Thomas with a resigned look. "You'd better go, like she says."

"But—but—"

"I'll take it from here." With a vaguely apologetic expression, Sarah shooed him off like he was a wayward cat. Thomas stalked away, down the creaky stairs that led out of the building.

53
ELIZA

Peter lifted Eliza out of the carriage without looking her in the eye, and the instant she and Mrs. McKinnon had gone on through the innyard, he staggered back, throwing out a hand for support and finding one of the horse's harnesses. He panted as though he himself had galloped the last sixty miles. One of the hostlers had to come and help him, and not until he was sat down in the bar with a glass of beer did he begin to feel like he could move and think again.

It was her. It had been her, all this time, and he had known it, but to have that confirmed only made him more uncertain now. What was he to do? *She* had left *him*. She had told him, all those months ago, that she was setting him free. And she had been with Pillar ever since. The thought of them together made the corners of Peter's mouth curl upwards in disgust. Would it have killed her to wait for him just a little longer?

The evening drew out, the firelight flickering in the corners of his eyes until his lids grew heavy. Peter was given a narrow bed in a corner of the inn and he tried to sleep, turning over and over on his hard mattress. But he felt as though his stomach was tying itself into tighter and tighter knots, the pain growing the more he tried not to think of Eliza, and at last he rose and went out, with the intention of checking on the horses.

The rain had dwindled to a gentle *pitter patter*, and snails criss-crossed the inn yard. As Peter was putting his arms through the sleeves of his dark coat, he felt a prickle at the back of his neck and turned to see a curtain fall into place in one of the upstairs windows of the inn. His heart rose to his mouth. Could it be—

He jerked his body around again in a twist that was almost violent and made for the stables. Whatever it was, he did not want to know. He had imagined it, in any case, just as he was imagining the sound of running footsteps behind him, and someone calling his name…

"Peter!" The person barrelled into him and he turned, and there she was: Eliza. She had a shawl wrapped around her head, and her eyes were too wide, and tear tracks shone on her cheeks. And she was speaking: he struggled to focus on the words—*she might be dead…*

"What?" he exclaimed, his voice echoing across the inn yard. Eliza clapped a hand over his mouth.

"I said I've hit her around the head. Mrs. McKinnon. I didn't want to do it—and I didn't know what to do after and I think she might be dead—and then I saw you through the window and oh Peter, Peter, Peter…"

He stood cold and stiff as she lowered her arms to his neck and buried her face in his coat. The lights of the inn seemed to bob up and down for a moment in his peripheral vision. And then he took her arms and pushed her back, a safe distance from him. "Come on. We have to go, before they find her."

"You'll—" Eliza gulped. "You'll help me?"

"Take my hand." Peter did not look at her directly—found he could not, not yet. "We'll have to go on foot—they'll raise the alarm if we take any of the horses. Come on, no time to lose."

And so, with joined hands, they ran out of the innyard and into the night.

54
SISTERS

Rebecca had to sit down for a while, after Sarah told her the truth. They came into her lodgings together and sat by the dying fire in silence. Then Rebecca, whose mind was still reeling, thought she had better repeat what Sarah had told her to make sure she had heard it right. "He's your *son*? Simon? Not your brother?"

So Sarah told Rebecca again about Edward, about how her mother had helped her to keep the secret until the baby was born, and about how afterwards, they had all carried on the deception that Simon was her brother, even after Sarah's mother had gone back home to Ireland, never to return. And Rebecca nodded, and the fire faded down into red ribbons, intricate and beautiful in the growing dark, because she had run out of oil for the lamp and could not afford anymore.

"It was easier not to tell anyone," Sarah said. "Even you. That way, I could keep my job in the factory. And Edward never stopped me from doing that—though he never gave me any money, either. Not until I met him again, recently."

"How could you do that?" Rebecca said faintly. She had drawn her legs up to her chest to keep warm. "When you knew about Eliza?"

There was a long silence, which was broken only by a drunken shout from the street outside. Rebecca got up to make sure the curtains were drawn, and while she was at the window, Sarah said, sounding a little choked, "I was scared. I didn't think I had a choice. You know what that's like, don't you?"

Rebecca stiffened, and didn't turn from the window. "It's not the same."

"You were going to break the strike." Sarah's voice was low and accusing. "You wanted to save your own skin. Tell me how that's different."

"It's different because I wasn't pretending to be someone else!" Rebecca swung around and glared through the darkness.

"And neither was I," Sarah shot back. "I never lied to you. Never lied to anyone, not really. Just let them believe what they wanted."

"It's not the same! For God's sake, Eliza—" And then Rebecca broke off, shocked into sorrow and silence by her own slip of the tongue. When she raised her eyes to her friend's again, she sighed. "I'm sorry."

"I'm not your sister," Sarah said, but she sounded resigned too, and as Rebecca came back to sit next to her on the hearth, they huddled close to each other for warmth.

"You should tell Simon," Rebecca said a long time later, when they were half asleep and the darkness had lightened to flickering shadows on the wall. "He should know he still has a mother."

Sarah shifted where she lay. "He has one, no matter if he knows it or not. And she's never going to leave him."

55
INTO THE DAWN

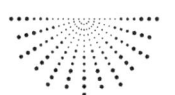

Peter and Eliza walked through the night. They splashed through muddy ditches and passed under rich-smelling trees, walked around sheds with sleeping livestock, and, once or twice, were chased across dark fields by barking dogs until their hearts were hammering in their chests.

He did not speak at all. She didn't either, at first, but as their breaths began to sync up with one another, their steps aligning into old rhythms, she found the words came more easily. "I'm sorry," she said, often. "I love you," was even more frequent. But Peter never replied, never so much as turned his head. He just kept tramping on, one foot in front of the other.

Eliza felt the tears fill her eyes, and one instant she would bitterly wonder if he would ever forgive her, while the next she would be eaten up with guilt that she had dragged him into this in the first place. She had made her choices, after all, a long time ago. She said all of this to him, too, through the course of their midnight march, and of course he said nothing.

It was near morning when Eliza finally gave up. She had been watching Peter's dark head against the brightening sky for so long that the sight sent her into a sort of a trance, and when her knees buckled under her from sheer exhaustion, she did not realise at first what was happening. Peter turned back and caught her before her head hit the ground. He tried to raise her to her feet again, but she pushed him away with her hands outstretched. Her left ankle was giving her trouble again, sending shooting pains up her leg. With her head down, she told him to leave her, thanked him for trying to help, and said sorry, once again, for all of the trouble she had caused.

They were in a meadow. Dawn was bleeding into the sky above them, and Peter looked down at Eliza where she was kneeling on the grass.

"I'm not going anywhere," he told her at last, his voice hoarse from lack of use. She did not raise her head. "Now come on, let's get moving."

He caught her hands and tried to pull her up, but Eliza pulled him down instead, until he was kneeling like her. She put her arms around his neck and hugged him close, and at first he was cold and stiff as he had been in the innyard, as though he were caught in a stranger's embrace.

But she was not a stranger. Because, Peter reminded himself, you cannot hate a stranger, and finally he pulled her back until he could see her face and cradled it with his hands and kissed every inch of it. "I hate you," he told her, as he wiped her tears away.

56
BLACK AND WHITE

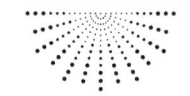

On the same day that Thomas lost his job as a clerk with the Edison Telephone Company, he arrived back at his apartment on Fleet Street to find the place ransacked from top to bottom. Papers had been scattered all over the floor and trampled underfoot; his wardrobe door was hanging off its hinges and the shirts inside torn or missing. Many of his books were missing, too, and when he searched among the desk drawers, he could not find any of the documents he had gathered about Pillar and Perkins, or the interviews he had transcribed with the various girls who had fallen prey to Edward Pillar.

It was lucky that he always kept a few spares with him. Without changing, Thomas checked the papers in his bag and went straight out again. He walked to North Audley Street, the heat of the city gathering close around him, carriages and pedestrians racing by and his thoughts racing to keep up.

Mrs. Besant looked hassled and irritated when the maid showed Thomas into her study. She did not rise to greet Thomas, just kept scribbling away as he told her what had happened.

"It must have been Pillar's men," he concluded, darkly. "Whether the father or the son, I'm not too sure. They made short work of the lock, in any case, and my landlady insists she didn't see anything."

"I did tell you," Mrs. Besant said, quietly.

Thomas frowned at her, his hands in his pockets as he leaned against the bookcase. With her head down, he could not make out her expression. "You mean—about the letter that I wrote?"

"What else could I mean, Thomas?"

"But…" He paused and shook his head as though to clear it. "You know that I am putting together a case against Edward Pillar to support the threats made in that letter. I have spoken to a solicitor; I am being careful…"

"Evidently not careful enough," Annie snapped, putting down her pen, and it was then, as she looked up, that Thomas saw just how angry she was. "It is lucky, you say, that you made copies of the important documents and kept them on your person. You don't seem overly concerned with the trespass on your property, on your possessions—"

"Oh, believe me, Annie, when I say that I am—"

"I haven't finished." Annie rose from her desk, and even at her small stature, she looked imposing enough that Thomas straightened, taking his hands out of his pockets. "What will they do the next time they visit your apartment, Thomas? What will they do if you publish this article about Edward Pillar? Do you think you will still be safe to walk around the streets?"

He watched her for a moment, confused. "*If* I publish this article? We agreed before that it would be worth the risk."

"We *did* agree that, when I had your assurance that you would keep your distance from the matchgirls." She fixed him with a hard stare.

"This is about Rebecca again, is it?" He could not help the weariness that crept into his voice.

"Not just Rebecca. Sarah, too. I warned you not to meddle, but you went with her to persuade Rebecca not to go back to work. As though you were friends."

"We *are* friends, of a kind! Is that so terrible?" Thomas spread his hands. "And how much worse would it have been for Rebecca to go back to work, and break the strike?"

"You will recall that I never wanted this strike to happen in the first place. However, that is beside the point. You…" Mrs. Besant sighed heavily. "You cannot help people and be their friends at the same time. I have learned this, Thomas. And I am tired of telling you that this is what is required to do our work. You ought to know by now."

"And what if I disagree? What if I believe that we are no better than these girls, that we ought not to hold ourselves apart from them when equality is what we are fighting for?"

Thomas had not realised how deep in his heart those words had buried themselves until they came pouring out. Mrs. Besant seemed momentarily surprised, too, but then her eyes flashed to meet his. "You are welcome to believe whatever you want, Thomas. But you must stand on your own two feet to do so. I will not shield you anymore."

"Don't talk to me like I'm a child," he snapped.

"Why not, when that is what you are?" Mrs. Besant stepped closer to him, and there was no fear or shame in her eyes as she surveyed him. "There was a time when I thought we were partners. But that was my mistake, since it seems all you ever wanted was for me to play your mother."

"That's not—"

"And I am already a mother, Thomas. I have my own children to worry about. My husband, too, who visited me just today to show his displeasure, once again, at the work I am carrying out here." Mrs. Besant ran her hands down her temples. "The work which only seems to grow and grow: the strike pay—the article—the public meetings—the letters to shareholders—the subscriptions. All this I have done, and more, and you accuse me of holding myself above these girls? I am their servant, Thomas. That is what I have vowed to be from the start."

There was a silence. Having finished her speech, Mrs. Besant watched Thomas for a moment more, and then turned away, as though he were not worth looking at anymore. "We are going to the House of Commons today, with a deputation of the girls. So you'd better take one of Frank's clean shirts. The maid can show you where to find them."

Thomas looked down at himself, at his wrinkled shirt, and said quietly, "Thank you."

57
MEMORIES

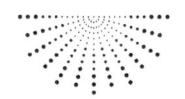

Edward Pillar did not visit the servants' quarters in his father's house very often, but he was struck today by how unnaturally quiet they were. Only a couple of servants were sitting in the servants' hall when he passed through, and they rose to their feet with grudging expressions. He returned the favour by ignoring them.

The housekeeper's room adjoined her office, and when he knocked, she called out hoarsely, "Come in."

The place was prettily decorated, with a floral-patterned armchair and lace curtains on the window, and impeccably clean. Mrs. McKinnon was reading a book in bed, with the sheets drawn up to her chin. Her eyes widened when she saw who her visitor was, and she struggled to get into a sitting position. "Master Edward—"

"Please," he said, gently, as he drew up a chair beside her bed, and sat in it backwards. "Don't exert yourself." With a glance at the bandage at the side of her head, "I've come to see how you are."

The housekeeper looked at him for a moment, and her expression softened. "You were always such a caring boy."

"We got quite a shock yesterday, when the constable told us what had happened to you." Edward drummed his fingers on the back of the chair for a moment, and then said, a little pointedly, "Have you remembered anything since? About your accident?"

Mrs. McKinnon looked at him regretfully. "I wish I could help you, Master Edward. I know you must be so worried about the girl. But the last thing I remember is setting down at Stony Stratford."

"You received quite a powerful blow to the head," Edward said, with a reassuring smile. "It is understandable that you feel some… confusion."

Alarm sparked in the housekeeper's eyes at this, and she raised herself up on her elbows. "I may not be at my best now, sir, but I will be good as new in a day or two, and I'm sure I will remember everything then."

"I'm sure you will," said Edward kindly. With a sweeping glance around the room, "At any rate, I think we may put two and two together. Eliza must have struck you over the head in order to effect her escape. We are lucky that, in her desperation, she did not do more damage."

"Yes, indeed, sir," Mrs. McKinnon said, with a shudder. "I do remember she had a look in her eyes, when we were in the carriage together: a look as though she might have killed me."

"How frightening that must have been for you." Edward winced, and affected deep thought for a moment. He could sense the older woman watching him anxiously. At last he ventured, "The strange thing is, I don't think Eliza would have been able to make her escape unnoticed. Surely someone would have seen a girl alone, after all? Particularly one as pretty as her."

Mrs. McKinnon's colour was even worse now than it had been: she looked white as death. "Yes, sir. You're right, of course."

"Which brings us to the coachman." Edward rocked back and forth a little in his chair, keeping his eyes on the housekeeper. "He never returned from his journey, though he was seen at the coach inn, as were you. Surely Eliza could not have managed to dispatch him, too? It all looks very suspicious, you must agree."

"Yes, sir…"

"So much so that the constable made inquiries and brought his findings to me. Is it true that this coachman was dismissed from his last position after a violent altercation with one of his fellow servants, and taken on here without a reference?" Edward raised his eyebrows, delicately, and waited patiently for the answer.

"Yes, sir," Mrs. McKinnon said, after a long moment, looking pained. "But it was Mr. Johnson's decision, sir, and not mine…"

"I am not interested in whose decision it was." Then, making an effort to soften his tone, Edward leaned forward again in his chair. "This coachman, as it turns out, knew Eliza from his previous place of employment. She used to work there, too, you see: I believe they were even promised to each other at one time."

Mrs. McKinnon's eyes widened as she took in the information. Edward continued, "And it looks as though they were communicating with each other. I found this…" He produced a newspaper clipping from his pocket, "… in the room behind the library. It is about the strike in my father's factory: I imagine the coachman must have sneaked it to her, somehow."

"I don't see how, sir," the housekeeper said, with some of her old firmness. "I was careful."

"Careful, yes, I'm sure you were. Careful enough that my father found out." Edward put away the clipping and smiled again at the housekeeper. "Mrs. McKinnon, you have been in our family for so long. We are all so grateful that you survived your ordeal. And you should feel free to stay under this roof for as long as you need to, until you have recovered."

Mrs. McKinnon's eyes followed him as he stood. Her voice trembling, she repeated, "For... for as long as I need to, sir?"

"Yes, of course," Edward said tenderly. "It is the least we can do, after all."

"Sir—sir, please, wait..."

He turned back to look at her. She had struggled up into a proper sitting position, and was panting, some of her hair coming loose to droop around her face. "You mustn't get excited, Mrs. McKinnon," he said. "You are still recovering—"

"Please," she repeated. "Please: you can't send me away. I never meant to betray you, but when your father asked me outright about the girl, I couldn't lie... He had suspected it for a long time. Please, Master Edward. I have known you since you were a baby at your mother's breast. I watched you grow into the young man you are today—I know that you cannot do this to me—please..."

There were tears rolling down her cheeks now, and Edward did not want to look at her anymore. "We will always be grateful for everything you have done for us, Mrs. McKinnon," he said as he walked out. "Now please, get some rest."

Upstairs, Mr. Johnson was hovering outside the door of the library. He looked as though he had not slept in days. Edward shooed him away before going in himself. "Father? It's done."

"Good," said Richard Pillar, looking up from the letter he had been writing. "That woman knows too much. It is the perilous thing about servants." Then, a more anxious edge creeping into his voice, "Any news of the girl?"

"None." Edward sank down into the chair opposite his father. "But I'm confident she will return, Father. Her sister is here, after all, and very much involved in the strike."

"Yes," Richard said, with a troubled look. "Speaking of the sister, you are aware that she turned down our offer to reinstate her?"

Edward tried not to look too smug. "Indeed, Father?"

"You needn't say 'I told you so'. Now…" Sealing the envelope, and putting it aside, Richard looked at his son. "What would you suggest I do next?"

"What would *I* suggest?" Edward could not hide his surprise. "I thought you didn't want any more input from me, Father."

"Well, things have changed, haven't they?" said his father, gruffly. "Of course, if you have nothing to say…"

"I would bring in the hands from Glasgow," Edward said, turning sombre in an instant. "The demonstration may have deterred some of them, but we can still transport a decent number here: enough to show our own girls that they may be replaced. We should arrange their accommodation ourselves and ensure that they feel protected."

Slowly, Richard nodded, and a smile spread across his face. "Then let's waste no more time."

58
STANDING UP

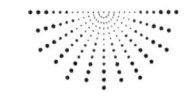

"If the right honourable gentleman would answer my question—"

"I have answered it. There are one thousand five hundred girls employed in the factory, but if the honourable member will furnish me with the names of a few who claim that they have been fined, then we may ascertain if there has been any breach of the law…"

"*I* will furnish the right honourable gentleman with a dozen cases in the month of June—"

Sarah, who was sitting beside Rebecca in the viewing gallery of the House of Commons, leaned over to whisper to her, "You'll talk about the fines, first."

"Of course," Rebecca whispered back, as she watched the debate below. The three MPs had been talking about

Pillar and Perkins for the past half-hour and did not seem to be getting anywhere. Down on the benches, the other gentlemen were restless, their voices rumbling, top hats shifting and pocket watches gleaming. Rebecca went on, "And then, our next demand is... a breakfast room separate from the main factory?"

"No, the one about the foremen," Sarah corrected, her voice rising ever so slightly, so that a few of the other girls sitting nearby glanced at them. There were about fifty of them altogether, in the deputation that Mrs. Besant and the Socialists had brought to Parliament. They had all dressed in their Sunday best, Sarah in a blue linsey frock with a high collar, and Rebecca in a chintz dress with a black bow tied around her neck. "You've got to give the demands in the order we settled on yesterday, in the Assembly Hall. Makes us look more organised."

"I wish you'd just go in my place," Rebecca muttered. "I know I'm going to get it wrong."

"*I* can't be the one to speak," Sarah hissed back. "I don't even work in Pillar and Perkins anymore."

"Then let one of the other girls do it."

Down on the benches where Mr. Browning had just taken his seat again, applause rang out again.

Sarah nudged Rebecca, so hard that she scowled and rubbed her arm. "*You* were the first one they dismissed," she said over the din. "The strike happened because of you. Don't shake your head at me, it's *true*. You—" She broke off as Mrs. Besant looked over at them, and fell silent.

Grateful for the brief ceasefire, Rebecca let her gaze drift around the viewing gallery again. The rest of the girls were arrayed on the benches on either side of them and behind. In the row in front sat the socialists, with Mrs. Besant and Thomas at the end. Rebecca could not help noticing that neither of them had so much as looked at each other since they sat down in the gallery, each scribbling their own notes.

"You're going to be fine," Sarah said into her ear, breaking her train of thought. "Now, give me the demands again."

Rebecca wiped her sweating palms on her skirt, and began to recite, in a whisper, "No more fines. No more deductions from the fillers' pay for paint, brushes or stamps. We settle disputes directly with managers instead of the foremen. And we get a separate room to take our meals." She glanced at Sarah, jerkily. "Did I miss anything?"

Her friend's pained expression was answer enough. "Let's go over it again."

∼

As it turned out, the whole affair was not as nerve-wracking as Rebecca had predicted. For one thing, it was just the strike committee that went upstairs to meet the MPs, rather than the whole deputation. The committee had been selected by Mrs. Besant, and consisted of twelve girls, including Rebecca and the Chapman sisters. Sarah had taken her leave to go back picketing and had given Rebecca's arm a squeeze as she wished her good luck.

For another, the office in which they gathered was far less grand than the Chamber downstairs, and the MPs far less intimidating when they were away from the benches. Rebecca said her piece as they all listened, and only once or twice had to glance at the notes that she had scribbled down earlier.

When it was done, general conversation broke out as Mr. Browning went around to speak to each girl individually. Rebecca intercepted Thomas as he was making for the door. "Aren't you going to stay for the photograph?"

He looked down at her, surprised, and adjusted his glasses. "I think I've been in the papers enough lately."

Perhaps she was emboldened by just having spoken in front of a dozen people—or perhaps there was something about the tired look in his eyes which made her press further. "This is your cause as much as anyone's, Thomas. I mean—" Her slip made him smile. "Mr. Barnwall. You've done the work for it, and you deserve the credit."

Thomas looked at her for a moment with an unreadable expression, and then his gaze drifted past her, to the other end of the office. Rebecca followed it, to where Mrs. Besant was talking with Mr. Conybeare. She frowned. "Did something happen between you?"

He was silent. Realising too late how her question might have sounded, Rebecca turned back to look at him. "I mean, did you have an argument?" She hoped he didn't notice her blush.

Thomas fidgeted with the collar of his shirt, which looked slightly too big for him. "Let's just say she's none too pleased with me at the moment."

Taking this in, Rebecca thought for a minute, and then said, "I know it's not my place…"

"That's never stopped you before." The fond look on his face made her stomach turn over itself, and as much as Rebecca tried to look annoyed at the interruption, she could not help giving him a small, foolish smile before she resumed,

"… but I think whatever it is, you should try to make things right with her. Mrs. Besant has done so much for us over these past few months. And working so closely together —" There was the blush again, "—I'm sure that you were bound to have a few arguments." Rebecca took a breath, and then rushed on, "But you're wonderful together, both of you. And you can't let—whatever this argument is— spoil it."

The fond look had vanished from Thomas's expression, and he was looking at Rebecca now with an expression of profound puzzlement. But before he could say anything, they were all being called to assemble for the photograph.

There was a small platform in the corner of the office, where the desk was, and Mrs. Besant and the other socialists arranged themselves behind it. With much fidgeting, chatter and giggling, the other girls took their places around and on the platform, and Rebecca, through no contrivance of her own, found herself beside Thomas.

They did not speak for a while—no one was supposed to, after all, let alone move—and just watched the man from the *Star* as he adjusted the camera. Finally, Thomas said quietly, without turning to look at her, "Ever seen one of those before?"

Rebecca shook her head a fraction. "None like that." Her eyes scanned over the various parts of the camera: the leather bellows, the case and the shiny wooden frames attached to it, and the tripod on which the whole contraption was mounted. Then it hit her for the first time, and she gasped. "I'm going to be in the paper!"

She heard Thomas's low chuckle. "And you're only thinking of this now?"

"I had other things on my mind," Rebecca retorted, and without thinking, struck out at his arm. He caught her hand, and hid it behind their backs, his other hand propped on the corner of the desk. His fingers twined through hers, his thumb grazing the underside of her wrist. And everyone went absolutely still and quiet, in time for the blinding flash of the camera that captured them all, matchgirls and socialists, and painted them in black and white upon the annals of history.

59
IMPOSSIBLE DREAMS

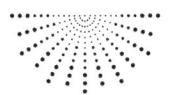

Thomas returned to his desolate apartment, barricaded the front door with a chair, and set to the task that he had been dreading all day: writing to his family.

Five years ago, when he had first come to London, he had never imagined it would all be so difficult. There were too many writers like him, filled with unquenchable thirst and impossible dreams. The most he could hope for, he quickly learned then, was to find some other way of supporting himself, so that he would not have to return to Ireland with his tail between his legs. Mrs. Besant had helped him find his first clerical job, and he worked in a series of different companies over the years, and lived in a series of different lodgings, each meaner than the last. And now… that little living was gone, too.

Dear Mam, he wrote, and then stopped, pinching the bridge of his nose. Through the small window behind his desk, he could see a dark blue sky descending over the rooftops of the city. A lump grew in his throat: this place was ugly and smoky, and he loved it with all his heart.

Shadows deepened around him as he wrote his letter. When the nib of his pen broke, he was grateful for the excuse to stop, and rose, stretching his arms above his head and then bringing his hands down to his hair. The sleeves of the shirt that belonged to Mr. Besant were dangling over his wrists. Thomas unbuttoned it, casting it away, and put on an undershirt he found under the pile of torn clothes in his wardrobe. He had thrown himself down on his bed, with the intention of sleeping for a few hours, when he heard a knock on the door.

In an instant he was up again, heart racing. It occurred to him that the men who had raided his apartment might be back—his eyes scanned the room around him for a weapon that he might use against them. But then the knock sounded once more, soft and tentative, and Thomas sighed at his own cowardice. He moved for the door, pushing the chair aside with a scrape, and opened it to find Rebecca standing on the threshold.

"I know I shouldn't have come," she said quickly, before he could so much as utter her name. "It's late, and I'm disturbing you, I know, but I was just…" Her eyes drifted past him, taking in the destruction of his apartment. "… worried."

"Er—come in, if you like," Thomas said, stepping aside to let her through. The instant her back was turned, his hand jumped to his hair, smoothing it down. She took slow steps, turning this way and that to look at the papers littering the floor, the stains on the carpet.

"What happened?"

"Pillars' men, I think. I'm not entirely sure. But it seems they wanted to scare me, or stop me investigating any further, or—what are you doing?"

"Helping you clean up," Rebecca replied, as she took off her coat and knelt to start picking the papers off the floor. Thomas watched her for a moment, and then shook his head vigorously, wondering if he had already fallen asleep, and this was some very strange—rather nice—dream. Everything was hazy and blurry. Then he remembered—

"My glasses." He went to the desk, rummaging among the mess there to see where he had put them.

"You look different without them on," said Rebecca, and there was a funny quality to her voice, but when Thomas looked at her, she did not meet his gaze. She had a sheaf of papers under one arm, and as she came to the desk to put them down, he turned, following her movement.

"Different how?"

"Younger," she said, after a moment's consideration, and then they smiled at each other.

Thomas found his glasses and put them on. Clearing his throat, "Well, I suppose that makes sense. According to some people, I'm still nothing but a child."

"Mrs. Besant?" Rebecca asked, as she moved towards his wardrobe. Taking his silence for confirmation, "I'm sure she can't have meant that."

"Then you don't know her as well as I do," Thomas said, watching her fiddle with the hinges of the door. "Annie means everything she says."

Rebecca stopped what she was doing, turning towards him. In the lamp light, her red hair shone gold. "But she cares about you… very much. I've noticed."

"She's like family," Thomas said.

"Then…" Rebecca's eyes were wide. "Then you don't…?"

Thomas straightened, crossed to where she stood. Gently, he took her hands and moved them, then closed the wardrobe door. "Rebecca. You should go home."

She nodded, looking a little dazed at his proximity. "I—I will. I just wanted to see if you were all right. You disappeared after the photograph—we were expecting to see you in the Assembly Hall, but you never came…"

"I'm all right," Thomas said, softly. They had been inching closer with every word that she spoke. But the first touch of Rebecca's hands still surprised him, when she reached up and took off his glasses. Her intention was clear, and it certainly was not her place to do what she did next. Neither was it his place to kiss her back, but he couldn't seem to help it. As her lips moved over his, he put a hand to her back, and felt the hardness of her corset. He drew her in, deepening the kiss, looping his arms around her waist. She smiled against his mouth, and he could feel her shivering, breathless and happy.

Thomas was the first to pull away: he knew he had to be, before things got out of hand. "I—don't want to do this with you."

Rebecca's eyes met his, uncomprehending. "What do you…"

"I'm sorry if I've given you the wrong idea," he interrupted, quickly putting some distance between them. "I just—seem to lose my head when I'm around you."

She looked away for a moment, thinking. Seeing her flush, biting her lip—Thomas took a step forward again and then caught himself, lowering his hands.

"You're beautiful, Rebecca."

She shook her head, still not meeting his gaze. "Don't say it like that."

"And I've never met a girl like you." Thomas took another step forward, and spread his hands, a few inches from her. She had to understand—he had to *make* her understand. "But if I behave like this with you, then I'm no better than him, am I?"

Rebecca did not need to ask who he meant. She just lifted her chin a fraction, and said, "What about what *I* want?"

"You don't want me," he replied, gently. "Trust me, Rebecca."

There was a silence. Then, shaking her head and avoiding his gaze, Rebecca went to collect her coat. "I wish people would say what they mean," she said, so quietly that he almost didn't hear her. Thomas followed her to the door, watched her hurry down the corridor and into the darkness.

60

GLASGOW HANDS

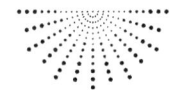

Mrs. Annie Besant could not remember what it was like to live a normal life. Perhaps her life had never been normal to begin with, but certainly in the last few months, she felt that she had seen every side of human nature. She had seen abominable cruelty and greed, and then, coming out against it, an outpouring of kindness and care which she could never have expected. Never before had one of her causes risen to the national stage in such a way. The strike had been something she dreaded rather than something she desired, but now, after two weeks of picketing, meetings in Mr. Charrington's Assembly Hall, newspaper coverage and public outcry, she knew it was the best thing that could have happened for the girls.

For this reason, she blamed herself for what happened on the day that the Glasgow hands were brought into Pillar and Perkins. She had been caught up in the angry tide at first, like the others, united in disbelief, that for the first time, the Messrs. Pillar had been true to their word. But the instant she arrived on the scene and saw the thousand-strong crowd pressing up to the gates of the match factory, she knew that it was all going to go wrong.

Perhaps it was the weather, too, that warned her. It was a dull morning, the sun a sickly splash of yellow, the clouds overhead locking in the summer heat. She could feel the weight of the air, pressing down close over their heads. Beside her, Thomas took out a handkerchief and dabbed the sweat on his face. Their eyes met, then quickly slid away from each other again. They had not spoken since their argument.

On her other side, a couple of the other socialists were talking quietly. Mrs. Besant glanced at her watch. *Five minutes to nine.* The crowd shifted restlessly. She looked around, and saw that on Mile End Road, more crowds had gathered as far back as Bow Church, some of them moving out onto the road to wave their placards at passing traffic. The occasional shout drifted on the air, but apart from that, there was only a low buzz of conversation.

At nine o'clock on the dot, the Glasgow girls arrived to work, and all hell broke loose.

They were escorted by police constables, who parted the crowd on either side of them. Looking over the heads of those in front of her, Mrs. Besant's heart went out to the girls: they looked a miserable bunch, travel-weary and frightened. Interspersed among them were the few East End girls who had not gone on strike, and they held their heads up with more defiance, secure in their own turf. Hisses issued from the watching crowd as the gates began to open to let the girls in. And then the hisses turned into taunts, and the taunts turned into screams of fury—"Blackleg!" "Scab!"—and before Mrs. Besant knew what was happening, the constables had started shouting, too, waving their truncheons.

She saw a moment later that several matchgirls had squeezed past them and were making for the gates, wrestling with the strikebreakers to stop them going in. The crowd swelled forward as though to follow them, and she felt herself pushed from behind, elbows jabbing into her sides—and then there was a push in the opposite direction, which sent her stumbling back, and she would have lost her balance had Thomas not grabbed her arm, holding her steady.

"We have to get out of here!" he called over the roar of voices, his eyes roving the crowd around them.

"This is my doing!" Mrs. Besant shouted back, struggling with his grip on her arm. "I can't just run away!"

The roar of voices grew louder, as the gates began to close again—and then people started throwing stones, and as Mrs. Besant watched a girl go down just inside the factory yard, she could not tell if it was one of their own or one of the Glasgow hands. The constables were still beating people back from the gates, swinging their truncheons this way and that, and at last Mrs. Besant threw her hands into the air, screaming at the top of her lungs, "Stop! In the name of God, stop!"

Her voice had the power to command crowds. But now, it all counted for nothing. There were too many people, their voices too loud, the chaos too perfect. Mrs. Besant turned to Thomas and clutched onto his arm as he cut a way out for them, through the throng.

∼

They struggled back down Mile End Road, Thomas leading the way, with his arm cast protectively around Mrs. Besant. He looked back a few times but could not spot any of the other socialists in the crowd behind them. A couple of carriages had stopped in the middle of the road, unable to move in the tide of human bodies, and the spooked horses reared up, sending people scattering under their hooves.

"There!" cried Mrs. Besant, steering him in the direction of Bow churchyard, and they pushed their way off the crowded street and in through the open gates. Others appeared to have had the same idea as them: Thomas could see a couple of girls hurrying up the path ahead, but it was quieter here, the roar of voices diminished so that they could hear themselves think.

"It's all over now," Mrs. Besant said, once they had both caught their breath. She was shaking her head, covering over a section of torn sleeve with her shawl. "You see that, don't you? The Pillars will regain a little of that public sympathy they have been craving. They will be able to pick and choose whichever demands they wish to honour."

"But perhaps they will still hire the girls back?" Thomas said, hopefully. The look, however, which Mrs. Besant gave him did not inspire confidence.

They were coming up to William Gladstone's statue, and the girls he had noticed earlier appeared to have stopped beside it. Then, as they came closer, he saw that one of them was lying on the ground, and they were trying to lift her up.

"Good Lord," Mrs. Besant said, in a low voice. "We ought to get help."

Thomas nodded—and then went utterly still. As Mrs. Besant turned toward him with concerned eyes, he told himself that it couldn't be: she had stayed at home, or her friends had gotten her away before things turned sour. But there Rebecca lay, by the marble plinth of the statue. He sprinted forward, kneeling beside the other girls to help them prop her up. Her head drooped in his arms, and he saw that a chunk of hair by her left temple was matted with blood.

"Thank you, sir," gasped one of the girls—Sarah, as she stroked Rebecca's hand, and then she turned and looked at him properly. "Mr. Barnwall!"

"What happened," he said, frightened by how pale Rebecca was. Her eyelids were half-open; he could see the whites of her eyes shifting beneath them, and her lips were moving.

"One of the coppers," another girl said, her voice bitter. "Must have hit her while she was trying to get away with us. She didn't say nothing, not till we were coming through here, and then she fell."

Thomas shook his head, and then, as Rebecca began to slide down, he secured his grip under her arms, hoisting her up again. "What should we do," he coughed out. "We've got to do something! What should we do?"

"There's a way out through the back of the church," came the calm, authoritative voice of Mrs. Besant. "We must get her somewhere safe, before she loses too much blood."

"I'll take her head," Thomas said to the girls, and they tried to lift her all together, but they lost their grip on her legs, and in the end he just took her in his arms himself, her head falling against his shoulder. When he looked at Mrs. Besant again, he found that she was staring at a patch of blood on Gladstone's plinth, with a funny expression on her face.

"There was a story one of the girls told me…" she began, in a strange voice, but then she shook herself. She hurried forward to follow Thomas, as he staggered under Rebecca's weight, and the girls ran ahead of them, and William Gladstone's red right hand stretched out as though it were pointing the way.

61
HIGHBURY

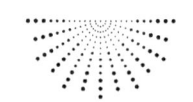

It was only eighty miles outside of London, which Eliza found hard to believe. Highbury was like something out of the pages of a book. The brownstone cottages, the village green, the columns of woodsmoke that trailed from the pretty chimneys and cast their fragrance on the narrow, winding streets below: Eliza felt as though she had been here all her life. In reality, it had only been two days since they had arrived here, but there was little intrusion from reality in a place like this.

Peter was more practical than her. It was he who had insisted that they give false names to the farmer who had let them ride in his cart, and then to the innkeeper when they were set down here; he who had made Eliza cover her hair with a shawl, so that she would not be so easily recognised; he who talked always of plans, of getting married and finding work on some farm.

She knew as well as he did, of course, that they could not stay here. They were too close to London, and the five pounds that Mr. Pillar had given Peter would only last them so long. A significant portion of it had already been spent on two nights in an inn. They would have to save the rest for travelling, and as neither of them had references, it was going to be difficult to find work.

So Eliza decided to live in the delicious present, to drink in every moment. For so long, she had been worried about the future, about what would happen if Edward grew tired of her and left her. But now that he was gone from her life, along with the child they might have had, she felt less than she had feared: a dull ache in her chest that came and went.

"I did love him," she admitted to Peter once during those days, when they were in their favourite spot: a footbridge over a stream. They leaned their hands on sun-warmed stone, and the water that bubbled over the rocks below them was crystal clear. On one side, a steep hill led up to Highbury proper, and on the other, a path led down to the small train station. It was invisible from the village, concealed behind the fold of a hill, but sometimes they would hear a magic whistle on the wind.

"I know," Peter said in reply, frowning down at the water. "You wouldn't have gone with him, otherwise."

Eliza watched him for a long moment. The shadow of stubble had appeared on his chin, and there was a fixed weariness under his eyes which she wanted to press away. She reached out and touched his face lightly. "I know it was wrong. But I thought you didn't love me the way I loved you. I thought my life was over."

Peter shut his eyes as he took this in, and if not for the warm, rough hand that came to rest over hers on his cheek, Eliza might have thought he really did hate her, just as he had said during their flight from Stony Stratford. But he said instead, tenderly, "Your life hasn't even started."

On the last day in Highbury, Eliza walked through the village to say goodbye to her favourite spots. Peter had gone down to the train station to inquire about tickets. They were going to go north, to uncertainty and hardship. But Eliza did not think about any of that, not yet. She just took everything in. She stopped in the green to watch the little boys kicking around a ball, and closed her eyes to feel the sun warming her face. She walked through the market, looked at the pretty jams laid out on one of the stalls, breathed in the scent of woodsmoke mingled with cooking meat and spices. Then there was the scent of ink and fresh paper as she passed the newsstand—Eliza could not help glancing at the newspapers on display, and then—

Her heart stuttered and stopped for an instant. She seized up the copy of the *Star*, staring at the photograph on the front page and sure that her mind was playing tricks on her. But there it was, in black and white, *Annie Besant,*

Thomas Barnwall and the Matchgirls Strike Committee, and below it, Rebecca's face, Sarah's face, the faces of other girls whom she recognised, all proud and beautiful and brave.

Eliza bought the paper before her pale face and slackening jaw attracted any more attention than she was sure it already had. She walked a little distance from the market, sat on a bench with her mouth dry with shock, and it was there that Peter found her some time later.

He sat down, and asked gently, "What's the matter?"

Eliza made a decision there and then. She folded up the paper and smiled at Peter. "Nothing. Did you find tickets?"

"Yes," he said slowly, still watching her. "There's a train to Birmingham in half an hour."

"Then let's go."

Eliza wanted to leave the paper behind. She tried to stop him pulling it out of her hands as they stood. But Peter was firm, and something in his expression changed as he looked at the photograph.

"Your sister," he said after a moment, raising his head with a look of wonder. "Is that really her?"

"She looks different, doesn't she?" Eliza smiled again, even as fresh tears sprung up in her eyes. "Come on, let's go to the station."

They started to walk, Peter with the paper folded under his arm. After a few minutes of silence, he ventured, "There's a train to London, too."

Eliza stopped in her tracks to stare at him. Quickly, she shook her head. "No, Peter, we can't. It doesn't matter. Let's keep to the plan."

"We don't have to stay long," he said, with a shrug, as Eliza continued to stare at him. "It looks like this strike is bigger than anyone thought it would be. And you're a matchgirl too, aren't you?" More gently, "This is your fight as much as anyone else's."

Eliza shook her head again. In the distance, they could hear the whistle of a train. "Peter." His name was choked on her lips, and she blinked away fresh tears. "Are you —sure?"

"If you're going, then I'm going," he said, and tucked an arm around her shoulders as they walked on.

62
TRAMPLED

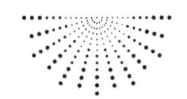

Rebecca dreamt that she had fallen in the middle of a crowd, and feet were trampling over her. Every time she tried to get up, or to see past the dark blur of bodies that blotted out the sky overhead, she would find herself rooted to the spot, a heaviness on her lids forcing her to lie down again, even though she knew that she could not stay here—she would die here, and Mum and Eliza would never know what had happened to her...

When she woke, the light in the room was different than that of her dream: it felt like evening. She could hear children playing outside, and Thomas was sitting at the table with his head in his hands. Wondering what could be upsetting him so, Rebecca wet her lips and croaked, "Where am I?"

His head flew up. Looking around, he had an expression as though he did not know how to answer her question. But finally he said, "Sarah's house," and looked at her again, with bloodshot eyes.

"You should get some sleep," Rebecca said, after watching him a moment, and he gave a strange sort of laugh. "You look terrible."

"So do you." His tone was light, but his expression was all earnestness as he came to kneel by her side. Someone had put her in an armchair, draped her with coats and shawls, and there was something soft behind her head. Thomas reached up and, ever so lightly, touched the bandage on her temple. "You're awake."

He had said it in a low and wondering way, and Rebecca turned her head to watch him as he pulled back again. The motion made her feel a little dizzy, but she did not want to let him out of her sight. "Don't leave me. Please."

Thomas was silent for what felt like a long time, and because he was looking down at her hand, she could not see his expression. But then he lifted it to his lips and kissed every one of her fingers. He kissed her palm and her knuckle, and then he moved in and kissed her cheek, his breath huffing in her ear. "I'm not leaving you," he told her. "Not ever."

Rebecca reached her hands up to the back of his head, softly stroking his fair hair as he leaned against her chest. "I hope this isn't a dream," she said, more to herself than to him, and then she heard how fast his breaths were coming, how every second one seemed to catch in a sob. Straightening up a little, she lowered her hands to his shoulders and held him back until their faces were level. His glasses were askew, and she could see the tears glinting in his eyes.

"I was scared, Rebecca," he whispered. "I thought…"

"Sshh." She straightened his glasses, traced his cheek with a light touch. "It's all right now."

Thomas let out a breath, half-sob, half-sigh, and leaned in again until he was hugging her close.

63
GHOSTS AND SHADOWS

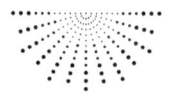

Jem Wilson watched the smoke curl out from under the door and, for a moment, debated leaving altogether and coming back another time. There was only silence within, and he had been privy to Edward Pillar's bad temper before. He didn't trust a man who kept his anger coiled up like that, only to have it strike at an unexpected moment. For Jem, everything was always close to the surface. Before madness had descended on the factory, and on London, and on the whole country, he had spent his days striding up and down between the workbenches of the matchgirls and keeping them in line. He was often angry, occasionally willing to demonstrate a point with his fists, but never without reason.

Pillar had seen that ability of his, and appreciated it, or so Jem liked to believe. For the past few months, he had enlisted him to carry out various duties which he could not perform himself. They mainly involved keeping people quiet. Edward Pillar, after all, was a ladies' man, and sometimes a girl's brother or father or lover might take against him, and from there, things could get ugly fast. It was Jem's job to keep them all in line, too, and his master paid him well for it.

Lately, however, Pillar's requests were getting a little more unconventional. Just the other day, he had sent Jem on the hunt for an Irish socialist who had written something untoward about him. When said socialist had made no appearance in his own apartment after dark, Jem, along with a few friends he had brought along, settled for tearing up the place instead. Pillar, instead of being angry when he heard this news, simply changed his orders yet again. He seemed to have an endless list of people who needed to be watched or dealt with in some way or another. Jem, for his part, was beginning to get tired of it all.

"Wilson? Is that you, lurking out there?" The voice of his master cut across his thoughts, angry and impatient, and Jem hastily turned the handle of the door, shouldering it open and stepping into the office.

"Mr. Pillar, sir."

Pillar blew out another skein of smoke, and tapped his cigar out on the desk. His icy blue eyes found Jem, flickered over him, and then away, as though he were somehow disappointing to behold. "Well?"

"I've seen her, sir. The girl, Eliza." As Pillar's eyes found him again, wide and eager now, Jem continued, with renewed energy, "She got off the train in Euston just an hour ago. A man with her."

Pillar brought his hand up, slowly, and took another puff of his cigar. "And where did they go?" he said a moment later, his eyes tracking the progress of the smoke upwards.

"I lost them in the crowds, sir. But I'd guess they've gone to Greengoose Lane, where the sister lives." Jem braced himself for an explosion, but Edward Pillar just turned and regarded him for a moment. On closer inspection, Jem could see that his eyes were bloodshot, glazed over with exhaustion. After a moment, the man smiled, which was more disconcerting than anything else.

"Quite right, Wilson. Well, we can do little else for the moment."

Jem turned as Pillar crossed the room to the door and drew it open. "Go to Greengoose Lane first thing tomorrow morning," the gentleman continued. "See where they go. And try not to lose them this time."

64
LOFTY FIGURES FALL

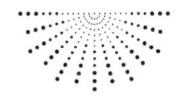

The day after the clash between the strikebreakers and the matchgirls, a deputation from the London Trades Council went to Pillar and Perkins. The strike committee came with them, including Mrs. Besant, Thomas, Rebecca and the Chapman sisters.

They sat in a large meeting room which Rebecca had never seen before, in the office wing of the building. It would have awed her once, to be in the presence of such important people, to have them all listen to her as she listed their demands. But now she had visited Parliament and spoken with MPs; she had had her photograph taken for the newspaper. The managers of Pillar and Perkins were not the lofty figures they had once been.

Richard Pillar was present, though his son was not. He looked tired, though his calculating eyes rested on

Rebecca as she spoke, and she knew that he had not missed a single word. Mr. Lethbridge was at his right hand, and kept his eyes fixed on his papers. Only a few times did she sense his gaze, and when she looked up to meet it, he would glance away again. Whether this was a sign of guilt or contempt, Rebecca was not sure. At any rate, she had much bigger concerns. She was representing eleven hundred women. She knew that she could not flinch.

After she had finished speaking, Mrs. Besant took over and talked at length about the work that she and her colleagues had undertaken, from their initial boycott of Pillar and Perkins' matches, to the interviews, to the strike. Thomas supplied a few words, his voice quiet and neutral. He did not say anything about his investigation of Edward, but Rebecca noticed that Richard Pillar sat right up in his seat, watching Thomas like a hawk for the entire time that he was speaking.

The sun rose higher in the sky, its rays penetrating the room so that it grew hot and airless. A protracted discussion between both parties, with many wasted words, kept them all in their seats until Rebecca could feel herself getting faint.

She was the one who had insisted on coming to the meeting, despite the arguments both Thomas and Sarah had made to keep her at home and resting. Now she could see the merit of those arguments, as the cut at her temple began to throb, and cold sweat wound its way down the back of her neck. She placed a palm on the table to support herself and looked up to find Annie Besant's solemn eyes watching her.

"Gentlemen," Mrs. Besant said, with a cough, as soon as Mr. Pillar's blustering allowed for a pause, "We have been here three hours now. I think we ought to call a quick recess."

As soon as Rebecca was out in the corridor, Thomas rushed to her side. His hand grazed her arm, his eyes studying her face. "Are you all right? You looked so pale in there I thought…"

"Not here," she said in a low voice, with a pointed glance at the door to the meeting room. Thomas gave a start, as though he had forgotten himself. He stepped back as the other girls emerged and passed them on their way out.

"I can bring you home. I mean—back to Sarah's house. You—"

"Thomas," she interrupted. His first name still felt strange on her tongue. "I just need some fresh air." She looked at him, at his glasses and messy hair, and felt a rush of affection, followed by that sense of disbelief which had seized her more than once over the past two days: disbelief that this could really be *hers*. "This is the most important day of the strike. You *must* stay here. You know that you must."

He gave a slow nod as he considered her words, even though it looked like it pained him. And then, as Mrs. Besant came out, speaking to one of the managers, Rebecca jerked her head in her direction. "Go on." Her eyes held Thomas's for a moment more, soft and intent, and then they parted ways. She went up the corridor, her head still throbbing, but her feet steady beneath her.

Outside the passage that led from the offices of Pillar and Perkins to the main factory, there was a courtyard, and Rebecca passed out into it with great relief. One hand on the stiff door, the other at her temple, she stumbled down the two concrete steps and came to a halt. The fresh air filled her lungs and relaxed her muscles. She had her eyes closed as she gulped down deep breaths, and it wasn't until she heard the crunch of gravel underfoot that she realised she was not alone.

At the other end of the courtyard, Edward Pillar was standing, and smoking.

He was far enough away that Rebecca had a moment's uncertainty as to whether it was really him. Then, seeing that it was, she was seized by an urge to step back into the building before *he* saw *her*. Her hand groped backwards for the door, then fell by her side as he turned his head.

Their eyes locked, and Rebecca was not so much conscious of the emotions that went through her, but rather of the sensations that they caused. Her eyes widened until they were straining her sockets. Her body began to shake. She felt hot, and sick. And then, as Edward looked away from her and vacated the courtyard through a door she had not noticed before, the tears came.

Later, she would wonder the same thing that she had wondered with Mr. Lethbridge. Did Edward turn his eyes from her out of shame, or contempt? Did he need to escape her words, or did he simply wish to rob her of the chance of uttering them?

65
EMPTY

As Eliza stepped into her old lodgings, the floor creaked just in the spot that she had been expecting, and the air smelled the same as she remembered. But her gaze was drawn to the bareness of it all: the discoloration on the wall where the Queen's portrait used to hang, the empty cupboard with the door that had never closed properly, and the armchair divested of its coverings.

"The landlady said that your sister left because she couldn't pay the rent anymore," Peter said, coming up beside her, and his voice sounded too loud in the quiet. Their train had been delayed last night, and they had been so late getting in that they had left it till morning to come and visit Rebecca. "Do you think it was because of the strike?"

"She must have been in trouble even before that," Eliza said blandly. She went to the window, twitched open the curtain and looked out at the hazy morning fog, over the rooftops. There was a lump in her throat. "After all, that's why I had to get a job in the factory in the first place. So that we could afford to keep living here. After Mum died—"

Something occurred to her then—a wild fear—and she turned to look at the chimney-piece, and rushed over. Her fingers trailed along its dusty surface, and she began to shake her head.

"What is it?" Peter said gently. "Eliza?"

"Mum's things." Her words were thick with sorrow. "They used to be here. I wouldn't let Rebecca touch them. I thought it was bad luck, that her spirit might be unhappy, or—or something. Her death was so horrible…" Eliza paused, looking at the dark impressions in the dust, each in turn: the shepherdess had been here, the locket there, and Dad's picture there. "It looks like they were only moved recently."

"Probably she had to sell them." Peter's voice was still gentle, but matter-of-fact.

"But before that…" Tears blurred Eliza's vision. "She must have kept them here, hoping I'd come back."

"And now you *have* come back."

But as Peter drew Eliza into an embrace, she shook her head again. "It's too late." For a moment, she was silent, as he held her, and then she spoke against his shoulder, her voice muffled. "This was a mistake."

"You've got to see it through now," he argued, drawing back. "Find Rebecca—"

"She won't want to see me." Eliza smiled sadly, her eyes soft as they gazed into his. "Let's leave, Peter. All we have here is the past. I've spent so long stuck in it, wishing my mum was back, wishing I didn't make the mistakes I did. Now it's time to move on."

He drew a hand down her cheek, wiping away a tear. "I'm sorry."

"It's my fault," she returned, softly, and drew her arm through his as they walked out.

They were coming down the narrow, creaky stairs when Peter tugged Eliza to a halt, and pointed ahead. The door to the landlady's parlour stood half-open, and they could hear that she was talking to someone. The tenor of the conversation sounded urgent, so much so that Eliza's eyes widened. She exchanged a glance with Peter, and silently they moved for the door.

But they were not quick enough, for when they came to the bottom step of the stairs, Sarah O'Brien emerged from the parlour, the landlady at her heels, and stared up at them.

"Well," she said after a long moment, during which no one moved. Her eyes rested on Eliza's, and she sounded a little breathless. "Looks like you've come just in time."

66
REGRETS

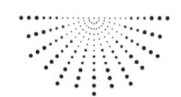

Edward found his father in the office after the meeting was over. Richard Pillar was on his hands and knees, scrabbling through the ashes in the fireplace. His son came to a halt, staring at him for a long moment before clearing his throat. "What are you *doing?*"

Richard gave a start and looked around with a slightly irritated expression. "He sent me a letter."

"Who?" As his father continued to poke around in the hearth, "I thought you never used that fire, anyway."

"I don't," Richard said, shortly. "Only once—a few months ago…"

"Father, come. Sit down." Edward took his elbow, guiding him to his feet and towards the desk. "You're tired from the meeting, you're not thinking straight—"

"Don't tell me that," Richard interrupted, but he took his seat anyway, looking past Edward's shoulder. "My thoughts are clearer than ever. All I can *do* now is think."

Edward felt a sense of trepidation, climbing within him. "Is it true? Did you really agree to all of the demands?"

"Not *all* of them." His father's voice was barely louder than a mumble. He dragged a hand down his forehead. "The fines are to be abolished. The foremen—to have a reduced role. And all of the girls are to be taken back, no exceptions."

"And are these not the most important demands?" Edward pounced forward, planting both hands on the desk. "I *knew* I should have been there. What were you thinking, Father? We had the upper hand after yesterday. We…" He trailed off, watching his father's expression, and then threw up his hands again, turning. "What is it you keep looking at, anyway? Is there something very interesting in the corner of this room?"

"Careful," Richard said, but there was no edge of authority to his voice. With a visible effort, he dragged his eyes back to Edward. "I am sorry. I could not have you there, not with Mr. Barnwall in the room. Who knows what claims he might make…"

"Who *cares*?" Edward broke in. "We can sue him for libel the second he puts pen to paper again! He is a penniless clerk, an Irishman no less; he poses no threat to us! He —*what*?"

Richard was shaking his head, slowly. "The fact is, Edward... well..."

"Well, what?"

"These things that have happened, over the past few months," his father went on, a little uncomfortably. "They are things that I would not have believed possible before."

Edward rocked back on his heels, taking that in. He glanced around to the corner of the office again, where his father's gaze had been fixed before. Quietly, "Then they have won."

"Edward." There was so much sorrow in his father's eyes when they looked at one another again that Edward froze for a moment. "I feel sometimes—that I failed you."

"Well, in this case, you certainly have," Edward snapped. "I trusted you, Father. I did not think that you would be so weak..."

"That is not what I am talking about." Richard closed his eyes, as though it were too painful to keep looking at him. "I mean to say that—your mistakes, your weaknesses, they have much to do with my own. I wanted you to be proud of this company, of this family, but perhaps..." He opened his eyes, glanced past Edward's shoulder again. "Perhaps I did not teach you the right lessons, as he said."

"As *who* said?" Edward was beyond anger at this point, his father's words bubbling within him and searing his mind.

"Arthur," Richard said faintly.

"I see." Edward gave a short, dry laugh. "Your colleague who has been dead for seventeen years is the source of this wisdom."

"There was trouble back then, talk of a tax that was going to be introduced." Richard's eyes grew even more distant. "Our girls protested against it and won us that victory. And Arthur—wrote me a letter. He was going to leave the company, sell his shares. He said that—we had lost sight of everything our fathers believed in. Our faith, our morals: everything."

"And then he died," Edward said harshly. "So what does any of it matter?"

Richard looked back at him, considering. "When you get older, Edward," he said after a long moment, "You begin to feel that some of the people you knew, who have left this world—are not truly gone. Arthur still speaks to me, I think. I saw him in the meeting room today, when we were deciding on the fate of those girls. And I knew what *he* would have done."

Edward was speechless in his disbelief. He looked around the office, looked at his father again, and shook his head. At last, he spluttered, "I am not going to stay here to talk of—of ghosts and nonsense with you. All I know is that you—*you* have made a grave mistake." He pointed with his forefinger, as he backed away towards the door, and

Richard looked back at him calmly, sadly. "And you will—you will regret this, Father."

67
HAND IN HAND

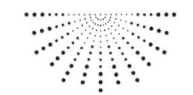

Sarah O'Brien had always been fond of talking, as Eliza remembered well from working with her, and it was some time before she or Peter could get a word in edgewise.

"We're not supposed to be here," Eliza said finally, when Sarah paused for breath after relating to them the visit to Parliament, the Glasgow strikebreakers and the meeting at Pillar and Perkins, all in quick succession.

"What do you mean?" Sarah rounded on them. In answer, Eliza tugged her shawl closer around her head. They were coming up Mile End Road, and though no one on the crowded street spared their ragged group so much as a glance, she could feel the skin prickling at the back of her neck.

"We're in a bit of trouble," Peter explained, in a low voice, with one protective hand to Eliza's back.

Sarah's dark eyes narrowed and flickered between them. "If I ask you what kind of trouble, are you going to tell me?" As they were both silent, she sighed. "Thought not. Come on!"

They followed her across the street, narrowly avoiding a carriage coming their way. "Where are we going?" Eliza gasped, rushing to catch up with Sarah.

"To Mr. Charrington's," said Sarah, over her shoulder. "The girls are all there, waiting to hear the results of the meeting at Pillar and Perkins."

The girls. Eliza swallowed, and forced the words out. "Is Rebecca there, too?"

Sarah looked back at her properly this time and did not reply for a minute. Eliza could feel Peter's eyes on her, as well.

"No," Sarah said at last. "I heard she left the meeting early. It's still going on, I think—it's been going on since morning. But one of the girls said she saw Rebecca coming out of the factory. When she didn't show up at Mr. Charrington's, I went to check her old lodgings, and that's when I met you two."

"Then…" Eliza did not know whether to feel dismayed or relieved. On the one hand, it had been the unbearable longing to see her sister—and not just to see her in black and white, but in the flesh—that had driven her back to London again. But on the other hand, meeting Rebecca would mean telling her everything, dredging up the depths of shame within herself. It was different with Peter; he knew it all already, and still loved her. But if Rebecca knew everything that she had done...

"I'm sure she's all right," Sarah said, though she did not sound entirely convinced of this herself. "Probably just went back to my house. Now." She turned on her heel, forcing them to stop on the pavement, and they saw that up ahead loomed the imposing facade of Mr. Charrington's Assembly Hall. They could hear the echoes of shouts from here; they could see the crowds swarming at the doors. Sarah crossed her arms over her chest and surveyed them. "I'm guessing you came back because you want to help?"

Eliza and Peter exchanged a look. He gave her a little shake of the head and turned to Sarah. "Yes, we do." His gaze drifted to the police constables that had been stationed at the entrance to the hall. Sarah followed it and looked back at them with a nod.

"Right then. Wait for me here. And try not to get in any more trouble."

As they waited, avoiding the gazes of passersby and trying to draw as little attention to themselves as possible, the sun broke out from the clouds and shone down on the street. Old puddles at the side of the road sparkled, and points of light gleamed out of the arched windows of the Assembly Hall.

"We should go back," said Eliza, after a few minutes' silence. Her gaze was trained on the door of the hall. "She might have forgotten about us."

Peter was looking around, with something like wonder in his face. Gently, he said, "She's your sister's friend, and you've been away for months. Do you really think she would forget about you?"

His words, however, did nothing to dispel Eliza's trepidation. The crowd outside the hall was growing larger as more emerged to join it, and now, instead of swarming, the figures appeared to be forming themselves into orderly rows. Placards and banners were raised up above their heads, and a rhythmic shout reached their ears, whose words Eliza could not make out. She had started to tingle all over, fear and anticipation colliding within her. *This* was what had been going on, while she was stuck in a room for weeks on end. *This* was what the newspapers had been talking about.

Sarah joined them again, flushed and out of breath. She handed Eliza a white apron and Peter a collecting box, both of which had been stacked under her left arm. "Here, now you'll blend in more." Her right hand was clutching that of a little boy—her brother, Eliza remembered, and his name came to her from that old corner of her mind which she had thought, once, to be lost forever.

"Hello, Simon," she said, with a tentative smile. She did not expect the child to even recognise her, let alone barrel forward and throw his arms around her waist. Eliza reared backwards in surprise, and then she hugged him back, and lifted him up, because there was something inexpressibly dear and familiar about his face, and because there was something wonderful in feeling seen, and accepted, and loved.

Then, over Simon's shoulder, she saw Peter watching them, and her delight turned to pure joy. It was as if she could see their future together reflected in his eyes. The longer he looked at her, with the child in her arms, the more his hope seemed to become absolute certainty, and that certainty wrapped her in its embrace, too.

It was with an effort that she put the child down and returned him to Sarah. Then she fastened on the apron, and Peter slung the strap of the collecting box around his neck, and they began to march with the rest of the great crowd, their hands joining and holding that promise between them.

68
MARCH

Rebecca clutched her untouched pint of bitter, and leaned closer to the neighbouring table, just as another roar of laughter went up. She wished alehouses weren't such noisy places. And what Mum might say if she could see her now! But these were fleeting thoughts, faint interruptions to the main refrain of her mind: *I will not let Edward Pillar out of my sight again.*

Because that was what she had done, she realised now, all those months ago. That had been her biggest mistake. Edward had expressed his interest in Eliza from the first moment that Rebecca had told him her name. But she had gone forth from that encounter and forgotten all about it. She had *let him out of her sight*, and he had worked his poisonous charm and turned her own sister against her.

Someone jostled her in passing by her table, so that a bit of her drink slopped out of the glass and stained her sleeve. But Rebecca didn't bother looking up or glaring at whoever it was, because the laughter had died down, and now she could hear the conversation going on at the next table over.

"Are you telling me that you lost them *again*?" Edward Pillar said to Wilson the foreman, who was sitting across from him.

"No, sir, only that the crowd on Mile End Road is so thick it was impossible to keep eyes on them. But I saw them all the way from Greengoose Lane to Mr. Charrington's Hall, and I think it's likely they've joined the march there."

"What march?" Edward repeated, with weary disgust. "Don't they know that it's all over?"

The words sent a prickle of suspense down Rebecca's spine. She had been outside Mr. Pillar's office for the entirety of his conversation with Edward; she had as good as heard the enemy admit defeat. But somehow, that was not the same as knowing that you were victorious, and not the first time, Rebecca wished she were back with Thomas and the rest. Then she would know the result of the meeting; she would know, once and for all, whether she should rejoice or mourn.

The stubborn refrain of her mind did not let her dwell on this possibility for long, either; it had not let her alone since she had seen Edward Pillar in the courtyard, and it did not seem likely to, at least not until she had found out what poison he was working now: what family he was seeking to destroy.

"I don't think they do know, sir," Wilson replied. He sounded bitter. "Or if they know they've got what they wanted, it looks like they just want to make more trouble. They're marching to Parliament, just like the matchwomen did in the old days."

"The old days," Edward snorted. "Of course, it all comes back to that. Well, Wilson, you know what to do."

"Yes, sir," replied Wilson, and Rebecca burrowed down in her seat as he passed her by, on his way out of the tavern. She let a minute or two pass before she worked up the courage to look around. But Edward Pillar had his head in his hands and did not see her as she slipped out in pursuit of the foreman.

69
A MISSING PEACE

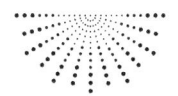

A cheer went up in Mr. Charrington's Assembly Hall when the results of the meeting were announced. Applause exploded in the galleries and echoed off the grand arches and the vaulted ceilings. The whole place was so large that it could seat five thousand. But as Thomas Barnwall looked around, he knew that there were far fewer than that number present right now, and he wondered why.

Mrs. Besant was smiling as she stepped back from the podium. She looked as though a great weight had been lifted from her shoulders. She shook hands with Mr. Shipton from the London Trades Council, with Sally Chapman from the matchwomen's strike committee, and with Mr. McDonald from the Fabian Society. It seemed a lifetime before she came up to Thomas, and then the polite smile was lifted from her face and replaced with one that was softer, and truer.

"Well, Mr. Barnwall," she said, "I must thank you for all the work that you have done with me over the past few months."

Thomas tried to smile. He really did. This ought to have been a triumphant moment. And with the memory of their recent argument brushed away like old cobwebs—Annie had said *with me*, after all, and not *for me*—he did want to feel glad.

She saw right through him, as she always did. And instead of anger, he saw kind acceptance in her eyes. "You're worried about Rebecca?"

Thomas nodded. "I haven't seen her, or Sarah. I don't know where they could have gone."

Annie tilted her head, considering. "I might have an idea." As he stared at her, she continued, raising her voice over the din, "While they were waiting for the results of our meeting, it seems a number of the girls set out on a march. An *unofficial* one, now, mind you. But they are to walk to the Houses of Parliament, following in the footsteps of the women who protested the match tax all those years ago."

All Thomas could see in his mind's eye was Rebecca marching, fainting in the crowd and no one being there to help her. "And—do you think this is a good idea?" he said, wildly.

Annie's eyes shone. "I think it is splendid." She reached out and squeezed his shoulder, then brushed down his coat sleeve. "And I think, Thomas, that you may be the only person in this hall who is not glad of it."

"I am glad," he said. "Of course, I am. I just, I'm worried about Rebecca, and…" Well, if she knew it all already, what harm was there in admitting it? He fixed his eyes on Annie's. "I haven't told her that I love her."

Mrs. Besant looked certain, unsurprised. "She knows." For a moment, as she looked at Thomas, and as Thomas looked at her, they felt together the weight of the unspoken and the unfulfilled. Her voice, when she spoke again, was so quiet and reverent that it was a wonder he heard it at all. "There are other ways, after all, of knowing these things."

70
WE'VE COME A LONG WAY

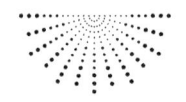

The water slapped against the Thames Embankment, in the wash of a passing steamboat. Eliza looked ahead, to the hundreds of matchwomen wending their way up the walkway. Around the bend of the river, she knew that the Houses of Parliament lay just out of sight.

"Hungry yet?" said Sarah from beside her. She was carrying Simon on her shoulders. On the long march from Bow, she and Peter had been taking turns, as the boy's short legs could not handle the distance as well as theirs could.

"Starved," Eliza admitted after a moment. Sarah grinned at that, and shaded her eyes against the sun, turning to look behind them.

"We've come a long way today."

"I can see the queen's palace!" exclaimed Simon, pointing ahead, and Sarah exchanged a look with Eliza.

"Well, what do you think? Will we drop in on her Majesty?"

"I'm sure she knows all about us by now." Eliza's voice was more serious. A moment later, she realised what she had just said. It was as if the intervening months had passed away in the last few hours that they had been walking, and she was just a matchgirl again. And she was not ashamed of that anymore, since she knew now that there were much worse things to be.

The significance did not seem to have been lost on Sarah, either. Her gaze lingered on Eliza for a moment before she spoke again, a smile still on her lips. "It's good to have you back, you know."

Eliza could not help the smile that spread across her own face in answer. "I think that might be the first nice thing you've said to me."

"Well. Don't get used to it." Sarah adjusted her grip on Simon's legs. "I should still be angry at you for what you put your sister through. Though I know…" She trailed off, and there was something guarded in her expression, so that Eliza could not guess what she had been about to say.

The Houses of Parliament loomed into view ahead as they rounded a turn on the Embankment. The traffic on the river was busier now, with barges and ferries jostling for position, and the occasional wherry winding its path between them. Several cheers went up at the sight of their destination, and Sarah lifted Simon down from her shoulders, because he was getting excited and wanted to walk again. Peter, who had fallen behind a little in his conversation with a friend he had met on the way, stepped forward again to offer to help with the boy. Sarah thanked him—but Eliza did not notice any of this. Her attention had been drawn away, towards the steps that led off the walkway and down to a landing stage.

A girl was walking down those steps: a girl with red hair and a black bonnet. Eliza saw her in profile first, and her heart squeezed and twisted in her chest. Rebecca—for it was her, she *knew* it was her—paused for a moment, surveying the river below. There was a man with her, whose face was turned away from Eliza, but who she thought might be Mr. Barnwall. He hurried her on, and they disappeared down the steps—but Eliza was already running, cutting through the crowd and ignoring the cries of protest from people she pushed out of the way.

She clattered down the steps, throwing out her hands for balance when she nearly slipped, and stumbled onto the landing stage below. "Rebecca!" The exclamation died in her throat as she took in the scene before her.

"Don't move," said the man. He was not Mr. Barnwall, but —Eliza could scarcely believe it as she saw the cruel gleam in his small eyes—Wilson the foreman. He was standing under the shadow of the walkway, the sound of tramping feet overhead filling their ears, and he had a pistol pointed at Rebecca, who stood only a foot away from him. "Don't make a sound."

"Eliza," gasped Rebecca, and Wilson clicked something into place on his gun that made them both jump.

"What did I just say?" His voice was low and dangerous, but there was a note of amusement to it, as though he was enjoying this. Without taking his gaze off Rebecca, he said to Eliza, "Get in the boat."

There was a wherry waiting at the edge of the landing stage, its curved bow bobbing up and down gently. The waterman had a cowl over his head, and was turned away from them, even as Eliza tried desperately to catch his eye. She took one halting step towards it.

"Hurry up," Wilson snarled, and then Rebecca burst out,

"Don't do it, Eliza! Don't go with him—"

Wilson crossed to Rebecca in one stride, caught her around the neck and pointed the pistol to her temple. "Another word from you," he hissed to his captive, "And I won't just kill you, I'll dump your body in the river where no one will ever find you."

Rebecca was shaking with terror; Eliza could see it. But with her eyes, she made the same plea that she had just uttered aloud. She stared into Eliza's eyes and *begged* her not to go. *He's going to take you away.* The words dropped into Eliza as though her sister were speaking into her mind. *I don't want that for you. Not now, not ever. Don't do this to me again, Eliza.*

Eliza took another step toward the boat. Overhead on the walkway, she could hear Peter shouting for her. She took another quick step, and Wilson nodded, shifting forward and keeping his grip on Rebecca. "That's more like it. Get in the boat, like a good girl, and I'll let your sister go."

Rebecca had her eyes closed now, tears winding their way down her cheeks. It wrenched at Eliza's heart. *I have no choice*! she wanted to shout at her sister. *Can't you see that? I can't lose you, either!* Downriver, she could hear the faint roar of a steam engine. An idea pierced the fog of her panicked mind.

"That's it," Wilson said, as she came to the boat. He edged closer—and that was when Eliza placed her foot on a slippery slat of wood and chose to let herself fall. She landed hard, twisting her shoulder painfully, and heard Wilson curse from somewhere behind.

"What's wrong with you?" He had to let go of Rebecca to haul Eliza to her feet again, though he kept his pistol trained on the former. Giving Eliza a shove, "Get in."

Eliza put a foot in the bow. It trembled under her weight. She could see the steamboat now, directly across from them, speeding upriver. Wilson came up level with her, his back to the river, and jerked his free hand at Rebecca. "Go on, go. You'd better run, before I change my mind."

Rebecca's bonnet had fallen off. Her hair was coming loose, strands sticking to her sweating face, and there was a trickle of blood winding its way down her temple, though Eliza could not see where she had been injured. But she stared at Wilson, and said, without so much as a tremor in her voice, "I'm not going anywhere."

"Have it your way," said Jem Wilson, with a tilt of his head.

The steamboat had passed them but made itself felt in its wake. Shallow waves chased each other across the river in rapid succession, coming right for the landing stage. Irate, the waterman scrambled to his feet to shake his fist at the helmsman of the steamboat, bellowing across the water. The wherry tilted dangerously. Wilson half-turned to see what was going on, and a wash of water came over the landing stage, snatching his feet from under him. He fired as he fell, but Rebecca was already running, and the bullet passed high over her head and through the walkway above.

Eliza had lost her footing, too, and was half-soaked by the time Rebecca got to her. Her sister pulled her out of the water and threw an arm around her shoulder. "We've got to go. Come on!"

They made for the steps, looking back once to see Wilson struggling in the river. His pistol had fallen on the landing stage, and he kept grasping for it, bobbing up and down in the water. "For God's sake, man, help me!" he snapped to the waterman, who moved to obey him, just as another wash of water came. The wherry tilted again—Wilson's outstretched hand was caught between boat and quay—and they heard a crunch of bone.

Rebecca winced, but Eliza felt a surge of savage triumph, and shouted, "Never mind your fingers!"

The last thing she saw, before Rebecca tugged her up the steps, was Wilson's face, red with fury as he shouted at them, and batted away the waterman when he moved to help him out.

Up on the Embankment, the march appeared to have passed on. What other pedestrians were there had scattered at the sound of the gunshot, and they heard fearful voices, high on the air. Rebecca hugged Eliza tightly, and then pulled away, just enough to put a hand to her sister's face, feeling the thinness of it. "I didn't think I'd see you again," she whispered.

There were a thousand things Eliza wanted to say—*I'm sorry* not least among them. But as she was opening her mouth to speak, she saw him over Rebecca's shoulder: Peter. He smiled at her, in weak relief that she was all right, and then she saw his knees buckle from under him—she saw the discarded collecting box nearby—she saw the red spreading over his shirt, and she knew that the stray bullet had found a target.

∼

Rebecca had run for help. The sun had set over the city, turning the waters of the Thames gold, and the sky behind the Houses of Parliament red. The rustle of skirts and the murmur of voices reached Eliza's ears, from the crowd that had gathered nearby, but otherwise she was unconscious of her surroundings. Peter was surprisingly heavy, and she had to use both her arms to prop him up. There was blood all over her white apron, and blood on her hands, too.

"Remember," Peter said, and she knew he was trying to speak to her in that firm, stern way he used to, but his voice was weak and rasping. Still, he did not take his eyes off Eliza, his black curly head resting against her chest. He had not taken his eyes off her in all the time that they had been stuck here on the Embankment together, however long that was; Eliza had lost track. It might have been minutes, or hours, and still no one was coming to help. "Remember… what I said. Your life's just getting started."

He tried to reach up to touch her, but his hand faltered. Eliza caught it, raised it to her cheek herself. "No," she said, and she liked to think that the strength in her voice made up for the weakness in his. She would not cry, not yet. "No, Peter, not *my* life, *our* life. You're going to be with me. We're going to get married." She really believed it. She had seen all the blood; she was not stupid. But miracles happened: she had survived, and Peter would survive this, too.

Peter did not contradict her. His fingers trailed along her cheek. The corner of his mouth lifted, and he gazed at her in that way she had always wanted him to, but did not want *now*, not anymore: he gazed at her as though she were the most beautiful and precious thing in the world. "Keep looking at me," he asked her, softly. "Right into my eyes. Don't look away."

He was going to be all right, Eliza knew, but of course she couldn't help feeling a little scared at that. "Isn't somebody going to help?!" she half-growled, half-screamed, and heard the crowd shift and mumble around her, and then the sound of running footsteps along the walkway -

Peter turned her chin gently, so that she was looking at him again. His eyes were shining with tears, and Eliza didn't know why the features of his face were blurring before her, because she was certainly not crying, not when there was nothing to cry about, not *yet*...

"Don't be sad again," Peter told her. "Don't be lonely. Not for me. Eliza..."

"I won't," she choked out, because she could not handle the despairing look in his eyes, and only when it was replaced with a smile did she feel that she could breathe again. Peter's hand dropped from her face to his side, and by the time help had finally come, his eyes were fixed on the sunset sky, and did not move again.

71
THE FALLEN

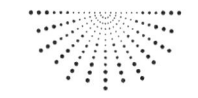

It was a tragic scene: a beautiful scene.

Edward Pillar watched from the crowd, in grim satisfaction, as Eliza wept and wailed over the body of her fallen lover. She tried to hold him up by the shoulders, but he kept slipping from her grasp. When he was carried away, she tried to follow, but her legs gave out from under her, and she fell to her knees on the walkway, sobbing her heart out.

Her sister, Rebecca, stood on one side of her, and the girl, Sarah, on the other. They didn't try to pull her to her feet, or to stop her from crying. And when the little boy came up, whoever he was, they let him tuck the shawl around Eliza's shoulders.

Edward knew that by tomorrow, the story would be in the papers, eclipsing that of the march to the Houses of Parliament. Jem Wilson would be found and caught.

Perhaps he had been already. It really was perfect. Edward had killed two birds with one stone, and his hands were clean at the end of it.

And as he left the crowd on the Embankment, melting away before anyone might see and recognise him, of course Edward felt a little tug on his heart. Who wouldn't, after seeing the woman they loved in such pain?

He did love Eliza. Or he *had*, at one time. But in his experience, love so often turned to hate. Eliza had grown to hate him, after all, just as she would grow to hate the boy, Peter, for leaving her alone. It all came around in the end.

For his part, Edward reflected, as he paid the driver and got into his hansom cab, he felt at peace. He neither hated nor loved Eliza anymore. She was just another broken person among many in this world, who would have to live her life with the feeling that she could have had something more. It was a feeling that he had always carried with him. And now, Edward thought, looking out moodily at the dark streets that passed the carriage window, someone else finally understood his pain.

72

THERE IS NOTHING LOST

Change at Pillar and Perkins' match factory did not come overnight. In fact, for a long time after the strike, the girls felt that they were back where they had started. The work was still hard, the routine unforgiving, and the fumes that emanated from the dipping-room as strong and deadly as ever. There were several more cases of phossy jaw, peppered throughout the months that followed the strike. Pillar and Perkins had been using white phosphorus as an ingredient in their match-making for years, after all, and they weren't about to stop just like that.

Eliza and the other girls whose work was confined to the boxing rooms were lucky enough to escape this particular malady, but they were not immune to the general gloom that had fallen over the factory. The fevered days of summer were gone, and the streets they had marched over were covered now with snow. Whispers of a killer roaming Whitechapel had become full-blown warnings, and as the dark winter nights drew in, no one felt much like going to meetings or concerts.

But small shifts in the atmosphere of the factory did, sometimes, make themselves felt. Jem Wilson had always been the most vicious of the foremen, and his arrest and subsequent trial—along with the conditions that had been settled with the company at the end of the strike—meant that his remaining colleagues were not as free with their fists, or fines, as they had been before.

Eliza could not say that she was happy, in those times. Life was more of a struggle than it had ever been before. The first month after the strike ended was one of heart-pounding suspense, as she waited for a reckoning that never came. Instead, Pillar and Perkins' management got in touch, offering her her old job back, and there was never a word about her history with Edward. Later, she heard that he had fled the country; Wilson had apparently given a thorough account to the police of the various tasks he had undertaken on Edward's behalf, and there was talk that the former housekeeper, Mrs. McKinnon, had done something similar. With Peter dead, and Edward's depravity exposed, the manner of Eliza's escape from Mrs. McKinnon—and Edward—was not dwelt upon, and the housekeeper, presumably to protect her reputation from further ruin, did not level any accusations against her.

No; Eliza was not happy. But as the year drew to a close, a small project began to fill up her spare time. Every Friday after she was paid, she would come back to Hackney, where she now lived with a few other factory girls, and add another portion to the savings jar that she kept under her bed. It gave her a kind of pride that she had never felt before, to see the small pile of coins and notes building up. At weekends, she would walk around the East End with her little scrap of paper, ticking off each name written there once she had visited the shop.

Don't be sad again. Those words always came back to her, whenever she was close to despair. Whenever the dark night seemed like it would never end, those words stopped her from losing herself in it. So she got on with the business of living, and found it was not so hopeless as she had thought before.

One day close to Christmas, when her project was finally finished, Eliza got permission to leave work early, and got her coat and hat from the cloakroom before going to eat dinner with the others. The new canteen was located in the office wing of the factory. It took up the whole ground floor, accommodating the thousand-odd women and girls whose food breaks had once consisted of snatched sandwiches beside their machines. The food was plain, but good. In the morning and afternoon, the canteen rang with laughter and chat, a wealth of sound which was much more welcome to Eliza's ears than it had once been.

"Is Rebecca leaving today?" Judy Chapman asked her, when they were halfway through their meal.

Eliza swallowed her forkful of potato and nodded. "I'm going to see her off at the station."

Judy looked delighted, and a few of the other girls leaned in to listen. "So they're spending Christmas with his family?"

"Maybe longer," Eliza said, with a shrug. She tried to look casual as she said it, though the thought of Rebecca being gone for so long, and so far away—farther than she had ever been from Eliza in their lives—gave her heart a little, painful twist. "His parents couldn't come to the wedding, so I suppose they'll want to make up for that."

As the other girls gushed to each other about how romantic it was, Eliza was surprised to find her hand sympathetically squeezed by Judy's sister, Sally.

"She *will* come back, you know," the older woman told her. "And Dublin isn't the other end of the world."

～

It was all arranged. The boat train for Holyhead was waiting in the station, the porter had already taken their luggage, and Rebecca's palms were sweating through her gloves. She kept glancing up and down the platform, raising a hand every time she saw a redhead in the crowd, only to drop it again when she realised it wasn't her sister.

Thomas wasn't much help. He was too busy listening to Mrs. Besant's plans for a matchgirls' drawing room to notice Rebecca's anxiety.

"It is not an 'institution' I have in mind, Thomas, with stern and rigid discipline, but rather a refuge for these girls, some of whom have no real homes, and no playground but the streets…"

"And when would this be built?"

"Well, it might take some time to get support for it, but Madame Blavatsky has expressed interest in the project. I will write to you once I have more details. But I think it would do wonders for the girls: a good-sized drawing room with a piano, a table for games, perhaps, a bookshelf for a little light literature… teach them to take pleasure in reading—"

"And maybe to be on time for important things," Rebecca interrupted, her last bit of politeness worn away by her impatience, and they both glanced at her as though they had forgotten that she was there.

"Oh dear," said Mrs. Besant, after a moment. "Perhaps your sister got the trains mixed up?"

"If I told her once, I told her a hundred times: the six o'clock from Euston," Rebecca muttered, and then, at the sound of the train whistle, she threw a desperate glance at Thomas. "I can't leave without saying goodbye to her."

"She'll be here," he said, but he looked uncertain. They could see that the carriage beside them was nearly full now, shapes moving past the windows to settle in their seats. Rebecca gave it a minute more: she looked up and down the platform one more time, and finally she said, with a lift of her shoulders,

"We'd better go."

Annie Besant gave them a kiss each. She kept her hands in Rebecca's for a moment, and Rebecca looked back at her, a little warily. Over the past few months, since she and Thomas had got married, she had heard more of the story of their long friendship, and sometimes she thought that Mrs. Besant must hate her for stealing him away. But when she looked at her now, there was nothing but kindness and warmth in the older woman's eyes. "You look beautiful, Mrs. Barnwall. It seems marriage suits you."

Rebecca blinked, still unused to the title, and looked down at herself. Out of the money he had made with his new book, Thomas had bought her a new travelling suit: a jacket with blue piping, cinched neatly at the waist, and a long, form-fitting skirt. Looking back up at Mrs. Besant, she stammered, "I don't—really feel right in fine clothes like this."

"It always seems like that at first." There was a knowing gleam in Mrs. Besant's eyes. "But after a time, you'll get used to it, and wear them just like you would wear anything else."

With a shared smile, they parted ways. Mrs. Besant waved at the couple through the window when they had settled in their compartment, and the train was just beginning to move when Rebecca jumped up again.

"I don't believe it," she said in a low voice, but a smile was spreading across her face, and with trembling hands she opened the window and leaned out.

Her sister, panting and flushed, was hurrying up the platform to keep pace with the crawl of the train. "You're cutting it fine," Rebecca said, sternly.

"Merry Christmas," Eliza gasped out in response, and reached up to pass a box into Rebecca's hands. "Open it when you're out of London."

Rebecca stared down at the box for a second, then back at her sister. "I… didn't get you anything."

"Doesn't matter." Eliza grinned. Her face had filled out over the past few months, so that she looked more woman than waif. "I'm sure you'll get plenty of presents from the Barnwalls." But she must have seen the flash of fear in her sister's eyes, for she reached up again to squeeze her hand, very briefly. Raising her voice over the din as the train picked up speed, "They're going to love you!"

Then their hands broke apart, and the platform and Eliza were yanked away into nothingness.

Feeling suddenly close to tears, Rebecca took her time closing the window, and sitting back down across from Thomas. She met his questioning gaze after a moment and gave him a closer view of the box. "It's a Christmas present, from Eliza."

"Very generous," Thomas replied, with a funny kind of smile. "I've got a little something for you, too, as it happens. Just a stocking-filler, mind you." Ignoring Rebecca's protests, he reached into his pocket and drew out a pink ribbon. Their fingers brushed as he passed it over.

Rebecca wound the ribbon around her hand, mesmerised for a moment by the pink against her pale skin.

"To tie your hair with," Thomas said, as though she did not know what a ribbon was for. Then, when Rebecca met his gaze again, he added, "You were wearing one just like it when we first met."

"I thought you didn't notice me then," Rebecca said, with a smile.

"I always noticed you," Thomas replied, and the look he gave her made warmth flood her cheeks. If their compartment had been a private one—if there hadn't been other passengers nearby looking disgusted at their display—well, Rebecca was not sure what she might have done. Unfortunately, it wasn't.

She didn't open the box until they were an hour outside London. Thomas was telling her about a new book he was planning to write. His book about the Long Depression, which he had returned to writing after the strike, had been more successful than he had expected, and now he wanted to write an account of the strike itself. "The only question is, whether or not to include the interviews with the girls involved with Edward Pillar. I know your sister, of course, will not want to talk about it, but I'm sure most of the others will feel safer now than they would have been before. After all, his conduct has been exposed to the world, and he is not likely to return to England any time soon..."

Rebecca made a noise as though she were listening, and gently took the wrapping paper from the box. It looked like one of the filling boxes from the factory. Inside, there was more wrapping paper, and Rebecca removed it gingerly. Then her hands stilled. Before her were laid out Mum's things, the things that she had sold long ago: the things that Eliza had never wanted her to touch. The silver locket, the porcelain shepherdess, and the daguerreotype of their father, which had a new frame. Her fingers traced each object, gentle and wondering.

She bought them back.

A light snow was falling outside, and tears were falling fast down Rebecca's face as she looked out at it. She saw her own reflection, shifting back and forth with the motion of the train, and for a moment she thought it changed, so that Eliza was smiling back at her instead.

"Rebecca? Well, what do you think: is it a good idea, this book?"

Turning back, she saw that Thomas was looking at her uncertainly. Rebecca wiped her eyes and smiled at him.

"I think it's very good."

73
CHRISTMAS

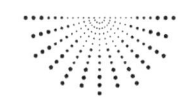

It had been snowing the day before, but Christmas Eve was dry and dark. Long clouds drew in and hung low over the city. The match factory in Bow closed early, and one by one the electric lights winked out, until there was just one left. Inside his office, Richard Pillar scribbled away, stopping every now and then to blow on his fingers. The charwoman had set a fire some hours ago, but he had not got up from his desk since then, and the flames were burning low in the hearth.

Elsewhere in the city, he knew that families would be gathering, carollers going from door to door, and church pews filling up with worshippers. But he knew that the work on his desk was not going to stop piling up just because everyone else was on holidays. *He* had to be *here* to see to it, or so he kept telling himself, at any rate, because it was better than imagining the great, empty rooms at home.

He had never realised before how much Edward's presence had directed the rhythm of his days. Troublesome though the boy had undoubtedly been, he had provided a purpose for Richard: everything, from his work to his social circle, had been set on the precedent that Edward would one day take over the company. And now that his son was gone, and not likely ever to come back, Richard, in the course of his daily routine, began to feel rather like a puppet, whose strings were being jerked around by some unseen master, whose motions provided an empty show.

There were still moments, as well, when he sensed his old partner's presence. But Arthur's visitations had taken on another quality now; where once he had warned Richard, now he did not speak at all. He just stood there, lurking in some dark corner at the edge of Richard's perception, and reminded him of what was coming for him.

An ember shot out of the fire with a crackle, causing Richard to jerk up in his seat. His heart kept thumping in his chest, long after the ember had burnt out on the carpet. With a laboured breath, he put a hand to his forehead and closed his eyes for a moment.

And that was when he heard it: the knock at the door. It repeated itself a few times, and when he was sure it was not some morbid manifestation, he called, "Enter."

The door to his office opened, admitting an older woman clad in black, whom he did not recognise for a moment. When he did, he squinted and said, "Mrs. McKinnon?"

"Mr. Pillar, sir," said his former housekeeper, bowing her head and sinking into a deep curtsy, and it was difficult to tell if she was mocking him or not. Then again, she had never been the type to do so before—but Richard's perception of the lower orders had been turned on its head so many times over the past year that he held nothing as certain anymore. "Merry Christmas to you."

"Merry Christmas," Richard repeated back faintly. He glanced at the clock over the mantlepiece: half past five. Earlier than he had thought, with the darkness outside his window. Looking back at Mrs. McKinnon, with a frown, "Er—what can I do for you?"

She looked back at him steadily. "I've brought you a visitor, sir." And, as the factory owner stared in bafflement, she stepped aside. A young woman entered the office, leading by the hand a small boy. She had short dark hair, and peered at Richard from under a heavy fringe, distrust and suspicion written all over her face. The boy was looking around at the office with interest.

"This is Sarah O'Brien," Mrs. McKinnon continued. "She used to work here, before she lost her finger in an accident back in March."

"Ah yes, I remember," Richard said, although he didn't. Accidents like that happened in the factory all the time.

Still, it was one thing to hear about them, and another to see the victim up close, with his own eyes. He looked toward the girl's left hand and could feel himself beginning to sweat.

"And this is her son, Simon," Mrs. McKinnon went on, and the boy looked around at the sound of his name, dragging his gaze from the bookcase to Richard Pillar. He was small and dark-haired, and there was a curious expression to his face... but it was when Richard saw his eyes that he went still in his seat.

"Come closer, boy," he said, quietly, and the boy obeyed, his mother following after. When he was opposite the desk, the boy leaned his elbows on the edge, and there was something about that casual movement—along with the icy blue eyes that he would have known anywhere—that was achingly familiar. Richard raised his eyes to the mother's face, and found his suspicions confirmed in her expression. For a moment, he could not speak or move.

"I think maybe," said Sarah, with an edge to her voice, "We should go now."

"Aye, perhaps you should," Mrs. McKinnon agreed, and when Richard looked at her, he saw the dark triumph in her eyes. "I just thought you might be interested in meeting them, sir."

He understood her: he understood her perfectly. He had dismissed her, a good and loyal servant, and this was her revenge. There was no end to his son's indiscretions. It seemed that he would always be followed by them, no matter how far away Edward was now. There were probably many more children like this one, whose mothers would jump at the chance to get to Richard's purse-strings.

All of this passed through Richard's mind in an instant, but he found, strangely, that he did not care. Darkness swirled outside his window, an empty house waited for him at home, and who knew how many more Christmases he might see before he passed out of this world. He rose from his desk as they all turned to go, and said, "Wait."

The boy had blue eyes, just like Edward, and just like Edward's mother. It was strange how things came back to you, when you thought them lost for good. Richard Pillar did not spend Christmas alone that year, not truly. For in his heart lived the knowledge that there was a child out there, and that the child might one day grow up to be a good man, and—that in the meantime, he might do something for him.

~

THANK YOU FOR CHOOSING A PUREREAD BOOK!

We hope you enjoyed the story, and as a way to thank you for choosing PureRead we'd like to send you this free book, and other fun reader rewards...

Click here for your free copy of Whitechapel Waif
PureRead.com/victorian

Thanks again for reading.
See you soon!

LOVE VICTORIAN ROMANCE?

If you enjoyed this story why not continue straight away with other books in our PureRead Victorian Romance library?

Read them all...

Orphan Christmas Miracle

An Orphan's Escape

The Lowly Maiden's Loyalty

Ruby of the Slums

The Dancing Orphan's Second Chance

Cotton Girl Orphan & The Stolen Man

Victorian Slum Girl's Dream

The Lost Orphan of Cheapside

Dora's Workhouse Child

Saltwick River Orphan

Workhouse Girl and The Veiled Lady

HAVE YOU READ

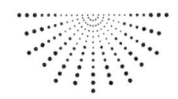

ORPHAN GIRL & THE BAKER

I'm certain that the thrilling history of the matchgirls has stirred your heart and kept you turning the pages to the final goodbye.

For another page-turner by Rosie Swan, read the story of little Hester Grace.

A sweet orphan girl scavenges for her next meal in the hustle and bustle of the Albert Docks. It is a shadowy and dangerous place for a young child, but amidst the darkness a secret love shines through…

For your enjoyment here are the first chapters of Hester's tale…

VICTORIAN ROMANCE

ORPHAN GIRL & THE BAKER

Rosie Swan

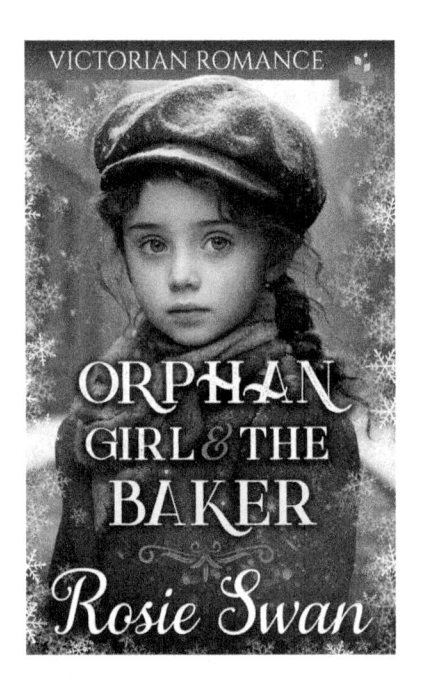

Robert Burrows had it hard as a child, though he knew that even when times had been hardest, there had been many in Liverpool who were much worse off than himself.

He had grown up as a middle child, sandwiched between a bossy older sister and a gentle younger brother, in Vauxhall, a neighbourhood whose very name was enough to produce a shudder in most inhabitants of Liverpool, as well as those of the rest of England. Back then, during the 1840s, the junction between Vauxhall Road and Scotland Road had been riddled with cellars and courts that were barely fit for one family to live in, let alone several. Many Irish families had ended up there, too, fleeing the famine that had been wrought upon them by the very same kingdom which now rejected them and shoved them into dark corners.

Conditions in Vauxhall had been so bad that political theorists had written whole books on the subject, and it was difficult for many to believe that in a city at the heart of the greatest empire in the world, in a port city of such vital importance as Liverpool in which so much wealth was produced, there could exist such misery.

Robert had survived those days, but only barely, and most of his family had not made it out. His sister had married well. His brother, mother, and father had all died, and the effects of each loss were not always felt at the time, when the business of living had to be attended to, but rather later on, when Robert was a bit older, a bit more comfortable, and, in essence, when he had the leisure of thinking of such things.

Unlike his sister, he stayed in Liverpool, and for most of the '50s worked hard as a baker's apprentice on a street near Albert Dock. When his master, Mr. Huxby, died, he had no children to inherit his bakery and so the place passed to Robert. For the first time in his life, Robert had a responsibility other than just surviving. He had a business of his own and also the possibility of improving other people's lives. The poverty in Liverpool was nowhere near as bad now as it had been during the '40s, but it still existed, and as often as he could, Robert would go down to Albert Dock to feed the orphans.

In 1857, a year after Robert had inherited the bakery, when he was twenty-one, he went down to Albert Dock and met a little waif named Hester Grace who, from that day forward, became Robert's shadow. She started coming around to the bakery every day. She would hang around on the shop floor during the day or knock at the back door of the bakery in the evenings when Robert was having his supper. He got very used to seeing her. She never begged, though she often looked so forlorn that of course he would have to give her something. She never stole; he tested her once or twice by leaving her alone on the shop floor while he went to get something, but when he got back, the pastries and breads would still be untouched.

Hester Grace, even if she had been clad in the finest silks and jewels rather than rags and scraps, would not have ranked among the great beauties of that day. At that time, what was considered most attractive in a woman was vitality and colour, and Hester had not much of either, though there was a fascinating changeability about her brown eyes. At times they were alert with intelligence, at other times full of melting softness. The perfect curls, too, which were recommended by the fashions of the day, were not available to Hester, and her black waves of hair, which she always wore loose around her shoulders and often without any covering, would make some passersby look at her askance, while others outright ignored such a creature as beneath their notice.

For a time, Robert was unsure of Hester Grace's age. He knew that, in the couple of years that had passed since their meeting, she had grown taller, and her black hair had gotten longer, but it was not until the year that war broke out on the other side of the Atlantic, the year of 1861, that Robert learned Hester's age, because she told him one day. She had just turned eighteen. She had never known her precise birthday, but she knew that it was sometime in April, and the day that she told Robert happened to be the same day that the papers were full of announcements of the Confederacy and the Union now being at war. Neither Robert nor Hester knew then how closely that distant war would soon intertwine with their own lives. Robert gave Hester a little cake, which she ate while sitting on the steps of the back door of the bakery, and he stood beside her looking out at the yard. They talked, as they always did, of nothing in particular.

∼

There was a book that Hester Grace had read once. It had been on the shelf in the schoolroom at Brownlow Hill Workhouse in Liverpool, where she had grown up. During lessons one day, she had sneaked the book under her shirt and read it that night in the girls' dormitory. She had lain curled up with her stub of a candle balanced on the bedstead and the dark roof above looming close to her face, as in the flickering light she scanned the print. There was no time for reading during the day at the workhouse.

Between school in the morning and working the looms in the afternoon, there was too much to do. The end of the book made Hester want to cry, but she was afraid of waking someone up, so she just let the tears roll down her cheeks in utter silence.

The next day, when the schoolmaster was looking the other way, Hester slipped the book back onto the shelf and did not look at it again. She remembered it, all the same, and a few years later when she had been about to leave the workhouse, she had gone back to look for it, only to find that it was not in the schoolroom anymore.

The book was about a little mermaid who fell in love with a human prince, and who longed to be with him so much that she traded her voice for a pair of legs. The bargain that the little mermaid had made with the sea-witch meant that she had lost her soul, and that for every step she took on dry land, she would feel like she was walking on knives. The only way to get her soul back again would be if the prince fell in love with her, and he could not see the little mermaid as anything other than a friend. At the end of the story, he married another woman, but the little mermaid got her soul back again and became a spirit of the air. That was supposed to be her consolation, but Hester couldn't see how.

Hester did not exactly feel like she was walking on knives whenever she was with him, her prince, who was really a baker called Robert, but sometimes she felt like she couldn't breathe, and sometimes she felt afraid of how quickly time seemed to pass when they were together. It made her wonder if one day this time that they had together might run out. That was why Hester liked to observe Robert every now and then, through the bakery window as he talked to customers, or from on top of the neighbour's wall as he walked up Cobbler's Lane. She would watch as he picked up the ball some children were playing with and threw it back to them, or as he stopped to help old Alice Smith carry her shopping. When Hester was not with Robert but instead watching him from a distance, time seemed to pass more normally. She could hear his laugh and see his smile, and she did not feel so afraid that she would lose those things someday.

Robert Burrows really looked quite ordinary until you had seen him smile for the first time. after that, even when he looked sad or serious, it was hard not to think of that smile. The possibility of it seemed to change his face completely. Once you had seen Robert smile, he transformed from a young man with a mop of brown, curly hair, to a handsome prince with light in his eyes, or so it seemed to Hester Grace, at least. She did not know whether anyone else saw him the way that she did. It wasn't until one day in October 1861, when a visitor came to Liverpool to see Robert, that Hester really began to feel, for the first time, in danger of losing her prince.

Hester was walking up Cobbler's Lane, towards the bakery, when she bumped into someone. She had been out scavenging in Albert Dock that morning, and she was still carrying an old sack full of cans, bits of rope, and other things. The stuff rattled as she ran headlong into a gentleman, and he started apologising right away.

"Never mind, sir," said Hester, bowing her head so that her hair came down to cover her face, and holding the sack behind her back.

"No, really, I wasn't watching where I was going." The gentleman sounded like he was from Manchester. Hester peered up at him curiously. He was fair and thin, with a receding hairline. He looked up and down the lane before going on, "The truth is, I'm a bit lost. Can you tell me if Burrows' bakery is anywhere nearby?"

"Yes, sir, it's right down that way," said Hester at once, pointing. "Happens I'm going there myself. I can show you." She hadn't really been planning to stop at the bakery, but this gentleman looked so gormless that she thought she'd better show him where it was, and if she got to see Robert into the bargain, then so much the better.

"Oh, that's very kind, thank you." They fell into step together and she sensed the gentleman glance at her. "So, do you know Mr. Burrows?"

"Know him? Oh, yes, sir, I often go around to his shop. He's been very kind to me."

"Yes, Robert is very kind." The Manchester gentleman cleared his throat as though embarrassed. "My name is Cecil Locksmith. I'm Robert's brother-in-law."

"Ah, so you're the one as owns the great warehouse in Manchester?" Hester exclaimed.

"Er, yes, that's right." Mr. Locksmith sounded more embarrassed than ever, so Hester decided it would be wiser to drop the subject of the warehouse. At any rate, they were approaching the door of the bakery. She stepped back to let the gentleman enter first, and, bafflingly, he did the same.

"Ladies first," he said after a moment, and Hester smiled and raised her eyebrows as she pushed open the door of the bakery. It was the first time in her life that anyone had ever called her a lady.

"Hester!" Robert sang out from behind the counter. A smile had broken out on his face as soon as he saw her, and when the gentleman entered behind her, that smile turned to a positive beam. "And Cecil! Well, this is a surprise!"

The other customers turned around to look at them, too, and Hester shrank back into the corner so that people wouldn't look at her too long. She wasn't exactly wearing her Sunday best. Robert served the last few customers before coming around from behind the counter to give Cecil a hearty shake of the hand. "Well, sir, so how do you do? I hope you had a comfortable journey from Manchester?"

"Very comfortable, thank you. I thought I'd drop in before my meeting and see how you were."

"I hope you didn't come out of your way!"

"Not out of my way at all. The meeting is just down on Albert Dock."

"How is Lesley? And how're the children?"

"They're well, all well, thank you."

Hester had started inching towards the door, not wanting to disturb the reunion now that her job was done. What happened next was the strangest thing. – One minute the two men were talking, and the next minute one of them, the brother-in-law, had buckled over, nearly overbalancing. Robert grabbed hold of him and struggled to keep him upright, his apron bunching up under Mr. Locksmith's weight as he exclaimed, "Help! Help! Won't someone help?"

The apprentice, Marcus, came darting out from behind the counter with a chair, which he and Robert managed to get Mr. Locksmith onto. The gentleman seemed to be half-conscious still. His mouth was open, and Hester could see the whites of his eyes under his lids, but his colour was awful, all white and grey.

"The meeting," Mr. Locksmith murmured, and made as if to get out of the chair. Robert put a hand on his chest to restrain him, leaving a trail of flour on the man's black waistcoat. "No. I'm all right, really. I just didn't eat very much today. and it was so hot on the train."

"You're not going anywhere until you've seen a surgeon," Robert said firmly. Turning back to his apprentice, who was hopping from one foot to the other in his agitation, he said, "Marcus, you know where Mr. Russell lives, on Lime Street? Go fetch him, please."

"Yes, Mr. Burrows," said Marcus, and took off his apron before rushing out of the bakery. As he was going, he turned the sign on the door from 'Open' to 'Closed'. From her corner, Hester stepped forward, the wares in her bag rattling.

"You said this meeting is down on Albert Dock, sir?"

Both men looked startled at the sound of her voice, as though they had forgotten she was there. "Yes," Mr. Locksmith said after a moment, and grimaced. "It's in the building next to the Dock Office, at the headquarters of a trading company, Fairbank & Co."

"Fairbank," Hester repeated, and then nodded. "I know it. I shall go send word you've been taken ill."

She turned and made for the door. Robert's voice floated after her as she was going, a faint, distracted, "Thank you, Hester."

∽

Marcus came back a half-hour later with Mr. Russell in tow. He was a good lad, Marcus. He had started apprenticing with Robert last year, at fifteen, the same age

Robert had been when he started here back in '51, when the bakery had belonged to Mr. Huxby, who had since died and whose wife no longer lived in Liverpool. The Huxbys had no children, so the bakery had passed to Robert and since then, it had been his to manage alone.

People often told Robert that he ought to get a wife who would help him run the place, but when Robert Burrows thought of marriage, he thought of his own parents. He thought of slammed doors and broken bottles. He looked at his brother-in-law, Cecil, stretched out now on the settee in the back room, and saw only a tired, faded man, a man who had tried and failed to make a success of himself. The last time Robert had seen his sister Lesley, when he had visited them in Manchester, she had looked worn out, too, and she had spent every spare minute trying to stop little Mary and Sam from bickering. On those rare occasions during that visit when she had actually spoken to Robert, it had been solely to complain about Cecil. So, in short, Robert did not look on marriage as something that would solve any of his problems, but rather as a grim eventuality that he need not think about just yet.

"I'm sorry," said Cecil after the surgeon had left. Robert looked down at the settee to see his brother-in-law watching him. "You had to close up shop on my account."

"It's one day, Cecil." Robert waved a floury hand. "It makes little difference. Besides, Marcus is going to see to it that whatever we didn't sell today is brought down to Albert

Dock. Aren't you, Marcus?" He raised his voice slightly so that his apprentice, lingering by the open door, had no choice but to hear him.

"But, Mr. Burrows, I don't like those children as run around barefoot and steals things."

"They don't steal. Most of them don't, in any case. They scavenge, and they often go hungry at this time of day." Robert watched with a half-smile as Marcus stumped out of the room.

"It seems things haven't changed all that much in this town," Cecil sighed, adjusting his position on the settee. "When I worked here, I used to hate going down the docks, same as your apprentice. I hated seeing the children going hungry. That was back during the '40s, of course. You'll remember, Rob, how bad things were then."

"I remember," said Robert. He walked around the table where he had used to eat all his meals with Mr. Huxby, a table that was only ever laid for one person these days, since Marcus took his meals at home. Untying his apron and slinging it on the chair, he said over his shoulder, "Maybe there aren't as many kids around Albert Dock these days. But still, you can't help feeling it when you see them."

"Is that girl, Hester, one of them?"

"Hester?" Robert repeated and turned back to face Cecil with a smile. He leaned one hand on the back of a chair as he thought for a moment. "She *was*. Now I suppose she still goes down there, but she's not like those other poor kids. She's clever, and she makes things."

"Makes things? What do you mean?"

"I mean, she, well, I don't know." Robert came around the table again, feeling he was quite out of his depth now. "She finds all kinds of odds and ends down at the docks. Sometimes she brings them around here to show me. Tins, forks, candelabras, even violin strings once. Ordinary things, mostly, but she makes something new out of them and tries to sell them. She can fix things, too, like that." He pointed to the round clock that hung above the door separating the back room from the kitchen. "It used to always lag a few minutes behind, no matter how much I wound it up. I let Hester at it and now it's always on the hour, every hour. Listen."

The large hand had just joined the small hand at four o'clock, and in the quiet came the distant chiming of the bells at St Nicholas's. Cecil Locksmith's eyes widened, and for a moment he looked as though he might even smile, but then his face settled back into its customary weary expression and he said in a low voice, "Extraordinary. Though, speaking of timekeeping, oughtn't your Hester be back from Fairbank's by now? Do you think she got lost?"

"I doubt it," said Robert after a moment. "She knows Liverpool like the back of her hand." With a glance at the clock, "But you're right, it has been a while. Almost two hours."

"There's nothing for it. I shall go myself and explain to them what happened." Cecil made to get up, but Robert restrained him by the shoulder.

"Mr. Russell said you were to rest."

"I have rested. And I've eaten, too, and that was all that was the matter with me, really."

Robert kept his hold on his brother-in-law's shoulder. Even if Cecil had been in his full health, Robert would have had the advantage on him in strength. As it was, he was easy to restrain. After a moment, Cecil gave up and squeezed his eyes shut.

"What's so important about this meeting, anyway?" Robert asked, letting go of Cecil's shoulder. As his brother-in-law threw him a withering look, he sighed. "That is, I mean, why should you risk your health for a meeting? You're evidently not well enough to travel."

"I told you, there's nothing the matter with me. Anyway, you only get one chance with Harold Fairbank." Cecil stared up at the ceiling, the expression in his grey eyes intense. "I have to get this deal."

They both listened to the ticking of the clock for a moment. "Are things that bad in Manchester, then?" Robert asked finally, in a low voice.

"Things are bad all over the country," said Cecil, and he seemed on the point of saying more when there came the tinkle of the shop bell. Robert sighed and got to his feet.

"I shall go and tell them we're closed," he said over his shoulder to Cecil as he went. "Though I don't know how they could have missed the sign on the door." He stopped talking as soon as he saw who was standing in the shop, and he came to a dead halt behind the counter. His hands jumped up to his hair, then down to his apron, wiping them there even though they were already clean as they could be.

A young lady was standing just inside the door, if young lady she could be called, for surely there was a title more noble, more worthy of the vision of beauty that greeted Robert's eyes at that moment. Her hair was brown touched with gold, teased into soft ringlets that framed her heart-shaped face. She was not dressed in the extravagant, loud patterns worn by many of the other young ladies of status in Liverpool. Her dress, instead, was plain blue trimmed with black, but something about the depth of colour and texture of the fabric told Robert that it had been just as costly as any of those other fine ladies' dresses. Her eyes danced with good humour, and the older gentleman standing beside her, evidently her father, wore the same expression, but Robert only afforded him a glance or two before looking back at the young lady. He thought, and the thought was met with a kind of rising panic within him, that he might never be able to take his eyes off her.

"Is Mr. Locksmith here?" the gentleman asked finally, his brown moustache quivering as he spoke. His eyes now had narrowed slightly as he considered Robert. "We were told-"

"Yes," Robert burst out, surprising himself with his capacity for speech. "Yes, he's here. I shall go and-" He looked back one last time at the young lady, who was smiling now, before he turned towards the back door. "I shall go and fetch him."

∼

It had taken Hester quite a while to find Mr. Fairbank. He had not been at his offices on the docks, and neither had his secretary there been particularly helpful. As soon as he spotted Hester coming up to his desk, he seemed anxious to get her out of the place as soon as possible. On her way there, she had stowed away the sack of scavenged items in her secret spot, in the loft of an abandoned warehouse, and she had combed through her dark hair with her fingers, but she couldn't do much about the fact that she had no shoes, or the fact that the streets of Liverpool were black with mud at this time of year.

"He might be at the post office on Duke Street," the secretary said, his eyes fixed on some point behind Hester, where a trail of muddy footsteps led across the tiled floor to the door through which she had entered. "There's a delivery due to come in this evening and he always checks at the post office in case of delays. Or perhaps he's at his solicitor's office in Toxteth. Or at his sister's house."

"And where is that?" Hester said, after an expectant pause. The secretary looked at her warily.

"West Derby Road."

"Thank you." She was about to leave when a thought struck her, and she turned back. The secretary looked pained. "Beg your pardon, sir, but wasn't Mr. Fairbank supposed to be in a meeting at this time?"

"He has no meetings scheduled for today," the secretary said, with a cursory glance at the black book on the edge of his desk.

"Alright," said Hester. "Well, I shall check all those places for him, then." And she proceeded to do exactly that.

The post office on Duke Street was closest, and though the place was so crowded that the windows were beginning to steam up, the postmistress told Hester that Mr. Fairbank had made no appearance there today. Toxteth was a bit of a longer walk, and by the time she got there it had started to drizzle rain. Hester tried the street door of the solicitor's office and found that it was locked. She peered up at the blurry grey sky and then bent her steps towards the north of the city.

There were many houses on West Derby Road, and she tried six in succession before finding the one where Mr. Fairbank's sister lived. Thankfully, the gentleman in question was there, and the maid told Hester to wait in the kitchen while she went to deliver her message about Mr. Locksmith. While Hester was waiting, the cook gave her some bread-and-butter, which was a good thing as she was starting to feel very hungry by then. The maid came back down and told her that Mr. Fairbank was very sorry. He had completely forgotten about meeting Mr. Locksmith today.

"He's going straight to Cobbler's Lane now to see him, and to make his apologies in person." The maid looked down at Hester's muddied feet and then added, "He's bringing the carriage. If you want to save yourself the walk, you can hop up in front. Better hurry, though."

Hester did hurry. She burst outside just as Mr. Fairbank was emerging from the front door, and she hung back a respectful distance until he had made his way to the carriage. She saw that he was not alone, but with a young lady in a dark blue gown trimmed with black, whom Hester assumed to be his daughter. Hester watched until they had disappeared into the carriage, and then hurried to sit up front.

The coachman was young, probably only around Hester's age, with a round friendly face and fair curly hair. He kept asking her questions about herself as they drove through the streets, but she did not pay him much mind. Her thoughts were full of Robert. He must be worried by now. He would think she hadn't been able to find Mr. Fairbank. She thought of the relieved smile that would cross his face when he saw them arriving at the bakery. She thought of the look of grateful surprise that she had seen in his eyes a few times before, each time a precious memory, as each time she had seen it, it had been for her and her alone. She wondered if she would see that look again today. She hoped that she would. She hoped so hard that it hurt something inside her.

Cobbler's Lane was too narrow for a carriage, so they stopped at the bottom of Dale Street, and the Fairbanks got out to walk. Hester thanked the coachman distractedly and followed after them, once again keeping a respectful distance. She did not know whether they knew she was there. She thought that they mustn't know, but then at one point Miss Fairbank looked back and saw her. She smiled and said something to her father, and Hester, embarrassed, ducked into a doorway before he could turn around and look at her.

She would just see that they got to the right place, she decided. She wouldn't go in and talk to Robert. He would have enough on his mind, in any case. Keeping a greater distance between them than before, she followed the Fairbanks down Cobbler's Lane, descending until the white dome of the Dock Office had disappeared behind the rooftops. She passed the rag-and-bone shop, whose bent-backed proprietor, Alice Smith, was sweeping up the front step, regardless of the rain. She passed the tiny bookstand and glanced down at the book covers just as she always did, inadvertently meeting the gaze of the old bookseller in the process. She smiled, but he did not smile back. He never did.

Hester drew up to the bakery just as the swing of Miss Fairbank's crinoline had disappeared inside the door. Mr. Fairbank followed after her, and Hester took up a position at one of the side windows, peering over a display of scones to the scene within. She saw Robert come out from behind the counter and wipe his hands on his apron. She saw the astounded look on his face as soon as he had clapped eyes on Miss Fairbank. He looked like a man waking up from a long sleep, his eyes very wide and blinking rapidly, the usual ruddiness of his complexion changing to a darker crimson.

Backing away from the bakery window, Hester suddenly understood why the little mermaid in the story had always felt like she was walking on knives when she was with her prince. Every step that she put between herself and Robert felt like it was straining tighter and tighter a cord that tied her heart to his, and yet there was no way she could stay and watch, not now that she had seen that look in his eyes. Hester kept backing away, almost limping in her agony, and did not notice what was behind her until she had knocked right into it.

"You, girl!" cried the bookseller, rushing out from behind the stand. Hester looked down at the books she had knocked to the ground and then back at the bookseller's livid face, before she took off running. His shouts echoed after her all the way up to the top of Cobbler's Lane...

Continue reading this unforgettable romantic saga...

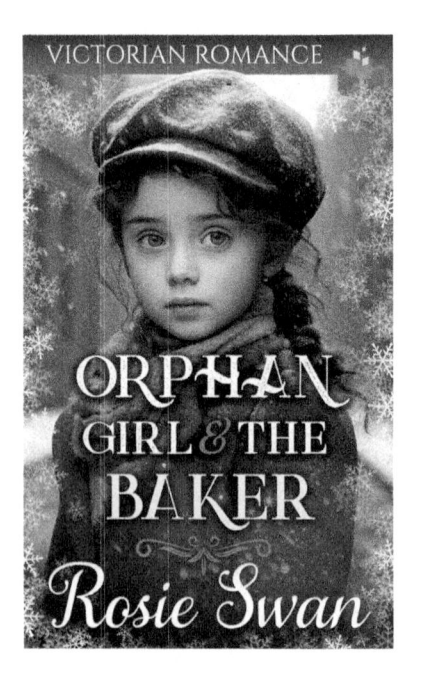

Read Orphan Girl & The Baker on Amazon

OUR GIFT TO YOU

AS A WAY TO SAY THANK YOU WE WOULD LOVE TO SEND YOU THIS BEAUTIFUL STORY FREE OF CHARGE.

Our Reader List is 100% FREE

Click here for your free copy of Whitechapel Waif

PureRead.com/victorian

At PureRead we publish books you can trust. Great tales without smut or swearing, but with all of the mystery and romance you expect from a great story.

Be the first to know when we release new books, take part in our fun competitions, and get surprise free books in your inbox by signing up to our Reader list.

As a thank you you'll receive an exclusive copy of Whitechapel Waif - a beautiful book available only to our subscribers...

Click here for your free copy of Whitechapel Waif

PureRead.com/victorian